RIVER RUN

BEYOND THE FIVE SENSES

CHRISTOPHER SEARLE is an English writer and the author of the Alternate Halesowen and Beyond series. An avid traveller of virtual worlds, he loves exploring; taking things slow to admire the scenery in worlds both grounded and fantastical. Such can be felt in his stories when it comes to crafting settings, and articles looking at video games.

SPACE RACE CHAMPIONSHIP

"Intense pain from being hit. Rocked from side to side as the 'craft tried to stabilise. Another hit. The capture. The panic. The elation of success followed by the sorrow of failure. Unsure of where his best friend was. Unable to reach him on the communications link. No-one to talk to but the attacker. Forced into the asteroids. Everything low within the 'craft. Nothing but rock and blackness to look on. Constant awareness of everything around him. Tiredness setting in. More failures on the 'craft. Ruptures within the spacesuit. Pain ramps up. Starts in more places. Lack of oxygen brings sluggishness to his movements. Hard rasps pierce his ears. He is determined to see this through to the end."

CHRISTOPHER SEARLE

FORESHORE PUBLISHING
LONDON

Published in Great Britain in 2025 by RiverRun,
an imprint of Foreshore Publishing Ltd
86-90 Paul Street
London, EC2A 4NE.
Reg. No. 13358650
www.foreshorepublishing.com
THE HOME OF QUALITY FICTION.

Set in Calibri Light
Typeset by Richard Powell
Printed and bound in Great Britain by 4Edge Ltd, Essex.
Copyright © Christopher Searle 2025

ISBN 978-1-0686132-9-6

Firstly, a big thanks to my dad, Martin, who sent the details of a publisher across to me, which started me on getting this book out into the world. By extension, a big thanks to my mom, Tracy, and sister, Rachael, as my closest family have kept me writing across these many years, providing ideas and helping correct a few errors in my writing.

The next goes to one of my oldest friends, Hayden, who inserted Star Wars Battlefront II into his PS2 for us to play at the end of 2007 and fueled my love of galaxies far, far away. Which started me on the path of making my own. Both Hayden, and my other oldest friend Claire, provided plenty of great experiences that have stuck with me.

Experiences mean the world to me, so a thank you goes out to everyone I encountered during my educational years. Those of Olive Hill, Staffordshire University, Leasowes, and Halesowen College. And a particular thanks goes to Jaspreet Singh from Halesowen College, who said I should start getting my works into the world, which is how I came to start my website all those years ago.

A thanks goes out to those of GRcade, the community I have spent many years with. Along with all the great experiences, there are many people who have helped me become a better writer, whether that be introducing me to new genres, notifying me about certain writing quirks, and being a nice place to discuss both writing and games.

And lastly, to anyone who has read any of my writing across the years. Whether that be my stories or articles. Thank you.

CHAPTER 1 – NEW COMPETITORS

"And it's that season again where we get hyped for the biggest event of the year. The official host of the season is back, so for the next four months of this year you will have me – Pyra Summers – talking you over the Championship and the rumours, stats, and official news that makes itself known. And since I'm back on the airwaves, you can be sure that first piece of news you all look forward to will be coming sometime this week."

Pyra Summers of Radio Racer [15/2-0085]

Two spacecraft waited together at the starting line within the cruiser's hangar bay. The improvised line was nothing more than two mini cruisers parked either side of the two 'craft.

The first 'craft was a Galaxy model – designation Y/26t. Oblong in shape, it had a rear rectangular section that fit around the control cabin's viewshield – which was also oblong in shape. The other 'craft was a Rotablade – designation G/0ld5n. A rectangular shape with rounded corners, it had a tubular rotating blade set either side that were as long as the 'craft itself. These were auto-defence weaponry emplacements, but were disabled for the moment. This 'craft also had an oblong shaped viewshield.

The two mini cruisers flashed their lights, and the pilots of the 'craft lifted them up and shot out of the hangar.

There was a lot of clutter that the two racers dodged around – the pilot of the Rotablade doing better than that of the Galaxy. Numerous lights marked the way for the racers, and as the 'craft sped past the lights changed colour.

The Rotablade was in danger of smashing straight into the hulk of a damaged mini cruiser, but a quick drop was all that was needed to avoid it. There was the issue of more debris beyond it, but the Rotablade smashed through all of it without a care in the world.

When the Galaxy hit this point, it rose above instead of going below, and seemed content to stay above most of the debris. It was forced back into the debris field when one of the sections of a cruiser floated into its path. It tried to dodge around the debris instead of going through it, which caused it to lose some speed.

The distance between the two 'craft had increased. The Rotablade was now within the outer limits of an asteroid field, effortlessly flying through them. After passing a few more, it was out of the field and hugging the plating of a cruiser as it travelled down the length of it.

The next light indicated the start of a structure that the racers needed to travel through. It was large, looking as though it was a cruiser in the process of being built. Or at least had been, as it looked abandoned considering the angle of it.

The Rotablade flew straight in, being completely aware of the girders that made up the structure. Despite that awareness, it didn't stop the 'craft from clipping one of them. The pilot was quick to react and saved it from colliding into a second.

The Galaxy had now opened up in speed, having hit the asteroid field. It made it through without hitting any, but there had been a few close calls. Then it was flying the length of the cruiser. The Galaxy had made sure to keep a larger gap between the two than the Rotablade had. When it reached the structure, it slowed down to enter, and kept that speed while traversing through.

The Rotablade was almost back to the starting cruiser, following the last few lights that created a winding path back to the hangar it had first started at. It was still paying no mind to the debris scattered around, and was able to bank and turn hard to avoid larger obstacles quickly. It slowed down to enter the hangar at the same time the Galaxy exited the structure of the abandoned cruiser.

It took about a minute more for the Galaxy to follow the path and enter the cruiser to land as well.

When both had landed, a results screen appeared with the time both had taken to complete the course.

"And it's a victory for the current champion!" a voice rang out.

The screens of light dispersed, revealing two boys sitting on chairs with a controller in hand.

"Will the current champion be beaten sometime soon?" the other of the two stated. "Tune in next time when we race in about... Five minutes?"

"The current champion will not be beaten," Tom Hughs said. "Not if the competition refuse to push their 'craft to the max."

"I just don't feel I can react fast enough," Lee Johnson responded.

"If you are used to the controls and the way something feels, you should be able to react no matter what speed you're going."

"And I always try." Lee looked around the room, picturing the race that had just happened. Then he looked back further to the last time he had pushed to near the max.

It hadn't ended well for him.

The game was a tie-in to the most popular event of the world they lived. One which happened once every five years. As it turned out, this was the year in which the next was to happen. Lee hadn't mentioned anything about it yet, but the news had confirmed the selection of the entrants for this year had happened. Within a week, those names would be revealed, and the hype for the event would begin fully.

"So, are we getting to a new race?" Tom asked.

"Yeah, sure," Lee replied. "But wouldn't it be great to be entered into the event for real?"

"As much fun as it would be, what chance do we stand without a spacecraft of our own?"

"We could get one easily."

"Nah... I couldn't see myself entering one. I'd be the youngest with the least amount of skill."

"Age is no proof of skill. You manage yourself great in the game, and you have the knowledge of flying that is sure to help. We have our pilot licences. It wouldn't be too much trouble to enter."

"Doing good in a game does not translate to doing good in reality, even with the knowledge we have. And we already missed the application date, even if we have the licences."

Somehow the more obvious reasoning for the questioning had bypassed Tom. That was fine by Lee.

He wouldn't want to spoil the surprise, after all.

As the next game was set up and the light screens that projected the game returned, Lee thought a bit more about the event. Both he and Tom were sixteen, so only remembered the last time it had happened. In fact, it was that year that the two had met.

Competitors could be anyone, so long as they were not affiliated with any company involved with the event. The mix of people from last year had been interesting, with some obviously being new to the whole idea of flying. The first event was always the same, and tested the full range of a pilot's skill. The other events all had something to do with the central theme of racing, with the final race being a long one.

The excitement around the event was always strong before, during, and after – lasting almost the entire year. And this year was sure to be an even better event than the last time, owing to the fact several new developments had been made in space-faring technology over the last few years.

The two hadn't made much talk about it yet, but Lee knew the day was coming up. The day they'd be caught up in the excitement and be talking about the Space Race Championship.

Casey Hughs lay on the king-size bed, looking up at the ceiling lost within her thoughts as a slow tune played. As ever, her thoughts were beyond the planet and out into the vast galaxy – wondering how her husband was faring.

Her husband – along with Kerry Johnson's – were members of the Craftile Armed Forces. The two had been in training for five years, and advanced to the positions they were in after three more. A year and a half back, a mission of great importance had come up. The two had been drafted into the crew for it, and they had set out. A year and a half had passed, and no word had come back.

She had no idea what the mission was, but she knew it had involved heading to the next system over, as the cruisers that had been assigned the mission had been fitted with enormous power banks that had been charged to capacity before they had set off. Everything the force used would have to be charged through those power banks, as the solar collectors would no longer be linked to the solar gatherer to receive a recharge themselves.

The one thing she did know was that he would be working with forces from Suati. The first explorers who had come to this system had learnt quite a lot from the people of Suati – once they had managed adequate communication with them. They had given the explorers the moon that had been Rotor 1, its planet having been destroyed by a powerful laser weapon from the next system over. The Suati had won that war, but it seemed another had broken out again, and they had called on the humans to help them.

She had enjoyed the years she had spent with her husband, but when he had first enlisted with the force, she had been cautious and worried. The worry had never left, even though it was just training and guard duty. She'd worked herself up into a frenzy when he had told her he was off on a mission outside of this system, but knew she couldn't stay mad at him. It was his dream, after all.

But still she worried.

The pace of the tune sped up before slowing down again. It came to a stop and a new tune played. This one had a jazzy beat to it.

Casey reached over and turned the music player off. She then sat up and looked at the time. Feeling it would be better to distract herself from her thoughts, she slid off the bed to her feet and headed to the kitchen – cutting through the storage room instead of following the corridor round to the proper entrance.

She knew Lee had come earlier, and he and Tom were probably still within the games room. She moved around the kitchen, preparing a meal for three, but still her thoughts lay with her husband, and what sort of action he was currently in.

"And tomorrow is the date we announce all those who have entered into the Space Race Championship. From what we have seen, the list includes several new challengers to go up against some of the previous entrants of Championships past. Fortunately, the champion of the last event hasn't put forth his name for this one, so there's no pressure in trying to beat him.

Pyra Summers of Radio Racer [17/2-0085]

Tom was sitting outside, lounging in a chair near the entrance of the house. He looked to the right of him at the empty landing field. He had a trainee licence for spacecraft, but had never owned one. His dad had, along with a mini cruiser, but both had been conscripted into the task force that had been sent who knows where. His mom preferred to walk places, but he was always wanting to fly. While his dad had had ambitions of getting to some action in the armed forces, Tom would rather explore new places. When he finally had his master licence, he'd apply for the explorer's guild.

For now though, he could relax and take things easy.

He faced the gate in the three-meter high fence that surrounded the property, and was surprised when it opened a second later. Lee walked along the path for a few steps before he noticed Tom and quickened his pace.

"Funny to see you out here when Radio Racer's currently announcing the competitors for the Championship," Lee said once less than two meters away.

Tom's eyes widened in surprise. He'd forgotten, having not paid much attention to the date when he had woken.

"Come on. Let's get in," Tom said, standing up and hurrying to the front door of the house. Entering into a small entrance lobby and turning right, he rushed inside with Lee following at a slightly slower pace.

The lounge was a simple design with basic white walls and carpet, with a red U-seat in the middle with a table against the wall at the U-seat's open section. The U-seat was named as it was nothing more than three two-seat sofas joined together with hinged tables.

The Lightmorph Media Display was already tuned to Radio Racer, with Mrs. Hughs sat at the U-seat listening in. Lee greeted Mrs. Hughs as he sat down opposite her.

"Six competitors have been announced," Mrs. Hughs informed them. "Three songs will be played between each announcement."

Tom sat listening to the current song, waiting for the end. Once it arrived, he listened more closely, hoping to hear a name he recognised.

The first to be revealed was a man from the city of Northington. He'd been a competitor before, but hadn't got through the free-for-all starting challenge. The second to be revealed was a female called Sally Evans. This was to be her first time competing, but she had a name to live up for as her sisters had once competed and had been in the final challenge.

"And our third competitor comes from Saltare," the host of the show said.

Tom felt a pang of excitement, curiosity, and shock as the thought of it being his name called out hit him. He turned to face Lee and found his friend trying to act uninterested in the name-drop of their hometown. The realisation then hit him as the host called it out.

"... Tom Hughs, son of a member of the Craftile Armed Forces, looks to be a strong competitor if his dad's record in training is anything to go by."

"You entered me," Tom stated flatly, still looking at Lee. He didn't want to see what his mom's reaction had been. "You entered me." A quick flash of a conversation hit him. "You even hinted at it a few days back."

Lee sighed and stood up. The host was still revealing the other competitors.

"Yes, I entered you," Lee said once stood at the opening of the U-seat. "Don't deny you aren't a great pilot. I know you have the skill needed to compete."

"I said before, though. I'm only good at Space Racer because I memorised the routes the game gives," Tom stated.

"Don't say that. You were top of the leaderboard within the trainee licence class we were a part of. And just because you memorise a route doesn't mean you can fly it without trying. It takes skill as well."

"But what about the equipment?" Tom asked. "What about the money needed to buy the spacecraft?"

"That's easy," Mrs. Johnson said as she entered from the games room. Tom blinked, wondering when she had arrived. He'd been outside since waking. "There's enough money to go around, so you can get what you need. If you want to go bigger, you just need to think about how to earn the funds. With the skills you have, I'm sure you'd be able to win at any Space Racer tournaments."

"But... What about... in the event?" Mrs. Hughs asked. "What if he competes and gets knocked out before he has a real chance of winning?"

"The fun's in the journey," Mrs. Johnson said as she sat down.

A new set of songs started playing, but no-one in the room was listening to them. Lee sat down again to face the two mothers, and Tom looked over at them, still in a slight daze from his name being called out.

Him. An entrant of the SRC.

The Space Race Championship was a big event, watched by many a person. It also called for great skill. As the host had said though, he should stand a chance if he was as skilled as his dad. He found some comfort in those words, and after a bit of thought was prepared to give an acceptance speech to the people of the room.

He stood up and walked to the spot Lee had stood before. "I might not have much in the way of real experience, but I do have skill," he started. "If I can get in a 'craft and give it a test run, I should be able to fly it and run rings around the competition."

"Well said," Lee commented.

"You'll do well," Mrs. Johnson added. "It's about the community of people you meet more than the winning. Just remember that."

Tom looked to his own mom to see her usual worried expression in place.

"You get to some action," Mrs. Hughs finally said. "I know that's what you want, so I'll let you have this chance to get some. Make your father proud."

Tom felt he needed to withdraw, and said he wanted to celebrate the news with a match on Space Racer. Lee agreed, with the two mothers saying they would prepare a celebration lunch.

Within the black confines of the games room, Tom booted the device up and created a single screen with the Lightmorph technology. He dragged two chairs to be in front of it.

"No virtual reality today, then?" Lee asked.

"I want to talk without the headpieces," Tom stated.

"Okay…"

Tom heard the uncertainty in his friend's voice and got straight to the point.

"Why wouldn't you ask me about something as big as this? Why surprise me with it?"

"I did want to surprise you with it, hence why I waited until the official announcement before saying anything. But I knew you would try to back down from it, which gave a more realistic reason. That was confirmed when I hinted at it a few days back."

"You… You got me there." Tom knew it was true. He'd backed out of plenty of stuff before. If he wasn't careful, he'd probably end up backing out of his dream of being an explorer as well. "I just… This is definitely something to get used to."

Tom had loaded the game and Lee had grabbed a controller. Tom then selected a randomised four races and began the event.

He still wanted to talk over the finer details, though. And as the racing continued, that's just what they did.

"You knew what he'd done," Casey said.

Kerry understood it wasn't a question. She had known about Lee entering Tom for the SRC, and she knew the two would be fine. Casey was a worrier. It was her calling.

And Kerry had a knack for being reassuring.

"The two will be together throughout the event. Lee knew that. It was part of the reason why he entered Tom."

"To... help?"

"Mostly, but because it will be an experience for both of them and great training toward their master licences." Kerry could tell Casey was getting worried again, and so added, "Tom will be great at this. He knows what he's doing."

"But Tom's right. What about the money? We can put some toward them, but it won't be enough on its own. Not for the best equipment possible."

"They don't need the best. Just good enough to compete."

Kerry checked on the food that was cooking in the oven after a few seconds of silence. When she stood back up, Casey asked another question.

"Do you think we should listen for the other competitors while they're playing games?"

Kerry drew a line through the black material on one of the surfaces and pulled up a screen of light to seven inches high. She quickly navigated to the live update of competitors announced.

"There have been twelve more announced since we've been in here. Eight are new entrants, two were entrants of the previous event, and two others are returning from the '70 and '75 events." She scrolled down a bit further. "It looks like there might be sixty in total."

She looked round to Casey upon saying that, and saw again the worried expression.

"What if he doesn't get through the qualifier? That many people..."

"I believe he can do it. So should you."

"I do! It's just the concern I have for him."

"You care for him very much. He knows that. He also knows if he does get hurt you will be there for him. I don't think he'll be taking many risks."

Casey didn't say anything more. Kerry had a feeling she was reassured, but would still worry.

It was her calling, after all.

"In celebration of the competitor announcements, it seems games rooms around the country are getting ready for mini-tournaments on Space Racer. From what we've been hearing, there will be free race competitions as well as full paid tournaments. Both are lasting for the two weeks of the holiday remaining, so get in while you can."

Pyra Summers of Radio Racer [19/2-0085]

It had been a full day after the announcement of the competitors, and Lee was looking forward to getting out for the day. He'd checked out the local games room – the community centre for gaming enthusiasts – the day before, asking if they could run a special event if the competitor for this town were to come in. The owners of the place knew the two, and said they would arrange a special event for this day. Lee didn't know what that event would be, but was interested in seeing what they had planned.

The traffic as ever was quiet in the north side of the town. Lee preferred it that way. The town was located near a large area of field as large as the city joined to Saltare's west. The planners for the town had originally only meant for the south side to be what it became, but the north side was added so the population of the town could be increased. And it had allowed another entry point into the space yard from the main route. As well as a college and a new shopping centre.

Walking through the parkland, Lee took the long way to reach Tom's house. Another good thing about the north side of the town was that almost half of it was greenery, which meant there were two other routes he could have taken.

Upon reaching the gated entrance of the Hughs' household, Lee sent the code to it from his PMD. He looked left and right to see who was around, then quickly entered. The Hughs owned a slightly smaller overall land area than that of the Johnson's, but the landing pad of both were very similar in size. If anything, the land his family owned was larger than what they needed, but it was best to be prepared for visiting relatives or friends that wanted to stay the night.

Mrs. Hughs answered the main door to the house quickly, having been alerted to his arrival from the gate. Inside, Tom was within the lounge, watching a film.

"You interested in heading to the games room in town?" Lee asked.

"Why not the one here?" Tom questioned, not looking away from the film.

"You can prove how good a champion is meant to be."

Now Tom looked away from the film. "You've arranged something else." He didn't look angry. He looked as though he was hiding a fire of competitive spirit.

"If you turn up, there's something special they have planned."

"I'm good to go right now."

Tom quickly fled and returned a minute later. He hefted his own PMD before pocketing it, saying as he did, "Did you get any details on the event?"

"There's definitely tournaments of Space Racer going on, so maybe they'll treat you as a returning champion. I have no idea."

After a quick goodbye to Mrs. Hughs, the two were back out and walking along the southern greenery route to reach the games room near the middle-east of the town. They were able to see the high-speed traffic flying through. Some dropped below to the slow lane so they could exit to the side routes, and as the two reached the games room Lee saw one of the vehicles that had dropped turn into the route they had just left.

Once inside, the two reported to the reception.

"And so, the prospective champion is here," the man said. "We've had single races going on while we waited, but now you're here we can begin."

He led them into the black area where a few screens of light were visible. A larger screen off to the side showed a map of where the racers were, along with small views of what each person within the games were watching. To the right of the black area was the bar, serving food and drink. Another screen of light stretched to the ceiling facing this area to allow those in the seating area to watch the games.

Once the race was complete and the lights faded out, the man called for all to gather so he could announce something.

"I'm sure you heard or saw the announcement of the competitors for the Championship," he said. "We have one here in our town. As such, today will be an event that anyone can enter, and we're raising the stakes. An entry fee is required to enter. It'll be our prospective champion in every game, with whoever enters playing against him. If he loses, the pot of money will be halved and equally given to those who beat him. At the end of the event, in six hours' time, whatever is in the pot will go to our prospective champion. The game is currently updating with new routes which will be placed in the rotation, so this will be new for everyone.

"The event will begin once the update is confirmed to be on our systems."

Those gathered started talking to each other, looking at Tom. A few even talked to Tom, who started showing some of his nervousness around new people.

Lee thought on what had been said, and what Tom had previously said about why he won on the game. Let's see if that really is true.

Lee indicated he was heading for the bar to get drinks. He claimed a table once he had them, and Tom joined him a minute later.

"I'm not so sure about this," Tom said. "I'm going to show myself up. You know how much I've talked about being the best while here before."

"I'll make this easy for you then," Lee said. "I'll join in for the first race."

"Really?"

"It'll be good to play against others again. And this will be the first chance to try out the new routes."

"Wonder how many new ones there are?"

"I couldn't really guess. There's been new developments recently, so I expect a lot of that will be included."

"Anyone wanting to enter the first race, please head over to the reception and stake your claim," an announcement rang out.

Lee quickly headed over and paid the entry fee of 500 grams. The monetary designation of grams was yet another addition from Suati. Most technological advancements that had been made since the humans had first come to live on the now-named Hortii had come from Suati in some form. It had been expanded on and made into their own thing since.

The first race was to begin shortly, and those who had entered for it were called to the floor. Ten chairs were set up, with one extra being in the centre. The hosts said that one was for Tom, who would be on the floor for all the event.

Lee sat on Tom's right, and the other competitors took the remaining seats.

Headsets on, the light-screens appeared on all four sides, bending inward at the top to create a 'roof' over each player. A controller in hand, Lee looked through the list of 'craft available. He had been right to think new ones would be added, and he had

14

a feeling Tom would be choosing the current latest. Lee felt he might do good with the 'craft Tom normally went for. Selecting the Rotablade, he selected a quick designation code and randomly selected the colour of the 'craft. The screen changed to a view of the hangar the race would start from.

It quickly filled up, with Lee looking at the racer line-up. Tom had indeed chosen the new 'craft, with an interesting designation. C/81mp10n. Lee wondered if it was a pre-made one for him, as he doubted Tom would want to draw attention to himself with what he had previously said.

The racer line-up disappeared from his view, with the sound of the hangar and the slight hum of engines making themselves heard. He was inside the Rotablade, looking out at the hangar. The lights of the mini cruisers flashed, and Lee lifted the 'craft up and increased speed. Tom had quickly built speed up, as had a few of the others. It seemed this new 'craft had the acceleration to make a quick start, but would it be able to handle well? He knew the Rotablade had good handling, and as he shot out of the hangar, he noticed the first light he needed to head for – situated a fair distance away at one of the spires of a cruiser. He built up the speed and gave chase to the leaders.

A flash within the cabin said that he'd passed the checkpoint, but he couldn't see the next. He noticed others turning to the right, and when he looked down at the scanner, he saw that the next one was... behind him and slightly right?

He killed as much forward momentum as he could to flip around to point directly at the checkpoint and reactivated the engines. As he shot forward again, he could see the leaders. Tom was out in front, having somehow noticed the second checkpoint beforehand. Tom passed it first, with two others doing so before Lee reached it. The racers could now see that a second cruiser was underneath the one they had started from. The third checkpoint was placed at the entrance of its hangar, and Lee guessed it was a full-length hangar that would have the fourth checkpoint at the other end.

Once inside the hangar, Lee quickly pushed the Rotablade to dodge to the left to avoid a parked mini cruiser, then all the way to its right side to avoid a line of them. He noticed Tom up above dodging around the girders that had been placed to stop racers from easily using the high route. It appeared he was the only one doing so.

At the end of the hangar, the fifth checkpoint was at another cruiser in the distance. A warning flashed up saying the checkpoint required a landing within. Inside the hangar, this cruiser had limited facilities. It was open to space, with the sixth checkpoint requiring a flight through the structure to the rear. The rest of the checkpoints led the way back to the starting cruiser.

Lee took a quick look at his position to find he was still fourth. He wasn't doing so bad. He wasn't getting top three, but it was better than he had been expecting. He slowed as he entered the hangar to work his way to the starting area. He settled the Rotablade to land and waited for the others to finish.

The light-screens faded, and Lee took the headset off. He stood up and heard Tom being congratulated on his first victory.

When Lee had arrived and told him of this opportunity to race, Tom had been apprehensive at first. As he'd said, he could show himself up and make himself look bad in front of those he usually competed with while here.

Now though, with five of the six hours of this event through with, he felt he was doing good. He had got through those reservations and had been congratulated on victory a lot. There wasn't any point in which he had faltered. Plenty of people had signed up for rematches against him, but at no point had he lost. He imagined that the prize pot was looking pretty large, and he was happy about that. He was happier about getting to talk to everyone he raced against, and though deep down it felt as though he wanted to run, he stood his ground to chat. He knew some of his awkwardness in interacting with people was showing through, but he couldn't help it, and no-one had questioned him on it.

He finished talking with two of those he had just raced and watched them out the door. Someone new walked in and turned to the reception. Tom headed to the table Lee had managed to keep, and sat down to take a drink.

"You're really on fire with this thing," Lee commented. "I doubt you'll be losing anything during this last hour."

"Thanks for the vote of confidence," Tom said.

"Just one question. That first race."

Tom had a quick think back upon mention of it and felt he knew what the question would be before it was asked.

"How did you-"

"-predict where the second checkpoint would be?" Tom finished the question. "There was nothing out in front and the cruiser was positioned in a way that made it look as though a checkpoint would be placed on that second spire. The way a long sweeping curve on a ground track would be presented, but with no way to cut across."

"You have a gift for noticing these things."

"It's just observation skills, really. Isn't that something everyone needs?"

As Lee replied, Tom turned back to the reception area. The female he had seen walk in had moved off to stand to the side of the black area where challengers were meant to meet.

He said, "That woman over there where the challengers wait." He waited for Lee to look. "She has the air of a champion, wouldn't you say?"

"Scared of some serious competition?" Lee teased.

"Nah. I'll probably beat her like I have everyone else. What I mean is – she has the air of someone who has actually been in a Championship before."

"Maybe she wants to race a new generation competitor," Lee stated.

"On a game?" Tom couldn't stop the sceptic tone from escaping as he said it.

"If she can't enter, this is the easiest way of sizing up the new lot. In fact, I'll enter again. It'll be fun, and hopefully I can put some of what I've seen here to use."

As Lee bounded off for the reception, Tom let his thoughts drift to the previous hours of racing. It had been easy, but he couldn't expect this level of competition during the Championship. As he progressed through, the challengers would drop until only the best remained. If he could get that far, he would consider himself happy to have been in the final. Even if not, it would be great to have taken part. He didn't give himself any hope he would win, as he wanted that to come as a complete surprise to himself.

The challengers for the next race were called, and Tom settled himself within the spot that had been his for these past five hours. At first, he had found the designation code resembling champion to be slightly unsettling, as it would add to his shame upon a loss. But after all these victories, he hadn't minded and felt good about it being there.

He really did feel like a champion.

Tom took a quick look left and right before the light-screens appeared and surrounded him within the game's environment. Lee was seated two seats away to his left, and next to him was the challenger he was sure had previously been in a Championship.

The race began, and he quickly took note of several identifying features that would alert him to the track they were on. He knew this one, having been on it quite a few times. There had been six new tracks added, and each one he had quickly noted the surrounding area for where the checkpoints might be.

The female had shot off the same as he had, and it seemed she would be some competition. That was fine by him. He could do with some.

As it turned out, she might have been fast off the line but was no expert in racing. He had a thought that maybe she was guessing her way through the controls, and while she was an expert at real 'craft, she had little experience on the game. It would explain several of the small mistakes she had made.

No-one else on the field gave much in the way of a challenge, and he finished first. He watched as everyone else finished, and was surprised to see that Lee had come third. When the light-screens dispersed, the female quickly left without saying a word. Tom ignored that and had a quick chat with the others.

After six more races, the event was called to a close. Those who remained gathered to hear the final tally of the prize pot. Over the six hours, 200,000 grams had been raised. It was an impressive amount but was still way short of what would be needed for new spacecraft. A used one could just about be squeezed into that amount, but a mini cruiser would still be needed. There was still a long time until the Championship started, but he wanted as much time as possible to train in a real spacecraft. He might indeed have a trainee licence, but it had been a while since he had last been in one for any serious amount of time.

He left with Lee, talking about the day but keeping quiet about his doubts.

He had a feeling there was something Lee was keeping quiet about himself.

"I can see myself doing well in a Championship, but I wouldn't ever want to enter one. It's a different experience to be the one who gets all the news and can talk about it. Seeing the bigger picture before anyone else. Being a competitor would reduce that down drastically, and I live for the bigger picture. That was certainly a good question, and we'll have another after this next set of songs."

Pyra Summers of Radio Racer [23/2-0085]

A few days had passed since the two had reported about the event at the games room, and Kerry was happy about the money they had earned through it.

They had since got it into their heads that maybe they could continue the winning streak, and so had set about entering into other paid tournaments the games room was now hosting. From what she had heard, Lee had started improving enough to get into the top three. She had also heard him once say it couldn't beat the real thing.

Money had been coming from members of both families, and even some friends had given some to the goal of getting better equipment. That total from the games room had doubled in the few days, continuing to grow with the wins Tom was racking up in the tournaments.

It was a wonder they still let him compete, she found herself thinking. He must have won every single one he'd entered.

She looked up at the sky to see the darkness creeping in. In an hour, it would be fully dark. By then, she had a feeling the two would have returned with whatever money they had won for the day.

Casey returned from the kitchen with some more drinks, and they sipped on them while waiting. Casey had insisted on getting the drinks this time, even though it was Kerry's property. She guessed that Casey was still worrying, possibly over what would happen if Tom finally lost a race. Kerry knew it wouldn't happen on Space Racer. He was just too good at it. In the Championship, though...

That was the problem.

Kerry's PMD chirped from the table with the screen lighting up. She pressed on the screen to activate the connection.

"We've finally been barred from the competitions," Lee's voice sounded. "We've still won quite a decent amount of money, but Tom's insistence on getting into them and winning has started to put other people off. It was a friendly encounter, don't worry."

Kerry couldn't help but smile at hearing that. She looked to Casey, whose expression had gone back to visibly worried, before looking back down and replying.

"I'm sure you can find another way to get some more, but if it comes to it, I'm sure the family accounts have enough to top the amount off."

"Pretty sure we're near enough a million now," Lee said quietly, and Kerry pictured him having looked around him before saying that. He might have been cheerful and a bit of a goof, but he was never careless.

"I'll take a look at some prices and see what extras I can add to the total. Tom will be staying here for the night, so return quickly."

"We're having a bit to eat in the northern shards sector before returning. See you soon."

The connection cut and Kerry looked up.

"Everything's fine," she said, seeing that the worried expression on Casey's face hadn't vanished. Quickly she picked the PMD up and scanned through some prices for spacecraft. "They can easily get a mini cruiser new if they settle for a used Galaxy model 'craft. Of course, the 'craft is the most important part…" She quickly did another search. "There's a few used mini cruisers available, so they can certainly fit a new 'craft in with the amount they have."

"It still doesn't seem enough, though," Casey said. "Not if they want to make this a regular thing."

"Leave the decisions up to them, and trust them to make the right ones." She gave a friendly smile, hoping to ease Casey's mind. Another thing to help with that would be keeping busy. "They're eating out, so we should think about eating something, too."

The two mothers were finishing their food when the boys arrived. Lee was holding a drink and took a sip from it as he sat down. Tom, Casey noted, seemed lost in thought.

"You are sure we can get everything we need?" Tom asked, and it seemed he had asked the same thing while they had been out, considering Lee's firm reply.

"We have enough."

A silence fell that Kerry broke.

"You have a million?" she asked.

"But can no longer get any more through the tournaments," Lee replied. "However, I don't think we'd need much more for what we need."

"The fact is you can get that stuff and move to the next phase."

Casey thought back to what was said earlier and spoke up.

"If you need any more, I can give it to you. After all, if it helps you to get better gear for the Championship, it will be worth it. It'll just be sitting there, otherwise."

"Thanks," Lee said. Tom added, "We'll head out tomorrow and take a look for ourselves. If we need more, we'll be sure to call."

"Now that we've sorted that," Kerry announced, "we can take it easy and take our minds off it for tonight. I suggest a game on the table once we've cleared things up."

The Johnson's certainly had a lot more space than was needed, Casey had always found, and it seemed that even they didn't seem to know what to do with it all. The dining room where they currently sat was located west of the kitchen, with the only entrance being to the kitchen. There were two lounge areas, with the group moving from the kitchen to the one opposite.

In here, a table sat in the middle with chairs around it. The Lightmorph technology was built into this table, and as everyone sat down Kerry pulled up a game of Four Point Fight.

The game progressed with the usual banter, with no talk on what was to happen tomorrow. Casey was wondering how the two would train for the Championship once back at specialist school, but they had the weekends for that. The two were focusing on the geography and history of this system and the one the humans had inhabited before. She wasn't interested in such things in such detail but knew the boys had fun with it, just as with the flying lessons.

"And with that," Lee proclaimed, selecting one of his pieces and directing it over to the last of Tom's, "I think you'll find no-one else can win."

Casey looked at the board. With Tom's last piece taken out, he was no longer in the game. She only had one piece left, though

Kerry had two. Lee also had two pieces remaining, but he'd left himself open. It was just whether either of the two other players could get lucky enough to take him.

Casey spun the number reel, landing her a four. She quickly took the opportunity to take the open piece of Lee's. Kerry had a spun a two, and backed both of her pieces away. Lee was unfortunate to spin a one, which brought a slightly concerned look to his face. He moved his piece a space, eyeing the board as he did.

Casey looked on the board as well and noticed that if she was lucky, she'd be able to take his last piece. Spinning for a number, she got a two. It wasn't enough to reach Lee, but she could start to make her way toward Kerry's pieces and try to take both.

Kerry noticed the move, and with the four she spun she backed one of her pieces away while advancing with the other. Lee was unlucky yet again with another one, allowing Kerry to take that piece and take him out of the game.

"I think you'll find you've just lost," Kerry jibed at Lee.

"I admit I got too ahead of myself," he admitted without his smile faltering.

The game didn't last much longer after that, with Kerry managing to place her pieces in strategic points to make Casey lose.

"That was a fun game," Kerry said. She swiped the board away and looked at the time. "Time to get some sleep, I think."

Kerry showed Tom to his room, Casey having chosen them earlier upon first arriving and putting their bags inside them.

Casey wondered what the two boys would come back with after their visit to the space yard. She didn't know much about the various models but knew they would.

And she'd be impressed with whatever they came back with.

"A few of the competitors have been seen up here in space, but whether they're using the 'craft they'll enter the competition with seems unlikely. No doubt modifications will be taking place throughout to make them better for the owner. With a total of sixty competitors soon to be getting up there, it's a good thing that space is infinite."

Pyra Summers of Radio Racer [24/2-0085]

Tom walked side-by-side with Lee on the way to the STRDC Spaceyard – as it was officially named. The company name was dropped to just call it the spaceyard. STRDC was an abbreviation for the Space Technology Research and Development Corporation, who had created the first spacecraft, mini cruiser, and cruiser back on Earth. They had then used them to travel the galaxy as part of the first exploration guild of Earth.

When they returned with tales on new experiences and improved technology, the invite became open for people to move to the second base of the STRDC to make it a true living colony. An entire cruiser had been filled with people, and when they returned to the system of the Suati, it was to find even more technological advancements had been made.

The advancements given to the humans from the Suati meant various new spacecraft could be made. New mini cruisers also started to be made, and the spaceyard was opened to the public for sales and also adapted to include ground vehicles. A new spaceyard was then opened in the south of the country to allow a wider range of sales to take place.

The spaceyard itself was nothing but vehicles and buildings as Tom looked around, feeling a nervous excitement that it was now time to take this to the next step.

To get his own spacecraft.

Lee walked out of the entrance hut that those who arrived on foot used to announce themselves, and indicated a larger building next to a row of Rotablade 'craft.

Inside, everything was a light yellow, with the partitions to the right being a darker shade. Lights indicated which were active and which of those were free.

The two walked to one of the available areas and looked in. Tom instantly recognised the person waiting for them, but it was Lee who spoke first.

"Hello, Matt. I see you've been moved to sales."

"Ar, it's good to see you two again," Matt replied. "You both been busy by the sounds of it. A competitor, eh?" he added, turning to Tom. "After seeing what you've done during the training sessions, I know you'll do good."

Matt had been the tutor for them both for a year as they progressed through the levels needed to set up their readiness for the master licence. He had then been replaced by a new tutor, and they hadn't heard anything about where he might have ended up.

"Thanks," Tom said. "But it all depends on how good of a 'craft I can get."

"Well, we can easily set you up. I'll take you out. Much better to look in person than just on a screen."

Matt led the two out and around the partition to another exit. This allowed them to get into the heart of the spaceyard – which was full of all manner of vehicles.

"No doubt you've been on Space Racer to see the new addition we've got," Matt queried. "Depending on how much you've got, you can have one."

"Just over a million," Lee said while Tom felt himself get slightly embarrassed. A million wouldn't be good enough, he knew it.

"Normally, that would, but I know you'll also be needing a mini cruiser. However, I know you two well enough to show you something, and hopefully you'll accept the offer I'm about to give."

Tom was interested at that and started wondering at the possibilities. The three walked through yet another building into an area that felt as though it was restricted.

Through another door back outside revealed a large boxy vehicle painted in yellow.

"Say hello to the double-size super cruiser," Matt announced.

A few seconds passed before Tom got over the shock to utter, "What?"

"A double-size super cruiser," Matt repeated. "It's a terrible name, but that's because it doesn't really have one. I'll let you in and we can talk more about it."

The three walked over to it, with Matt pressing a button revealed by pulling back a covering. A small shunk sounded as a climbing step pushed itself out from underneath the entrance. The docking grate was currently closed, with the entrances for people on both sides of it.

Matt climbed up first and pressed another button, and after a second the door slid into its housing. Climbing up the rest of the way, he allowed entrance for both Tom and Lee.

The hangar bay was decked in a light steel-blue with a darker shade of blue being used for the walls.

"The double-size super cruiser," Matt said for the third time. "So-called because that is a combination of the two names used to describe it while building it. During development, it was either known as the super cruiser or mini double-size. When it was complete, it still didn't have a name, so that's when it was named the DSSC. The only one that's been built, as a prototype."

"You were hoping to get it tested during the championship, weren't you?" Lee asked.

"We were hoping to be able to get one of our staff into the Championship to test it, but that plan never went anywhere and now it's probably going to just sit here and put the whole mini cruiser 2.0 project on hold."

"And that's where we come in," Tom suddenly said. "You called us here to see if we'd like to try it out."

Matt told them to follow him, taking them to the rear end of the DSSC, where a ramp allowed them access to the floor above. Out of that room and into a corridor, they followed this into the control bay. Four seats set out in a square and all pointed to the viewshield, the controls were neatly set out across the front of it.

"You know how to control a mini cruiser?" Matt asked.

"I know," Lee said. "I haven't had any experience, but I've read enough that it should be easy enough."

Lee took the pilot's seat with Matt beside him. Tom was behind Lee.

"Start easy, and just lift off," Matt instructed.

Lee managed it easily. The DSSC slowly rose, and from the sensor that Tom could see beside him, they had risen to the eight-meter safety limit.

"Before we continue, do you have a place we could head to and land?" Matt asked.

"Both of our houses should have landing pads large enough," Lee said.

"And do you want a Space Kicker to try out?" Matt asked, referring to the latest 'craft available to buy.

"Yes," Tom readily said.

"I'll call one up, then. Docking grate control is that one there." Matt pointed the control out as he called a colleague from his PMD.

Within a minute, a second colleague was on board with the Space Kicker now sat in the hangar.

"Take us over to your house then, and get ready to send the acceptance code to your gate."

"Tom, you can handle that," Lee said.

In no time at all the DSSC was hovering over the Johnson property, and Tom was sending the code while Lee was on call to his mom telling her not to worry about what was about to land.

The code accepted, the DSSC landed with Lee having to only make some small adjustments for it to comfortably fit on the landing pad, and the three walked back to the hangar bay.

Now Tom could admire the Space Kicker in person. It had looked a good design from the game, but in person it looked a lot better. Shaped pretty much like a slice of pizza, most of it was an isosceles triangle with a small part of the point removed to create a small straight. The rear had been pulled out a bit to make two straights instead of one. The canopy shield was shaped like a small version of this irregular pentagon, but it functioned the same as the usual bubble canopies.

Lee and Matt were at one of the exits with the door retracted. Tom's mom had just been helped up inside, and Lee's mom followed a second later.

"This is huge," Mrs. Hughs commented.

"It's great," Mrs. Johnson added. "But how much is it going to come t- Is that the Space Kicker as well?" She ran over to stand next to Tom and started to admire the 'craft. "The dark blue looks real good on it," she said as she started to walk around it. "Modern canopy... Those have to be modern engines... It all looks good, but the question of cost remains."

"The STRDC are happy to loan the DSSC to the two for the duration of the Space Race Championship," Matt stated. "The Space Kicker will come to just under a million grams, which the two say they can cover."

He said he'd give everyone a quick tour. The two forward rooms of the lower level were large but empty. The starboard aft room was smaller than the two forward ones, but also empty. The port aft room was where the ramp up to the second level was located, along with a few seats. The upper floor lounge area was slightly larger and also held a few seats, this time with a table. There were three other rooms up here – not counting the control cabin and engine access.

All of them were back to the hangar, where a discussion was taking place about things that could be improved about it. Matt had said hardly any of the rooms were furnished because they had wanted to just focus on the build of the thing. Now it was going to be getting some actual use, fittings and furnishing could be added.

"Those forward rooms seem out of place," Lee said. "If the docking grate is open, those doors are going to be closed. If a problem arises, there's no way get over to the other side."

"We had thought of that, but never got further with the planning. If anything, one of those rooms could be made into a workshop for mobile 'craft repairs, but we're at a loss for what else they could be."

"I'm sure as we get a feel for it, we'll come to understand what could be put there."

"And speaking of getting a feel for things, how would you like to take a proper test spin of it? And Tom could get a feel for the Space Kicker and see if it's a good fit for him."

Tom looked up at that and felt excitement bloom. "Of course, I would," he enthusiastically said.

"We taking it up to space?" Lee asked. "Or just to high atmos?"

"I think staying within the atmosphere would be a good idea to start," Matt said. "If Tom would like to get into the Space Kicker, we'll take off and tell you when you can go."

"Okay."

Tom watched as the group moved back to the aft to take the ramp back up. He then quickly hopped onto the Space Kicker and pulled the lever back to open the canopy. It lifted three quarters upward, then slid over the last quarter that would always remain fixed. Once inside, he pressed a button to bring the canopy back into closed position. He knew the lever was covered now, and wouldn't be able to be used unless he removed the lock.

A small vibration hit him as the DSSC's engines fired up again. As he waited, he looked at the controls and familiarised himself with the layout. It was simple enough to understand. A lever to control speed, along with the buttons to set a maximum, placed above and below the screen that showed both current speed and set maximum. The control stick on the left that handled pitch and roll. The control stick on the right managed the strafing on both the Y and Z axis. Other buttons he was less familiar with, but he wouldn't be needing them.

"Tom? You receiving?" Lee asked through the speakers.

Tom managed to find the right controls for the communications and activated his own microphone. "Yup. All set here."

"Good. The port docking grate is lifting now. Head out and have fun."

Tom used the right control stick to lift the Space Kicker, remembering he needed to retract the landing claws but failing to remember which button it was. He saw a light on the board was flashing at him, and next to it was a switch. He flicked that and heard the slight mechanised noise as the landing claws lifted into their housings.

He set the speed with the buttons and flung the lever forward. He'd forgotten how fun it was to fly for real, and as the enclosed hangar disappeared from around him, he quickly snapped a roll. He could see the ocean below him and was surprised how fast that DSSC was. It would certainly be a real help for some of the challenges of the Championship.

If he knew what they were.

He had a few more minutes flying around, marvelling at the Space Kicker's own sense of speed. When Lee called for him to come back in, Tom flew back to the DSSC and ran a ring around it before settling beside the hangar opening. He strafed the 'craft inside and landed.

"Inside," he reported. "What a great little 'craft. It's mine, for sure."

"Great," Lee exclaimed. "Stay inside while we land, and then payment and such can be handled."

Tom felt confident that he had a good chance of winning. He had no idea if Matt was showing favouritism to his two former trainees, but this was the best possible combination he could imagine. He still didn't hold any real hopes of winning the Championship, but he knew his chances were high for such a victory.

CHAPTER 2 – NEW EXPERIENCES

"The Basic 'craft can work for this Championship but being the oldest model available it would need some serious upgrades to make it a worthy competitor. From what I've seen around, there are a few that have been flying around in training. I just can't see any of them being that great when it comes to the racing."

Pyra Summers of Radio Racer [31/2-0085]

The sale of the Space Kicker had been made, and though they were allowed to keep the DSSC parked at either of their houses, Lee had to take it over to the spaceyard to pick someone up each day of the week so they could see him in action. He didn't mind, as having a co-pilot on a cruiser – even one this small – was always a good idea.

Tom had been training within the atmosphere, but this time they had gone beyond the ocean and to the desert that made up the other half of the planet. They were able to stay out for most of the day due to supplies loaded in the lower aft rooms. Lee was grateful to note that Tom was picking up quickly on more advanced skills. He was able to pull them off almost all of the time, and Lee hoped he'd be able to do the same while in space without a true point of reference for which way was down.

On the final day before the education break ended, one of the spaceyard workers had said they'd keep the DSSC for when they were next able to train, and in the meantime keep working on improving it. The Space Kicker had been landed at the Johnson property, but Tom hadn't wanted to end the training yet.

While Lee and Mrs. Johnson watched from their garden, Tom had taken the Space Kicker out to the open field and pulled off a series of loops, flips, and spins. At one point he had even dropped below where the two watchers could see him, and for a second Lee had feared Tom had tried something daring and failed to pull it off, but then the Space Kicker had risen again, and Tom had pulled in for a landing. The two had talked about the training and what they would do next into the night, but knew they would be back to school the next day.

And today, they walked to the specialist school. It was the first time they had been here since the Championship announcement, and while a few of their classmates had been at the games room, Lee felt a big deal would be made about it now everyone was together.

Standard education had been an okay experience for him. He'd found it fun. Advanced education had been a trying time during his second year; he had got through it with Tom – as they had both been together for most of that time.

Upon entering the room of their class, they were greeted with applause. Classmates were hoping the best for them. They wanted to know what spacecraft Tom had, what sort of things he was training for. It was again attention he usually avoided, though he was handling it better than before, Lee noted.

It took a while before the session started, but occasionally questions were still asked of Tom. The next session was a free-talk session, where students could talk with their tutors. Tom and Lee were called in for a discussion about how they were planning to manage their time training with their education, and they had said the training wouldn't disrupt the time they spent in school.

For the rest of the break, Lee made sure Tom read up on all of the Space Kicker's controls. There were a few tricks Lee was sure Tom had forgotten about, and he wanted to test him later on.

The boys, as Kerry had expected, arrived as soon as school had finished, and Tom had sat in the Space Kicker and lifted the 'craft in the air for some more training.

Kerry heard Lee speak instructions to Tom, and Tom managed to perform them with only a bit of fault.

"Pull up and try it again," Lee said patiently. "Remember, as soon as you drop pull back on the left stick. Make it a quick one-two."

The move was meant as a combat dodge. As soon as a pursuer saw you move down, more often than not they would track. That allowed you a second to quickly pull up and away from the point where the lasers flew. Kerry knew there were other variations of the move, including a boost back up after dropping.

Normally a 'craft would have had engines running around it, hidden within its body to control the varying directions. As such, they had been a meter or more larger than the Space Kicker. The Space Kicker was the first to use the new technology that – if she remembered right – were called repulse-pads. They were more efficient to use, allowing the exact amount of power needed to be transferred and used to give pinpoint accuracy of movement. She had followed the development of this 'craft through her husband, who had given her updates on how it was progressing since he had been planning on buying one himself.

As she watched Tom and his Space Kicker thundering through the air, she felt that pang of wanting her husband back. She was sure he'd have loved seeing his son and his best friend's son working together, as she was sure the two were doing wherever they were.

"Alright!" Lee cheered. Tom's whoop of joy sounded through the speaker of the PMD.

Tom had successfully performed a roll and snapped to the side mid-roll to push himself skyward first time.

"Can we try some faster stuff?" Tom asked. "I want to see how fast this thing really goes."

"We'll need the DSSC for that, and I'm not getting it back until the weekend," Lee stated. "I've got something lined up when we do get it back that you'll enjoy, but for now, that was a good session. Come back in."

Once Tom had landed, the two said quick byes to each other and Tom left. Lee turned to face her with a smile on his face.

"He's doing as well as I expected," he said. "I bet he doesn't realise that, but I really don't want to tease him about his being good only in the game talk he was spouting during the holiday."

"He'll realise once you get out in space. Which..." Kerry looked up to see the darkening sky and the shining light twinkles of the stars. "You'll be doing this weekend?" she queried.

"After that fun thing I mentioned, yes."

"Let's get in and I'll make us something to eat," she said, guiding him inside.

But not before one last look at the stars. Fight well, but be safe, she wished, hoping that wherever her husband was he knew she was thinking of him.

"We're starting today off simple enough. It's the weekend, there's some tunes lined up ready for a relaxing atmosphere, and then we'll be breaking out a surprise in the form of a guest. She's been taking over the radio waves with her singing talent, and she is gracing us with an appearance all afternoon. This is sure to be an exciting day."

Pyra Summers of Radio Racer [35/2-0085]

Tom had continued going to Lee's house for the rest of that week to fit a bit of training in, then arriving home for food talking excitedly about what he had been doing and what he hoped to do. Casey listened to the stories but carefully chose her words when replying. She never wanted to make it sound like she was trying to restrict him in his actions, but she wanted to know he would be safe.

One day, she would finally stop worrying about everything. She had to keep telling herself that. She knew she went overboard, but could never help it.

At the start of the weekend, she felt a sense of unease. It would be the first time Tom had ever been up to space. She wanted him to be safe while up there. She knew he could take care of himself, but it was a weird experience of first amazement and then a sense of disorientation that you could never be rid of. Or at least, that's how it had felt to her during her first experience in space. She had a feeling Tom would handle it better.

"Enjoy yourselves," Kerry said to the two boys, who were sitting on the open starboard hangar entrance. She and Lee had arrived in the DSSC ready for Tom and Lee's weekend training. This time it would be the Johnsons staying at the Hughs' household for the weekend.

"We will," Lee answered. "And we'll be safe. Actually," he looked to Casey then to the garage behind her, "you wouldn't happen to have any spacesuits, would you? Safety first, and all that."

Casey quickly turned and went inside, looking around the shelves and boxes. She emerged a minute later with a spacesuit in each hand. Both were grey in colour, with a black box attached to the back. She handed them up to the two, with each grabbing hold of one.

"We'll be back in a few hours," Lee said.

"That should be plenty of time to fill with some shopping around Crystal sector," Kerry said. "Keeps us out as well."

Casey felt she'd much rather be out, and so agreed. She needed to stock up on a few things anyway.

The two boys retreated inside the DSSC, with the docking grate closing over the hangar entrance a short while later. The super cruiser then lifted as the two mothers watched, and once above the eight-meter limit, it shot away.

"They'll be fine," Kerry reassured. "Now come on. Crystal sector awaits."

Tom watched from the co-pilot seat as the DSSC slowly started rising toward cloud cover. He was surprised when it stopped. The spacesuits that his mom had given them were on the seats behind them, and Tom wondered what they were doing with them if they weren't heading out to space.

He questioned Lee on that and got the reply that they would soon.

"First we're going to do something that'll test your skills," Lee stated. "You'll be in the Space Kicker, matching speed with the open hangar. You'll then be trying to land inside at speed."

Tom's eyes widened upon hearing that. "Are you sure I can do it?" he asked with scepticism. Even despite that, he could feel excitement at being able to try it.

"Sure," Lee said cheerily. "Just remember how to effectively use the right stick. Get down below and into the Kicker and let's try it out."

Tom lifted from his seat and headed down below. Once inside the Space Kicker, Lee said the portside docking grate would remain open while they practised.

Tom lifted his 'craft up and out of the hangar. Once a short distance away, he flipped over to watch the DSSC start to accelerate away. It turned and followed a wide path to pull up beside him.

"Okay," Lee said. "Remember, the key is matching our speeds when the time comes to enter. We need to keep updating each other of our speed, otherwise, this could go wrong."

Tom looked down at his shield to see it at full. It would handle anything that hit it, but once it ran out, he'd have to be careful until it could be recharged. He didn't want to have emptied it in just one day.

He affirmed and told Lee to start up first. He watched as the DSSC started moving away, then pushed the lever all the way forward to bring his 'craft up to speed.

He increased his speed slightly to catch up with the DSSC, and the gap between the two vehicles slowly decreased. An exchange of speeds was given, allowing Tom to give it a bit more speed to quickly close the gap, then reduce speed slightly to be matching the DSSC.

Tom nudged the right stick to the right, and slowly he edged inside. He managed to get to the middle with no trouble, activate the docking claws, and put it down while reducing the speed to zero.

"That was easy," he complained. "I thought it would be harder."

"This was just a test," Lee said. "The harder part comes now. I'm reducing speed a bit to let you out, then we'll do this again while adding in a new factor."

Tom lifted off, managing to just avoid clipping the side of the DSSC as he shot out of the hangar, then turned and matched speed with the DSSC, which then dropped.

"Come and get inside now," Lee said, and Tom could hear the slight goading that worked to encourage him.

Pushing the left stick forward, he tilted down and manoeuvred to the side of the DSSC. It was shuddering slightly in the wind, making it harder to be accurate. Tom increased his speed and overshot where he needed to be. Quickly correcting that, he made to enter inside, but the DSSC pulled up. It took a second for him to realise why.

Pulling the left stick toward him while at the same time dropping his speed, he avoided splashing straight into the ocean.

Rolling himself the right way as he increased speed and flew upward again, Lee called to him that he needed to be quicker, but for this time they'd be rising slightly higher. The warning light telling him to swap to the atmos power drive appeared, which meant they were nearing the highest point the kilo power drive was capable of reaching.

"Let's try this again," Lee stated. "Keep alert at all times for any changes that might be coming. Begin."

The DSSC tilted down and tried as best as possible to keep a straight diagonal down to the surface. Tom quickly set to match that line and keep his speed. He inched forward as best as he could, and when within access of the hangar quickly nudged himself inside.

Turbulence struck, and the Space Kicker hit the floor before Tom could quickly correct for it. He activated the landing claws once pulled away and quickly slammed down to the floor again. This time, the magnetics within the claws held him in place.

He felt the DSSC level out and slow to a stop.

"Very good," Lee said. "A slight loss of reaction to the sudden change, but you handled it well enough."

Tom let out a ragged breath before answering. He felt himself slightly shaking. "Once more," he called. "I can do it without touching anything."

It took two more attempts before he did what he claimed he could do, and the only reason he had failed was the turbulence. There was no way of anticipating it, so the easiest thing to do was get inside and land as quickly as possible.

"Record time," Lee congratulated. It meant little, but Tom accepted it anyway. "Now we're going to where you want to be. Get out again and activate the atmos power drive."

Tom silently hissed "yes" before acknowledging what Lee had said.

The Space Kicker was out of the hangar fast and was heading up for space before the DSSC had started turning around. The atmos power drive calculated the speed needed to break out of a planet's atmosphere, though all 'craft and cruisers already had the necessary information for Hortii to make that calculation quick. By the time Lee caught up to him, the Space Kicker was ready to break out.

The simple word "go" was said over the communication link, and Tom pumped the lever forward and was pulled back into his seat as the speed of the 'craft rocketed him upward through mists of white. That white then turned back to blue before fading to black.

The atmos power drive swapped back to the kilo power drive, and Tom looked out on space for the first time. The blackness was empty and infinite, and he felt queasy after the trip up. He blinked and looked down at his speed. He had been continuing to travel without realising it. He cut the speed down to zero, then jumped at a slight crackle as communication returned.

"How you feeling?" Lee asked.

"Weird," Tom replied. "Lost in a void."

The DSSC appeared in his field of view with the port entrance of the hangar open. "Get inside and right yourself, then we'll continue."

With something to now focus on, Tom was able to bring the Space Kicker near to the super cruiser to land. Lee told him not to lift the viewshield until he stated, so Tom watched as the docking grate closed. A few more seconds passed before Lee said he could exit the Space Kicker.

As soon as Tom had walked up the ramp, he saw Lee sitting on one of the chairs. He sunk into one facing Lee and asked, "How come you're fine about this?"

"I've already been in space before. Twice now, maybe three. Once was just a short period, but the others were for hours at a time. My dad said being in space is hard at first, but the longer you spend out in the void, the easier it becomes."

"Just like anything else," Tom said. After a few seconds, he added, "I'm ready to head back out."

"Already?" Lee asked in slight disbelief.

"The sooner I start getting used to it, the better."

"Okay."

Tom could hear the uncertainty in his friend's voice, so stated, "I'm fine. I just needed a bit of a rest."

Once back out in space, he felt he was handling it slightly better, and guessed that maybe it was just the transition to space that had upset him. He pulled off a few of the tricks he had been practising in the atmosphere, and found the more he did them, the easier it became to handle the weightlessness that was affecting his movements, though he still struggled with the orientation.

Lee called for him to return, and Tom was able to use the scanner to scout out his position and head to it. He had to spin the 'craft to get it in the right position to enter.

Once inside, he headed for the control bay to see Lee headed for a long cruiser in the distance. Lee looked behind him to see Tom stood looking out the viewshield at the cruiser.

"The pride and joy of Hortii," Lee stated. "The Surveillance Cruiser. And we'll be staying there for something to eat."

Kerry hid her smile as best as she could, looking at the tins of vegetables as she put her PMD away. Lee had just called to say they wouldn't be returning. He'd be treating Tom to a bit of luxury in the Surveillance Cruiser. She didn't want to break the news to Casey just yet and was glad the other hadn't been around to see her take the call.

Crystal sector was so named as the routes that made it had been shaped like a gemstone. To the immediate north and south of this sector were the shards. This sector had once been just one, but the split to three was meant to encourage smaller businesses to open up. It had certainly done that.

Casey came into view with a basket of goods, announcing she was finished and wondering if Kerry had too. Making no mention of Lee's message, she said she had. Having paid for the food, they decided to go somewhere to eat. There was a café the two enjoyed nearby, so with sandwiches in hand the two sat at a table and listened in on the music playing. Occasionally the two talked about what they'd be doing later, and while Casey talked about various games to play once the boys were back, Kerry felt she may as well get it over with.

"They won't be back," she stated. "Lee called earlier to say they'll be spending the night on the Surveillance Cruiser, ready to get out as soon as possible the next day."

"Oh," was all Casey said.

Conversation stopped, and filling the void was the announcer of the radio station giving a dedication to someone who had requested a song. The people sat in the corner clapped as the song started and they all shouted a Happy Birthday to someone sat at that table. Kerry looked around to see six teenagers all in a celebratory and rowdy mood.

"Don't mind them," the server said as he passed. "It's the owner of that shop next door's son and a few friends. He's returned for a few days from the north."

"Farmer, is he?" Kerry asked.

"Yeah. He works hard and provides for his dad well enough. They'll be off once his dad closes for the day to celebrate further." He turned to Casey. "Your son's in this Championship, right?"

"Yes," Casey replied.

"Here's hoping he does well," the server said before walking off.

Kerry looked at the time on her PMD. "We'd best be going, I think."

"You think the boys are enjoying their time on the Sur-C?" Casey asked, using the short form of the Surveillance Cruiser.

"Oh, knowing the number of food courts on it, I'm sure they're enjoying it."

Lee had enjoyed seeing the reaction of Tom to the Surveillance Cruiser's interior. The hangar bay was the standard fare of grey-blue, but it was the width of the cruiser to allow access from both sides. Being built on top of the main body of the cruiser allowed for more space within. Two layers held the guest accommodation, food courts and entertainment venues. Along with being the first place guests to the planet would visit, it also served as a secondary base for the Craftile Armed Forces. The lower level was fully in control of the CAF and mostly served as a training base. It was never officially recognised as a base so as not to compromise the entire cruiser if ever an invading force came.

As for the food courts, Lee had convinced Tom to visit one that catered to the Suati. On the second of his visits to the Sur-C, his dad had taken the family to the place. Lee had enjoyed the food on offer, as well as the design of the place. Tom had commented on the design – that of how a Suati diner looked – but hadn't much liked the food.

Now the two were back out in space and having run through the same docking while moving procedure as in the atmosphere, Lee was now running Tom through the power drives available to him.

"The drive you've been using at the minute is the kilo power drive," Lee stated, looking out at Tom who was idling in the Space Kicker. "And also, the atmos power drive to get up here. For faster travel, you have the mega power drive. This drive allows for faster traversal through space. We'll test it by doing a lap around the entire planet."

"Okay," Tom's voice sounded through the speaker. "I know how to activate it, so just give the word."

Lee instructed Tom to position next to him, then on his command up his speed to 01:00 KPD. Then, once Lee had hit the set speed and Tom reported he had, Lee gave the command to swap drives. On the board, the only noticeable change was that the KPD had changed to MPD. Then the DSSC started to build up a greater speed, with the current speed readout catching up to the change that had taken place. The numbers rolled down fast, then started increasing again until it hit the speed of 01:00. By now, the two 'craft were almost finished with their loop of the planet, and Lee had instructed to head straight for the Sur-C without swapping drives.

As he had expected, Tom had voiced his surprise before remembering what would happen and then voicing concern.

"No need to fear," Lee calmly said.

Tom went ahead with it anyway, and another shout of surprise sounded through the speakers as the emergency breaker kicked in to decelerate him back to 01:00 KPD.

"That's exactly what I was concerned about," Tom said with a dry voice.

"Just testing the systems," Lee stated. "And if you're serious about winning, you'd better get used to that feeling. And if you can do so at faster speeds, all the better."

"Wouldn't the fast speeds be for the mini cruisers to deal with?" Tom asked. "That one event last time had the competitors docking with their mini cruiser before blasting away."

"That was then. It could be that challenges this time need the user of the 'craft to manage such a speed themselves. That can be something we'll work on throughout if you want."

Mentally, Lee added that to his list of training. When back home, he would be looking at previous events for inspiration of what the challenges would be and devising time trials and such for Tom to try. He would do his best to help him be a viable competitor.

"Anyway, we'd better head back in. Get in here so we can rest up."

"Wait... I thought we were going back down to home?"

"Nope. We'll be staying here during the Championship anyway, so I thought we should have at least one night testing the services out. The rooms included. Don't worry, I've already sent word as to what we're doing to our parents."

Lee heard a slight breath, almost a sigh, before Tom said, "That's good, then. But next time, can we go to a normal food court?"

"Yes, we can."

Tom was less impressed with the hangar of the Surveillance Cruiser the second time he saw it, but he was still fascinated by the various 'craft and mini cruisers around. In training for the licences, they had only ever used the basic model. He knew of the other models from the game, but the mini cruisers were hardly featured, and so it was these he had looked upon the most.

Once the DSSC had landed and the two were out in the hangar, Tom looked out at the hangar entrance they had used. The energy filling in the gap allowed the hangar to keep its air pressure while still allowing things in or out. On a cruiser as large as this, it would be inconvenient to need to open and close the docking grates and keep the hangar empty of people every time someone wanted to enter or leave. The atmosphere gauze was a great piece of technology fitted onto all cruisers for that purpose. Tom wondered if it was also a part of the DSSC.

The two walked to the forward end of the hangar, which was closest to where they had landed, to head down to the reception lobby. Just like other cruisers, there were ramps to traverse between levels.

Tom let Lee do all the talking, and a guide was called forward to take them to their room. They moved further forward down the cruiser and turned off the main path. Stopping outside a room numbered 1612, the guide inserted a code into both their PMDs that would allow them ten hours access to the room.

Inside the room, a small lobby gave them access to an LMD on the table, with two doors to the left and one on the right. Lee walked toward the right-side door and looked in.

"Bathroom," he commented. "Which means those are the beds," he added, pointing to the left. He then walked to the middle of the room and sat down on one of the tables, activating the Lightmorph Media Display across the table. "Game of something?" he then asked.

"Sure."

The evening air was breezy, so Casey had sat outside once again.

"Everything's fine," Kerry called from inside the house.

Casey dropped her PMD to her lap and looked over her shoulder. Kerry was walking out with two glasses of blackberry.

"It's all fine," Kerry said again.

Casey took a glass absently and had a sip. She then looked up.

"You've been on the Surveillance Cruiser before. What sort of things are there?"

"A whole lot of stuff. You'll be seeing for yourself soon enough."

"I will?"

"You'll be up there supporting the two, right?

"Of course. I just..."

"You're thinking further again, aren't you?"

Casey had indeed. Thinking back to where her husband was. Back to what he was doing, and back to the unknown. And also, the feeling that her son would be going away as soon as he had his master licence.

There were times where she tried to distract herself from the thoughts. For some reason, it wasn't working today. Though she had an idea of why that was.

"I know what you need," Kerry said. "You shouldn't dwell on those thoughts for too long. How about a game?"

Casey finally looked down. "Worth a try," she said.

She had once found it difficult to do much, in the early days, having been constantly fretting over what her husband was up to so much she had sat for hours at a time doing nothing. It had taken a while to break from it, but the threat of it returning had always seemed there.

She was glad to have Kerry by her side.

The two PMDs were connected and a game started up. She had a good time playing, and it was another game in before either of them noticed that darkness had fallen.

"It's near enough a win for you," Kerry stated, "so why don't we call it quits and head in?"

"Yes, you're right. About both things."

"Both?"

"Everything is fine. I shouldn't be worried."

As she walked in, she knew tomorrow would be time enough to start trying to not let it affect her.

"Yesterday was great, but today should be better. We have yet more guests – including one of the competitors of the Championship. They were also a competitor of the last one as well, and they'll be here giving some tips for the new entrants. For now, though, we're starting off with some great tunes to get you raring to race."

Pyra Summers of Radio Racer [36/2-0085]

Lee awoke to find himself satisfied. The bed had certainly been comfortable. He was confident that when the time came for all of them to be here, they'd feel at home. Or even better than home, considering the facilities.

In the lounge room, Tom was already up and waiting.

"Breakfast," he stated upon seeing Lee.

This time, Lee had brought them to a regular food court. This one had a difference in that it was designed to look like it was outdoors. The tables were wooden benches usually seen in outdoor food venues, with the food counter designed like an outdoor bar. The ground had artificial grass, along with a few trees and bushes around.

"Wow," Tom had said upon first seeing it, and Lee wondered if he'd found his favourite place to eat here.

They had collected food, sat down at one of the benches, and started eating it when the lights flickered and then an announcement sounded.

"We are currently in a state of emergency. We ask that all guests remain where they are until the emergency has passed. For the safety of everyone, the hangar is closed down and access to it is forbidden until the emergency has passed. Thank you for your understanding."

Silence followed the announcement. Small conversations started up. Lee tucked back into his food. He looked up to see Tom's concerned expression.

"What?" Lee queried.

"We can't be under attack," Tom said, "so what sort of emergency is it?"

"We won't find out unless we ask, and we can't do that until the emergency has passed. Best not to be concerned."

"What about the DSSC, though?"

"You don't think they wouldn't have guards posted in the hangar? They care about security here."

"I meant... Well, we can't go out for training, can we?"

"No, we can't. It doesn't matter much. We've done the basics, so it's just a case of thinking what challenges are available and running timed runs."

"We'll still be doing ground runs, right?"

"I don't see why we couldn't come up to space for an hour on occasion. After all, training on the ground isn't going to do good in the Space Race Championship, is it?"

Tom laughed, and Lee was glad to hear it. There was no point treating any situation as serious until it was clear it was. The Championship wasn't a serious thing, and neither was the current emergency on the Sur-C.

Tom had gone for second helpings, and halfway through his eating of it, a new message sounded through the announcement system.

"We thank you again for your patience and understanding of the current situation. Restrictions have now been lifted. The emergency has now passed. We hope you enjoy the rest of your stay."

"Well," Tom said. "That's great. Time for practice."

Lee was watching one of the people leaving the food court. She had an air of familiarity about her, but he couldn't quite place it.

"Finish your food first. And after that, we'll head somewhere else before heading out."

"Where?"

"You'll see," was all Lee offered.

The fact was, he knew of where the access to the CAF visitor's entrance was, and if anyone knew what had happened, it would be them.

The conversation went quick, with the guard stationed at the visitor's entrance saying that a blip in the system had caused the emergency to be called, but after an hour of trying to trace it and nothing else happening, they had decided that it couldn't have been the first sign of anything serious.

"How's the training going?" the guard asked.

"Alright," Lee answered. Tom had been showing his nerves again and hadn't spoken once during the entire conversation. "We're going to be doing timed runs and stuff so he can get used to managing speeds and manoeuvrability."

"He'll do well, I can tell. He has what makes his dad great at his position."

"Speaking of..."

"No word," the guard stated. "We're hoping for the best, but when the remainder of Talon Force returned, they said the fighting was fierce, but no serious casualties had been taken."

"Talon Force..." Lee quickly recalled what his dad had told him about the special operations unit known as Talon Force. He then remembered a recent mention of them. "Didn't they return half a year ago?"

"Indeed."

"They were almost wiped out."

"I'm not one for saying bad things, but that was their fault. Didn't know when to retreat until it was too late. Right in the thick of it, heading straight for the largest action."

"Figures," Lee said. "Well, we'd best get back to training."

On the way back to the DSSC, Lee thought a bit more about Talon Force. They were known for ruthless tactics and used any means necessary to achieve results. Obviously, they must have tried to end whatever was happening as soon as they could and failed at that.

Hopefully, the Craftile Armed Forces out there hadn't suffered too much from those actions. And hopefully, Mr Hughs and his own dad were still out there fighting to win.

"There's danger up ahead. Swap down to the kilo drive and get ready to dodge."

Tom flicked the switch to swap drives, and this time he felt more in control of himself than the last time he had experienced the sudden deceleration. Since this was role-playing, there wasn't really anything in his way, so he made a quick drop once the kilo drive had kicked in. He then showed off a bit by performing a series of quick dodging manoeuvres and followed that off with a zero-flip – named as it required quickly cutting the engines while angling up to then reignite them once in position.

It felt a lot different performing it in reality than on the game. Tom shook his head with eyes closed to rid himself of the odd feeling. Opening his eyes, he noted the DSSC had come into view.

"You alright?" Lee asked.

"Yeah... Doing that just took something from me. I'm okay now, though."

"Stop showing off, and we'll roll again."

Tom once again increased speed and swapped from kilo power drive to the mega power drive.

"Too fast!" Lee shouted.

Tom looked down at his control board to see that his set speed was 02:00. He was about to correct it, then thought of what speed he could achieve at maximum. Quickly he increased speed to 03:40 and watched as the actual speed number increased to hit the set speed.

As he travelled along at the highest speed, his scanner picked up numerous things. One of those things was the other planet orbiting East Star – Donaldo. All the planets in this system were named by the Suati, but Tom's understanding of the language employed by them wasn't that good. It might have had something to do with water, he wasn't entirely sure.

He was curious, and so swung his 'craft in the direction of the planet to take a look at something entirely new. He had no idea if Lee had been to a different planet, and so he'd be the first of the two. Plus, it was good experience for when he became a true explorer.

The mega power drive kept him going up until he was almost at the edge of Donaldo's gravity well then continued to work upon hitting the atmosphere.

He was engulfed in a swirl of dark clouds. He could hear rumbles within it. Disengaging the MPD, he let the 'craft slowly coast back to 03:40 KPD.

He broke out of the atmosphere to look upon a storm. Bright red flashes made themselves known in the sky – filling the darkness with blinding light. There was no rain, which made the storm dangerous. Even more dangerous was the wind, that seemed as though it was trapped within the cloud cover and was buffeting the 'craft everywhere it could. Even at his maximum speed, Tom was struggling to keep the 'craft stable.

It was a wondrous moment to have experienced, but this wasn't the place he wanted to be. Not at the minute. Not while he was alone with no backup and no easily reachable repair station.

He set the atmos power drive to calculate what was needed for a quick breakthrough to space while continuing to look upon the storm and the planet. He had to dodge out of the way of a flying creature, though he didn't get a chance to see it in detail.

A beeping announced the atmos power drive was charged, so with a bit of difficulty, he managed to pull upward and let the drive do its work. The 'craft shook as another blinding flash of red erupted. A warning light showed, with his display saying that the 'craft had lost some power.

The Space Kicker returned to space, and Tom quickly set it to maximum speed. He noted that the maximum had fallen to 02:80. He seemed to have lost more power than the 'craft realised.

Once back to using the mega power drive, he thought about the planet. His surprise at first seeing it. The worry of the danger that the storm possessed. There were plenty of other feelings he'd had as well, but he needed a while to fully understand them.

He noticed that his scanner was showing a mini cruiser falling into line with him. It took a second to realise Lee had been waiting for him.

"Just what do you think you were doing?" was the first thing Lee said when the connection to him returned.

Tom found himself with a guilty expression that turned to excitement at telling his best friend of the experience he'd had on the planet.

Lee listened to the story with interest. He had expected Tom might have done something like that but was still unhappy with the impulse that had driven Tom to do it.

He knew about Donaldo and the two words of the Suati language it was made up from. Tom's limited understanding of the language meant he couldn't be forewarned that the planet had an unforgiving storm constantly destroying anything that stayed too long.

Storm Drain was a pretty good name for it. No matter what the Suati had tried, they had been unable to work out how to survive with technology in such a harsh environment that could easily drain the energy from all devices. As such, they had named the planet Donaldo [do-na for storm; ald-o for drain] and never set a course near it again.

He was sure that he'd heard a rumour of a research station, though.

"I'm sure it was an experience," Lee said once Tom had finished. "And I'm sure you'll be telling it again once back home. Drop to the KPD and get on in here."

The journey back was quick, with the DSSC left once again at the Spaceyard. Tom had spent no time in telling those of the 'yard his story. Matt was particularly interested in how he had handled the fierce conditions of the planet, and so at least half an hour had been spent with Tom talking in detail about the experience.

Lee had no doubt that he'd have a lot more stories after the Championship. And he'd be telling them all in great detail.

Tom flew the Space Kicker back while Lee walked it back to the Hughs' house. When he walked through the gate, Tom was already telling the two mothers about his experience on Donaldo.

Lee sat down and listened in, smiling. This Championship was already giving Tom a lot of new experiences, and Lee hoped he'd be able to have some in the future.

CHAPTER 3 – FORCEFUL INTERVENTION

"The start of the third month approaches, and we have word that every one of the competitors for the Championship have been seen out in space. Some are even staying on the Surveillance Cruiser for the entirety of the time between now and event's end. Now that's commitment to training."

Pyra Summers of Radio Racer [41/2-0085]

Lee had seen Tom training all this week, and he was confident that he had the skills.

Once Lee was back at his own house, he had started looking back on the previous Championships that had happened and made notes on them. He couldn't set up the extravagant set pieces the Championship normally used, but he had planned on running through things a checkpoint at a time – instructing Tom to dodge out of the way of any obstructions. They both knew Space Racer and the events that were on that, so Tom was able to use his knowledge of that to improvise.

As well as that, they had again boosted up to the mega power drive to get Tom used to the sudden decelerations and accelerations swapping between drives caused. Tom was used to the feeling now, as well as the feeling of weightlessness from space. It was a great thing to see.

Tom had wanted to go back to Donaldo, but Lee had said they shouldn't risk it. Besides, he had reminded Tom, there was little point in exploring until after the Championship as racing was what they needed to focus on.

They'd had little time to train during the four school days, though it was helped somewhat by the fact they were allowed to use their licence training session to get up in space and train for extra time.

The next weekend was here, and both were in space once again. The DSSC was in position ready for Tom to fly through its hangar. Lee could see Tom waiting from the front of the viewshield. He confirmed that he was ready to go.

"Okay. Remember it's a dodge underneath, then a hard turn to go through the hangar. And go."

The Space Kicker moved forward with increasing speed, then made a drop at the last second. Lee quickly swapped to the rear camera to see it pulling around to enter the hangar. Swapping to one of the cameras within the hangar, he watched a blue blur appear for a second on the feed.

Looking up, the Space Kicker had pulled up in front of the viewshield.

"How was that?" Tom asked.

"As good as could be expected," Lee said. "Now would you be able to do roughly the same thing except approach from below?"

A pause of a few seconds, in which Lee had a feeling Tom was doing some calculations. "In two tries I think I can."

It took him three. On the first try, he overshot and ended up boosting over the DSSC instead of through it. On the second he scraped the upper lining of the hangar and had slammed to the floor trying to correct it. On the third try, there had been a moment where it looked like he might have failed but managed to pull it off.

"Yeah!" the exultant exclamation came through the speaker. "This really is great. I really must thank you for entering me into this. It's the most fun I've had in ages."

Lee smiled at that. "You're welcome. This is good fun for me as well. We'll give it a few more runs before heading back down."

Lee recited the next checkpoint he had in mind. This one involved something similar to what Tom had done during Space Racer, but instead of strafing around the fittings of the hangar roof he needed dodge around several smaller 'craft. That couldn't be done, but Lee was leaving it up to Tom to create a pattern of random shifts before flying through the DSSC's hangar.

"Going good," Lee stated, seeing the pattern of left, left, right.

The Space Kicker then strafed left sharply before driving a long right. Lee watched as it continued on for longer than it needed.

"Pull off!" Lee exclaimed, but only received crackles from the speaker.

Lee watched as it finally faltered in its constant speed, then stopped. It stayed still for a minute.

"That… wasn't meant to happen," Tom said in a questioning tone.

"Are you sure everything's fine with it?" Lee asked. "Do we need to return?"

"All reading fine."

"Scanning for static pulses," Lee informed, having thought on the next reason for a failure. "Irregular patches around, and some thin streaks…" It was an odd combination. The patches were uncommon but not unusual. The streaks of static meant someone had been firing a special type of laser infused with the stuff.

Hitting one of those streaks alone wouldn't be enough to cause issues, but enough of them in close proximity would.

"Move away from the area," Lee advised. "Too much static, and I think someone might be training using CSP lasers."

"Aren't they meant to be prohibited to security forces only?" Tom asked.

"I think they might be, but it's always possible a friend of someone in security is helping that friend train in a more active way."

The Space Kicker moved away from the area, with the DSSC following suit. The two set up a new checkpoint to practice from, but no sooner had Tom started than Lee shouted for him to abort.

"Static streaks inbound! Get inside quickly!"

Lee kept his eyes locked on the scanner, now tuned exclusively to look out for static, and just about heard Tom say he was inside when the streaks passed over the central point of the scanner.

The lights flickered slightly, but that was the only effect the static had on the DSSC.

"I recommend we head back down," Tom said. Lee hadn't heard him enter. "Even if we aren't being targeted, I don't think we're going to get much more done today unless we were to head out further."

"I'm sure the crew of the Sur-C are tracking the static appearances, but I'm still reporting it."

"As you should. Land at mine and I'll get a full diagnostic run on the Kicker when we land."

"Good day training?" Kerry asked as Lee entered.

"Someone seems intent to make space a static wasteland," Lee commented. "Other than that, he's doing great in performing all these moves."

"That doesn't seem a nice thing to be doing, but there could be plenty of reasons."

"There's two months until the Championship starts. Seems a bit too early to be trying to sabotage it, don't you think?"

Kerry thought it through. It was never too early to do something like that, but doing it too much would surely get whoever it was noticed. It was possible that whoever it had been testing how much they could get away with.

"I'm sure it won't happen tomorrow," she said with a reassuring smile.

"I'm still going to contact the Sur-C and get them to monitor everything going on."

"You don't think they already are?"

"Maybe it is a random occurrence, and I shouldn't be thinking too much about it. I just can't shake the feeling that we were being targeted."

"What does Tom think?"

"Don't think he's thought beyond the fact training was stopped early."

Kerry hoped the next day would be less action-packed than today. There was no reason for what had happened today to happen tomorrow. Not if security had already found out who had been firing the charged static pulses.

Tom looked up to the night sky, the breeze of the silent night sending slight chills across his skin. Outside, sat in one of the chairs, he could reflect on the training.

Everything had been going well, and aside from the events of today being a one-off annoyance, he felt happy at everything. Tomorrow he would be back in space and zipping around the DSSC in a load of patterns. He knew it all. He had the control of the Space Kicker down fine. He needed a bit more challenge.

He supposed he'd just tell Lee he wanted to freestyle a bit. Have a bit of fun. Lee wouldn't mind. Maybe they'd even have a chance to head inside the Surveillance Cruiser again. Tom wanted to explore more of it, having only seen two of the food courts within and nothing of the other entertainment.

"Are you okay?" Mrs. Hughs asked. "Come inside. It's too cool to stay out for long periods."

Tom looked around to his mom, who once again was looking worried about something. He suspected it was more about why he was out here than anything else, and stood up to head in.

"Just thinking about tomorrow," he said.

"So have I. Why not have a break? You've been at it too long."

"Two weeks isn't that long, but I do think a break would be welcome." He saw a smile break on his mother's face, so was quick to add, "After tomorrow. No training for a week. It'll allow Lee to find more patterns and events to test me on."

Mrs. Hughs' face fell slightly as the smile dissolved, but Tom had a feeling she understood that tomorrow had already been planned for, and was back to her usual state.

She really did need to start worrying less, but he knew how hard that would be for her. There wasn't anything he could do to prevent that. Unless he quit the Championship, of course, and that was very unlikely to happen.

"It's not just about having the fastest 'craft. There's a lot that goes into the Championship that will test a competitor – both within the 'craft, outside it, and also how good their teammate is. I underestimated two of those three things last time, and I intend to use what I learned from that last Championship here."

Katie Daniels speaking on Radio Racer [42/2-0085]

"If you want to…"

Lee was certain this turn of events had nothing to do with yesterday's events, that Tom just wanted a day to mess around. Maybe it was the way he had set up the training. He hadn't allowed much variety for a few days.

"Go ahead," he conceded. "I'll watch from here."

Watching as Tom flew around, Lee looked out on the vast array of space. As ever, a number of 'craft were around, as were a few mini cruisers. Not a single one of them looked to be training with any sort of weapons.

He couldn't shake the feeling of being targeted.

Looking back to Tom, the Space Kicker performed a drop into a zero-flip, with it flying upside down for a while before another zero-flip righted itself.

"You can't do such fancy tricks in that thing," Tom called out in a goading voice.

He had a feeling Tom knew what was on his mind and was trying to diffuse those thoughts much the way Lee had diffused many situations before.

"I don't think any passengers I had would be happy if I tried."

"You a taxi service now?"

"I could take a lot of people in this thing, that's for sure." Lee scanned the area around them again, then set the scanner to check for static.

He tried to shake the feeling of being targeted. It was just paranoia at play. He had to keep telling himself that.

"Well?" Tom's voice broke him out of his thoughts.

"Well... What?"

The sigh Tom gave was audible through the speakers. "Nothing's happening or going to happen. Just relax and enjoy yourself. This isn't you."

It wasn't. He was never usually this worried over something. He was right to be cautious, but nothing had happened yet. He felt visibly relaxed and muttered thanks to Tom.

For the few hours they remained out in space, nothing more exciting happened than Tom's over-ambitious freestyle in space.

"Okay," Lee called. "You want to head inside the Sur-C for something to eat before heading back down?"

"Great." Tom's voice sounded a bit strained as he manipulated the controls to perform another weird spin. "Let me get inside and-"

"Tom?"

Nothing appeared to have happened except for the silence. Tom was still lining up for his entry into the hangar. Lee waited until he was almost at the DSSC before opening the hangar grate.

Or it would have opened, had he not noticed something.

"Who are you?" he asked into the silence.

No response.

The link that should have been connected to Tom had instead been hijacked and connected to an unidentified person.

Lee looked through the viewshield. There was nothing from this side. Feeding power to the engines, he started to turn the DSSC. Halfway through the turn, he realised that things had gone quiet up in this area of space.

The power flickered. The health monitor then blitzed to life showing a wave of static had now infected the systems of the DSSC.

"Tom! Move!" Lee called into the microphone, knowing it was pointless to try.

He scanned across space again, looking for who was doing this. He focused on Tom, who was waiting, possibly for him to open the grate so he could enter the hangar and they could quickly make planetfall.

He didn't seem to be looking out for any sort of immediate danger, so it must have come as a surprise to him when something slammed straight into the side of him. It had looked like a Falcon model 'craft.

And it looked modded to a military spec.

The power of the DSSC flickered again. The static that had infected the systems was eating the shield energy away. Once it was gone, the systems would start failing.

Lee put the DSSC into a flip and built up speed. He'd try to collect Tom before anything else happened to either of them, then make for the ground.

After that, he would be contacting the security of the Sur-C to try and track the person down. It had to be the same one.

A mini cruiser pulled in front of him. Lee pulled on the left stick to avoid it while dropping speed to make a sharper turn. His right hand pushed the lever forward to gain maximum speed again once past the other mini cruiser.

He fumbled the controls to swap the scanner onto the main screen. Only Tom's Space Kicker was visible on it, which meant these two were dangerous.

Being hidden from scans was never a good sign.

Tom felt the impact on his right side as he slammed against his restraints.

Who is this? Tom wondered, looking to his right.

A 'craft he remembered as a Falcon had flown straight into him, using its forward point as an anchor, and continued to push him further away from Lee.

If you want to control me, I'll control you.

Tom threw the lever forward to inject maximum speed. He checked his set speed to see it was too low. He hit the button to put it to the highest number, then initiated the swap to the mega power drive.

Whoever had him in a lock hadn't expected it, and Tom was free. He didn't want to drop yet. He had no contact with Lee, just the unidentified hijacker that had stopped them from communicating.

He should have listened to Lee.

Yesterday had been a sign of something.

He had no idea what they were up to, but he had to find someone to help.

He tried signing out from the current link but found access blocked. He couldn't swap out to a new channel, or even close it down. Everything else was still functional, so he had to plan this fast.

He could see exactly where the Surveillance Cruiser was. He could line himself up while still under the MPD, hit the danger point to quickly revert down to the kilo power drive, and hopefully end up in the hangar where he wouldn't be followed.

It was the only shot he had, short of heading down to the planet while trying to avoid the disabling static shots.

"Don't bother trying."

Whoever had spoken had done so through the link. It sounded like a woman who was serious in her actions.

"I know what you intend to do."

Tom couldn't back down from the threat. He had to do it.

Everything was set. He'd be entering into the portside hangar entrance, and he hoped he could kill his speed fast enough to stop and land before anything got damaged.

Looking at the scanner, something caught his eye on his board.

His set speed was slowly dropping.

He hammered on the button to bring it back to maximum. Nothing happened.

Swapping from scanner to health monitor, he noticed the drain on his speed was from the damage previously caused. He dropped the set speed manually to 02:00, which was still a good enough speed for what he had to do.

He felt the speed drop to what he had set, then he felt it drop altogether.

The engines had swapped from MPD back down to KPD early.

"I told you not to try it," the voice stated, "Now, are we going to be civilised about this, or do I need to rough you up some more?"

"You can't talk about being civilised," Tom growled. "This isn't civilised."

"What I have to say is for your ears only."

"I'll only listen once I know my friend is safe."

"We only want you split for this duration. Once you listen, you can be reunited."

Tom could see the Surveillance Cruiser. It wouldn't be long before he was inside. His plan had to change though, and he was willing to bring the landing claws out as soon as he passed the threshold of the entrance and slam the Space Kicker into the ground to stop.

Once again he was slammed into his restraints as the Falcon 'craft impacted against the side again. Somehow in exactly the same place as before.

This time it was the Falcon who jumped up to MPD speed, managing to account for the speed at which Tom's 'craft was going.

All Tom could do was watch as the Surveillance Cruiser shrank as he was pulled further away from it.

"What do you want to talk about?" Tom stated in a resigned voice.

"The Space Kicker and the Super Cruiser have been putting up a good show of fighting, but it seems whoever these other two have finally worn them down. Security teams have been dispatched to both locations, and we'll be keeping you up to date on the latest updates as they happen."

Kerry turned the sound down a bit and looked across at Casey. Her head was buried in her hands and she appeared to be trying not to burst into tears.

It wouldn't be right to say anything to try to make this better, so Kerry retreated to the kitchen to make two lemon teas.

Back in the lounge, the sound had been turned back to full. Casey took her cup of lemon tea without a word. Her eyes were red.

"The reading from the Super Cruiser is that it is being drained of power. Whoever is driving it has seemingly been diverting power from every system they can into the shields to make sure they aren't overwhelmed by a complete shutdown. Meanwhile, the assailant of the Super Cruiser is managing to put up a good fight against the security team."

Kerry took a sip from her lemon tea, hoping to everything she could that Lee could work something out. He had to. It was what he was good at. With the security team helping, he had to survive.

"Meanwhile, despite doing everything they can, the other team are having trouble finding the Space Kicker. All tracking has disappeared from it, but the team is confident they can stop the two."

Casey lifted herself slowly from the sofa and walked away. Kerry followed after her. She found Casey outside looking up to the sky.

"They will get back safely," Kerry said in a quiet, reassuring voice. "I know they will. The security teams will do everything they can to save the two and disable their attackers."

Casey didn't say anything.

Kerry put an arm around Casey's shoulders and joined her in looking up at the sky.

Do everything you can to return safely. I want you back here safely.

If Kerry wished it, it would come true.

It had to.

Lee was grateful that the security teams had arrived. It had given him a bit of relief against having to juggle the task of nursing the shield energy while at the same time dodging the attacks from whoever was in that mini cruiser.

He had only one option remaining. He had to get down to the ground as soon as possible. If he didn't do so now, it would be worse to attempt it with unreliable systems.

Another strike landed on the engines. This attacker was managing a mini cruiser too well. There had to be some automated weapons on it.

He watched as the shield energy blipped with the new reading being too low for comfort. The static infection had stopped natural regeneration of the shield and was working too fast that the fitted systems had to be prototypes. It was that, or not everything had been tested.

Once he got down to the ground and to the spaceyard, he'd be asking about that. He couldn't blame them, of course, since he was the one doing the testing. And no-one would expect this much static to be used against it.

The choice of static weapons meant this was a scare tactic. It was either that or a diversionary one. Which was worse, he couldn't think of now. Any hope of rescuing Tom had fallen flat, and he knew that a security team would be looking. One had come for him, so it was fair that one would be going for Tom – if the engagement had been followed by those on board the Surveillance Cruiser from the beginning.

He risked using the mega power drive to shoot him closer to the atmosphere, which lasted just a few seconds before failing.

A blip of the readout.

Zero percent shield energy.

The lights within shut off. The monitors wiped themselves of all information. The DSSC was gripped by the atmosphere, and Lee felt the gravity bringing him down. He pressed buttons and flicked switches across the board with nothing happening. He tried the sticks and found he had no control.

He tried everything he could again, trying not to look out the viewshield at what was coming to meet him.

All the systems were dead, but there was still a bit of power left around.

Looking around, he jumped through the entrance into the main part of the cruiser, and tried navigating to the smallest room of the left. Without the gravity generator working, he was now subject to the gravity of the planet, which had meant the simple walk to the room was a climb upward.

Pulling himself up to the entrance, he climbed around and inside the room. Lying on the floor that was meant to be a wall was the spacesuit that had been left there. Attached to the back of it was the power unit.

Smiling to himself, he picked it up and climbed back over. He carefully dropped onto the back of the seats and worked to keep himself stable as he moved back to the board.

Pulling off one of the panels, he scanned the wires and ripped one from the housing. He pulled the panel from the power unit of the spacesuit and pulled the energy storage from it. Attaching the wire into it, he jumped back into his seat and reached out to pull the left stick toward him.

Now righted, he had about a minute before the power zeroed again. He needed to make a decision on where to go and fast.

He smiled again. Fate was certainly being kind to him.

He pushed the lever to hit maximum speed, turning slightly to head in the direction of the spaceyard of Saltare. He kept the DSSC as level as possible, only dropping on an acute angle to hit the ground.

There was no chance he'd be able to stop and land. He strapped himself in again and braced for the uncontrolled drop that was to come.

❖

"You're a competitor in the Championship."

It was statement, and Tom treated it as such.

"Yes."

"Then you'll be wanting to know the challenges that are coming."

"No."

"Don't lie. Everyone wants to do their best at it, so naturally, they want to know what's coming up."

"Not me."

Tom had no idea if it was true, but he didn't want to admit it. Not to whoever this was, anyway. He'd labelled her as bad news, but this was going a bit too far. It was near enough controlling.

He looked down at his monitor and swapped back to his scanner. Several blips had now entered the picture. He tried getting a reading on who they were when the scanner failed. He swapped back to his health monitor. His shield energy reading was zeroed. He had no idea how long ago that had happened, but it was probably when this had first started.

That piercing point wouldn't have been able to strike if his shields had been active.

"Don't lie," the voice repeated. "I'm trusting you with this information as you're a newcomer. The final challenge, if you can get that far."

The way she had said that last part made it sound as if she didn't believe he'd even get through the opening round.

"I don't care at this point. Just let me go."

"Oh, no. You're not going anywhere unless I say so."

"Then say where!" It was desperation at this point in time. He couldn't see any way out. He tried again his mega power drive, and this time it worked. The two 'craft started rotating in a circle.

A powerful blast at close range shorted his engines out. Somehow, her engines hadn't. She took control again, and after a minute he saw the first rock float by.

They were now inside the asteroid field.

Tom felt his heart beat faster. There was a slight ragged breath to his voice when he said, "Why here?" and he heard the fear in his voice.

"If I'd known you were such a wimp, I wouldn't have taken pity on you. Then again – better to be prepared."

Tom hadn't even noticed the reversion back down to the kilo power drive, but certainly noticed when an asteroid came within view to his left.

He grabbed onto the right stick and forced it to the right. No resistance was offered. When he looked to the right, he found the Falcon that had been there no longer existed.

"Enjoy your final challenge," the voice said.

A buzz then filled the speakers. Tom scrunched his face when he first heard the noise, keeping his eyes as slits to see what he was doing. He found he could now shut his communication module off, and did so.

The buzzing stopped. He rubbed his ears which had the remnants of the buzzing still within them, then looked around to see space rock everywhere.

His outward lights still worked, and when the light flooded the area it revealed even more space rock that had been hidden from the lack of light.

He couldn't remember which direction he had been brought in here. He looked around but found only rock around him. His forward engines came to life again, and he quickly had to power them down back to the kilo power drive then dodge around a large piece of rock before coming to a stop.

He tried his communications module again but shut it off after a second when the buzzing started up again. He looked down at his health monitor to see a failing 'craft.

There was only one thing he could do.

He picked a direction at random and powered the engines to maximum.

"The Super Cruiser is heading toward the spaceyard of Saltare, having managed to right itself. We have no idea how much power it has remaining, but that's a lot field it can use as a landing buffer. The Saltare spaceyard is where it came from, so this Super Cruiser is returning home. Up in space, it seems the mini cruiser that had been attacking it has now disappeared, along with the Falcon 'craft that had been controlling the Space Kicker. The security team that was in charge of that hunt are now certain they went inside the asteroid field, and that the Space Kicker is still inside."

That did cause Casey to start crying.

Kerry spoke calmly to her, encouraging her to at least leave the house. Getting away from the news would be good, but that wasn't why Kerry wanted her out.

Lee was heading to the spaceyard. That was also where the two should be going to offer support once he landed.

As they left the house, a large boxy shape could be seen up in the sky. It dropped rapidly. Kerry didn't want to watch the descent and followed the route to the spaceyard with Casey in tow – who didn't seem to have noticed the imminent crash of the DSSC.

She certainly heard though, as did Kerry. A loud thump on impact just outside the spaceyard on the large empty field of grass. Its weight had stopped it from bouncing, but the sizzle of it dragging itself across the ground could be heard.

The crunch of the barrier as it got ran over resounded on the air, then silence.

Kerry called for Casey to hurry, and she did. It seemed she knew what was going on after all.

As they hit the entrance, Kerry rushed an explanation of who they were to the guard, who seemed to understand.

There was a flurry of activity inside as workers hurried over to the site of the crash to see what had happened. Kerry and Casey joined them, and after passing through a building and out onto the grounds again, there the super cruiser sat.

"Back!" someone called. "Everyone back until the situation is clear."

"Is he okay?" Kerry said once she reached the front.

"He'll be out in a minute. People have gone in to see how he is."

Kerry let out a relieved breath. She didn't look to Casey while waiting. A figure emerged from the open hangar entrance and jumped down. A teen was supported by people still on the cruiser, who was then passed to the one on the ground.

"I'm fine. I'm fine," Lee said as he was guided over to the two parents.

Kerry ran over to him and took him from the man.

"He's a good mind, this one," the man said. "I was right to trust him with that thing."

"I linked the power pack from the spacesuit to give the cruiser some last-minute power to at least get a grip on the situation," Lee said as though it wasn't worth a mention. "I just want to know who those attackers were and what they want."

"We'll talk about that inside," the man said.

The four of them walked to another building not far from where the DSSC had stopped. Inside the lobby filled with pale green colours, the group sat down.

"We have a bit more information than what the news crews are letting on," the man started. "From what the long-range views have been able to reveal, it looks like both of those vehicles are from the Talon Force collection. All identifiers to mark them as such have been scrubbed, but that amount of auto-lock weaponry clearly marks it as such. All of that collection of vehicles was thought to have been destroyed when Talon Force were disbanded, but obviously a few have escaped into the wild."

"But why would Talon Force want to disrupt the Championship?" Lee asked.

"It's not Talon Force. Not as far as we're aware. But we are unaware of the motive."

"Try scare tactics. A good place to start."

"Yes. Scare tactics. But this has gone beyond that."

"How?" Kerry quickly put in.

"Until we get more information, we won't know for sure. But we do know these two were operating yesterday as well."

"That's it, then. They've got some idea that Tom is one to watch. That he's a strong contender. They're trying to..."

Lee held back on what he had been about to say, and Kerry was glad he had. Casey looked completely broken.

The two had only remained outside for a minute before they had headed back in, and the lemon tea had helped a bit. Maybe another one would help.

"Is there a kitchen around here?" she asked.

The man pointed the door out, and Kerry stood up. She tried convincing Casey to come with her, but Casey wasn't moving.

"He'll be alright," she whispered. "Tom knows how to handle situations. He'll make it out fine."

Again, she wished it to be true. If she wished it, it would happen.

"So, Matt," Lee asked in a quiet voice, aware that Mrs. Hughs still remained huddled within her seat. "Do we know if Tom is indeed being targeted?"

"I'm afraid it's possible." He held his hand to up his ear, listening to something through his earpiece. "There is no sign of the Talon Force 'craft, though the team are on guard and waiting for if he emerges from the field. A two-man team has entered with powerful scanning equipment to hunt your friend down and return him."

"Good. I hope he's doing okay."

"He should be. Might be a bit tense, but he should be okay."

"Speaking of okay, how's the super cruiser?"

"You did great with it. It's been saved from heavy external damage, so only the underside plates need fixing up. That's already happening as we speak. The internal systems are being restored, with static resistance being strengthened. It's unlikely whoever attacked today will try the same tactic again, so it does seem a bit moot to be doing it, but better safe than sorry."

Mrs. Johnson arrived with a tray of lemon teas. She passed the tray to Lee, took a cup, and held it out to Mrs. Hughs. Mrs. Hughs looked up and took the proffered cup.

For a while, they sat in silence, all possibly locked in thoughts hoping that Tom was doing great. Lee left them to it and took a walk around the spaceyard.

As soon as the DSSC was fixed, he'd be out there looking for Tom. He needed to for his own mind as well as both families. Tom had once helped him out in a big way. It was time for Lee to do the same.

It was clear Tom was trapped out here. It wasn't just a case of picking a direction and sticking with it. The disorientation within the field of rock staggered him, and as he travelled around rocks, he had a hard time finding which way he had been going.

As each hour passed, he was getting more on edge. The field was huge, with no easy way out. He wanted to find that exit but felt as though he was circling the field. Though the rocks were different, it felt as though they were all the same.

He rolled the 'craft to dodge around another of the rocks, forcing the 'craft down when he saw another one right in front of him.

"That's enough," he growled.

71

He dropped the 'craft further, thinking that maybe he could find an exit by heading straight 'down'. He still had to be watching everywhere he could for more of the rocks, but he found doing this was more manageable than flying forward.

It was slow going, though. He bounced the 'craft around rocks that the sensors picked up underneath him, feeling more on edge than he had while going fast. The woman who had attacked him had to be out there still.

Waiting.

The health of the Space Kicker was fading all the time. His shield energy was no longer the only thing that had gone. Both atmos and mega power drives had completely failed. The ejection for the docking claws had now forced them to stick on, though the magnetics within them no longer worked. His was thankful his life support system was still working, but even that was failing.

Checking again, it was now lower than twenty percent. He wasn't going to chance it. Opening the rear storage, he pulled the spacesuit out and tried as best as he could to pull it on while still managing the controls. Once he was sure it was fully operating to give him oxygen, he diverted the remaining power from the 'craft's life support into his engines.

With the engines able to operate that bit faster, he angled the Space Kicker in the direction of his drop, and within a few minutes noticed the absence of rock.

I'm in the clear!

Something slammed straight into the side of his 'craft. He slammed straight into the side of the 'craft, bounced off, and hit the other side.

He'd forgotten to put his restraints back on.

Looking around, he failed to spot a problem. There was no-one around. There was something coming out of the right side of the Space Kicker, though. It looked like sparks.

His health monitor flashed one more report that he never got the chance to see.

He was now truly flying by eye alone. With massive damage. And no way of seeing his attacker.

Tom gunned the Space Kicker as fast as it could in what he hoped was the direction of Hortii.

Casey hadn't said much since coming to the spaceyard. She hadn't said much since before then. Her boy was lost in space and very likely not coming back.

She desperately wanted him to come back.

She was nursing yet another lemon tea that Kerry had made. The taste of it was calming, but after so long her sense of calm had been shattered by not having any news. She felt she'd no longer break down as there was nothing left to break.

Space was an empty void, which was pretty much how she felt at that moment.

"Result!" Lee exclaimed.

Casey blinked, wondering what had him excited.

"You have to let me take the super cruiser. I don't care if it isn't fixed."

She appeared to have missed something but didn't feel the need to find out what. Any news that interested her would probably be repeated.

"I'll be back. And I'll have him."

Casey looked up to see Lee standing over her.

"I promise," he said, then left at a run.

It took a long time for Casey to realise what was happening and why Lee would risk himself in an unfixed vehicle to head out to space.

"Has he been found?" she asked in a flat voice.

"They've still not been able to get a full scan on him," Kerry said, "but he has emerged from the asteroid field. Things aren't looking good, but everyone is doing everything they can to help him. Lee will bring him back. Once they return, I'm sure a break is just what they will need."

A small ray of hope allowed itself into her heart. It couldn't break through the void, but it was slowly eating it. She knew the void would only collapse when Tom was back safe on the ground.

"Situation report," Lee called once the crew of the Surveillance Cruiser had redirected his call to the security team now stuck in battle protecting the lone Space Kicker.

"We're doing everything we can," one of the team stated. "Only trouble is even with six of us this one is tricky work."

"One?" Lee asked. "The 'craft or cruiser?"

"The Falcon. We suspect the mini cruiser might be waiting somewhere to strike."

"What I'm going to do will cause them to react. Be sure to protect me as I collect the Space Kicker."

"Okay, Mr. Johnson, sir."

Lee knew his dad was recognised among the security teams. Half of it was made up of members of the Craftile Armed Forces, which was also another plus.

Lee accelerated toward the still moving Space Kicker, which suddenly shunted sideways as a CSP missile struck the opening in the body.

"You were right, sir. The mini cruiser has come into play."

"Get three of your team onto it for distraction. I'll handle getting the Space Kicker to safety with the remaining three."

"Will do, sir."

His dad had garnered a lot of respect from these men, and they were showing it in return to Lee. So long as he didn't mess up any orders that would get them hurt, he felt they'd keep that level of respect for him.

It would have been enjoyable for him to have command had the situation not been so serious.

"Are we able to confirm the pilot as active?" Lee asked.

"Unconfirmed, sir. We have reason to believe he is only half aware of his actions."

Lee didn't like the sound of that.

The DSSC was now ready to try for its first collection. The portside docking grate was now open, with Lee edging the speed of the super cruiser ever so slightly to get it alongside the Space Kicker.

"Whoa!"

Lee felt the impact as something exploded within the hangar. Lasers off to his left indicated the three security members had reacted fast to draw the Falcon away. Lee concentrated on focusing on the camera which would show the Space Kicker outside.

"Abort!" rang through the speaker.

Lee pulled upward.

Another missile had come out of the darkness.

"The Falcon is no longer in play," a report sounded. "It managed to quickly dock with the mini cruiser. Repeat: Mini cruiser is now primary target. Protect the super cruiser with everything you've got."

Lee looked at his scanner to see gravity was near to pulling the Space Kicker down through the atmosphere. He had one more try before the very risky manoeuvre of getting it inside while wild turbulence shook them both.

"Keep that mini cruiser as far from us as possible," Lee said. "There's only one chance while still in space. I want that chance to go as smoothly as possible."

An affirmative came through, but Lee barely heard it. He lined up for the next shot at getting the Space Kicker inside. He kept the outward camera in focus so he didn't have to look at what damage had been caused.

The Space Kicker was now in view.

Lee pushed the right stick to slide around the Space Kicker.

Another explosion.

Whoever these people are, they've gone beyond scare tactics, Lee thought as he fought to right the super cruiser.

The Space Kicker was now trailing smoke. The faintest tinge of blue meant they were now inside the atmosphere. Lee alerted the security team of that, hoping they could keep the mini cruiser in space.

"Good luck," was the last thing Lee heard before signing off. He didn't need the distraction of open communication.

The DSSC rumbled and shook. He could see the Space Kicker veering away from him in an erratic pattern. Up, down, side-to-side. It started to tumble through the air, and Lee was sure Tom had been knocked unconscious from the blast of that missile.

"If you wish it, it will happen," Lee repeated a saying that had been passed down in the family, and hoped and wished with everything he had that he could pull this off. It needed to be done quickly and without causing any more damage.

That would be tricky.

The Space Kicker had started dropping rapidly, and though they were over open water, Lee didn't want the Space Kicker to make a splashdown. Recovering it from the water would take time.

Locking eyes with the screen showing the side the Space Kicker flew, Lee focused on that alone as he inched closer, fighting the turbulence all the way.

The super cruiser dropped below the Space Kicker. Lee knew he wouldn't be able to right it in time, so did the only thing he could think of. Angling the portside hangar entrance upward, he swooped upward to claim the Space Kicker inside.

Continuing the movement, he rolled the right way back up as the docking grate closed. He then activated the communications back to the security team.

"Success," he reported with a dry voice.

He felt every part of him tensed, his body cold with the adrenaline rush of action. He blew out a tired, ragged breath and ran his hands through his hair as the reply came.

"Well done. Unfortunately, the mini cruiser bolted once you'd entered atmosphere."

"Did you follow?"

"No. We mean that literally, sir. It bolted. Somehow, that mini cruiser has a bolt power drive fitted to it."

Lee sighed in frustration. The old sci-fi films used to mention a state of space travel called hyperspace. The bolt power drive was as close to that state as the Suati had managed.

And it didn't leave any trace of where it might have gone. Trying to follow in the direction it had left from wouldn't do any good as direction changes could be programmed into the computer before the bolt engine was activated.

"They scarpered as soon as they fired the missile, right?"

"That last one? Yes, sir."

"They knew their time was up. Firing that missile was probably their last act of — if I'm following their actions correctly — forcing the feeling of fear of space."

"Is he doing okay? The pilot?"

"Since we know there's going to be no more attacks, I'm going to check. I'll keep you updated."

"You've done your dad proud today. He'd be very pleased to know what you did."

"Thanks."

Lee knew he couldn't feel proud yet. His best friend was still in an unknown state. Tom had helped Lee out of tight situations before.

It wouldn't be right if he didn't realise that Lee had just repaid that debt.

Kerry lowered her PMD with shock.

She didn't want to tell Casey the news, but it had to be done. Walking back inside, Casey remained where she had been for these long hours. Even the news of the rescue hadn't done much to get her active. Kerry had been unsure on exactly how to help but knew that not revealing the news would be worse than keeping it from her.

"Lee has rescued Tom," she started, looking carefully at the reaction of her friend. "He's already been admitted to the hospital. He's in a bad way."

She debated whether continuing with the rest of the story. It had to be told, she knew. Casey had looked up with lost, pleading eyes. She wanted to know.

"Lee did his best, but things looked serious up there. They went from charged static pulse lasers to CSP missiles, and as a last resort fired a burst missile before bolting. Lee and the security team did everything they could to hold the attackers off."

"Can we visit him?" Casey asked.

"Not until he wakes."

Casey let loose a strained wail, sounding like an injured pup. Kerry took it as the build-up of feelings being let loose after total constraint upon them for so long.

It summed up how she felt as well.

CHAPTER 4 – BLOCK AND BREAK

"After all that excitement from a few days ago, it's once again quiet up in space. The attackers have disappeared, with no new information coming to light on them. We haven't heard much about the condition of those who they had attacked but can confirm there is no serious injury. Restrictions have been lifted, so those that are training can get back at it. We hope to see the survivors of the attack back up here soon."

Pyra Summers of Radio Racer [02/3-0085]

Intense pain from being hit. Rocked from side to side as the 'craft tried to stabilise. Another hit. The capture. The panic. The elation of success followed by the sorrow of failure.

Unsure of where his best friend was. Unable to reach him on the communications link. No-one to talk to but the attacker. Forced into the asteroids.

Everything low within the 'craft. Nothing but rock and blackness to look on. Constant awareness of everything around him. Tiredness setting in. More failures on the 'craft. Ruptures within the spacesuit.

Pain ramps up. Starts in more places. Lack of oxygen brings sluggishness to his movements. Hard rasps pierce his ears. He is determined to see this through to the end.

Rock is no longer in sight. A blast shakes him up. His head hits the back support.

Somehow on the ground, he's following instructions from Lee on performing tricks. Now plummeting towards the ocean and water. Before he hits the scenery changes again to space. There's no danger.

Suddenly back within it. His awareness allows him to note the security team and a vehicle he is familiar with. A blast strikes. He is flung forward into the control board.

Tom wakes up in complete darkness. The light softness of the pillows and the covers does little to relax him.

Sitting up, he feels woozy. Unstable.

"Careful," a voice said.

"Where am I?" Tom asked, hearing the panic in his voice. The memory flashes were still vivid in his mind, and he had no memory of how he had got here. Just because everything was soft didn't mean the welcome would be.

"You're in the hospital," the voice answered. "Your friend brought you here immediately after he rescued you."

Tom blinked. "He did?" Lee had rescued him? From all of that? His best friend had looked out for him. Had risked himself. This was even more than a simple school fight. Not only had Lee repaid the debt, he had surpassed it.

"Indeed. They've been awaiting the news of when they can visit you. Everything is normal from what we can see. We've fixed up a few minor injuries, but there was nothing serious. You've been resting ever since. Now you are awake, we will slowly return the lights to normal."

"Right…"

Everything was normal? He had been blasted over and over again, nearly suffocated through lack of air, and everything was fine?

He heard the person walk out.

He was alone again.

His sense of panic had lessened, but it felt as though a part of him was still out there, being beaten by continuous missiles.

He felt around him. His hand landed on a table. Shuffling it around, he knocked into his PMD. Grasping it, he brought in front of his face and pressed the on button.

The light made his eyes water, forcing him to close them against the onslaught of light. Through the slits he made of them, he took note of the time. Placing his PMD back down on the table, he tried not to think of what had happened.

It was a long hour in which the lights slowly returned to standard output. He tried not to think of anything, but everything brought his thoughts back to the dangers of space. Even how hungry he was feeling and when he'd be able to get something to eat.

He was sat up and eating when Lee arrived with both mothers. Tom thanked Lee as soon as he could, and Lee wasted no time in launching into the story of the rescue.

Tom listened while eating and was fascinated by what it held. Lee in command of a squad from the CAF? A daring capture within the atmosphere? It sounded too good to be true. But Tom wouldn't say anything about such, as he enjoyed the thought that such events did happen.

"You're going to have to stay here for a day, they've said," Lee stated. "But once you're out, we can get back up there and continue the training."

"No."

Tom looked up to the excitement on Lee's face draining away at the simple word. Confusion took its place.

"What?"

"We agreed. We take a break for a week after that day. We stay on the ground for now."

"Yeah…" Lee scratched the side of his head. "I'd forgot about that. Whenever you want to get back up, say the word."

The rest of the visit flew by, with Lee saying that the Space Kicker had been taken to the spaceyard for some serious repairs. The DSSC now had a plan in place for all of those spare rooms which would be worked on during the break. All of them had been worried about him.

He couldn't express his happiness at having them here but felt a loss when it was time for them to leave.

It left him with nothing but his thoughts. Thoughts of a place he didn't want to be.

"Is Tom okay?" Matt asked as soon as Lee stepped inside.

"He's fine. Just needs a break from flying."

Lee still felt bad about trying to pressure his friend into heading back to training after his ordeal – however lightly he had put it. He'd got caught up in the excitement of seeing his friend well and revelling in the story of the rescue. Tom needed time to relax and Lee should have seen that.

"Good to know. Everyone needs a break from something now and then."

"I still want to know what he's really thinking." Lee stopped next to Matt. "He seemed pretty reserved during our visit."

"Give him time." Matt turned and indicated the exit out to where both vehicles waited. "The super cruiser is now working well. The strength of it is definitely the strongest point to take forward with new models."

"And the Space Kicker?" Lee asked.

"Bad. I don't think I've ever seen a puncture within the framework as bad as that."

Outside, Lee looked upon the Space Kicker. The entire of its plating had been removed. The right-side plate had a large hole pierced through it, and the thing that had caused it looked to have messed up the inside. Cables had been cut in half, with a few having been fully removed and scattered around. An entire section of the main internal components had also been damaged.

"We feel the stress of action has caused most of it," Matt explained. "Everything will have to come out of it. There's nothing that is salvageable from it. Just as we've given you the DSSC for testing, we'll also give you a new upgraded Space Kicker. I know we really shouldn't, but you've done a lot of good in testing this, and from what I heard, you've been a great leader."

Lee looked away from the damage at that remark.

"Where did you hear that?"

Matt gave a cheery laugh. "Soon as the Craftile security team returned to the Surveillance Cruiser, they were talking about how the son of Steve Johnson was just as great as the man himself."

Lee knew he'd done a good job with the commanding of the forces, but he felt himself conflicted with emotion at hearing that. He felt great joy at being as good as his dad, but the sorrow of missing his dad tried to cut into that. His eyes watered and he closed them.

"I'm just happy to have been a help," Lee said, opening his eyes again and wiping them.

"I'm sure they'd be happy to serve beside you if ever you wanted to take that command," Matt commented.

"I'll think about it," Lee responded in a small voice. He knelt beside the Space Kicker to look inside again. "Is everything here being taken elsewhere to research?" he asked.

"Can't make a stronger 'craft without looking at what needs to be strengthened. We know of the two areas that need work the most, so it shouldn't be long before you have a new 'craft to play with. I have a feeling that a version two of the Space Kicker will be out much faster than the other models."

"Makes sense, since all the others only had version twos made after no new 'craft had been built for a while." Lee checked the time as he climbed back to standing. "I need to get back, but I'll be here again tomorrow. Hopefully with Tom."

"Be happy to see you, any time." Matt waved him a goodbye, which Lee returned.

Walking back, Lee had time to think on the events again.

As soon as he'd signed off from the security forces, he'd contacted the hospital to let them know what had happened. They had said to land in the urgent care department and they would sort everything. Lee hadn't wanted to leave Tom alone, but when he had set the DSSC on autopilot and rushed down to the hangar, it dawned on him that he needed to.

He had focused purely on the Space Kicker and getting Tom out of it. Somehow, it had landed on its claws even if the magnetics had no longer worked. The viewshield had been pushed up easily, meaning the locks had failed on it. Lee had pulled Tom from the seat and lifted the cracked helmet away from his head. He hadn't responded to anything Lee had tried, and once the DSSC had landed and the emergency unit had entered to relieve him of Tom, their eyes had widened upon entering.

It wasn't until returning to the hangar after making sure that Tom had what he needed that he'd understood those reactions. The missile that had been fired into the hangar hadn't been a charged static pulse.

Aside from the warping in the walls and the blackened surfaces, nearly everything had been fine. Until he looked up to see cracks had formed everywhere. A closer inspection of the floor had revealed those same cracks.

But it had held, and the damage to the hangar had quickly been dealt with once Lee had taken the DSSC to the spaceyard.

Only as he had walked back on that night had he realised that maybe the emergency unit hadn't expected to walk in on a place that looked like it had been bombed.

That night, Mrs. Hughs had stayed over at the Johnson's house, where his mom had continued giving reassuring comfort to her. Mrs. Hughs had continued to stay at their house throughout. Lee felt she didn't want to be alone, and wondered if that was how Tom was feeling as well.

Tomorrow the two would be back together and never need feel alone again.

Casey lay on the bed, eyes staring up at the ceiling.

Tom was safe. He was healthy. She was still worried.

After the break of however many days, he and Lee would be back up in space and risk being targeted by the attackers again. She wouldn't be able to convince the two not to go up. Not with the Championship still going ahead as planned. And it would be going ahead. No-one else had been attacked. The attackers hadn't even been seen since. No-one seemed to realise they had been targeted because of the Championship.

Casey knew that was the truth.

Though the Talon Force connection had not been announced, it had somehow leaked out. The only speculation that had made itself known was that someone from Talon Force had been turned on by Adam Hughs and wanted to strike back through the only method available to them.

It was absurd to think of. Adam wouldn't ever attack anyone who wasn't attacking him. He was professional like that. But not everyone knew him as she did, and not everyone listened to the truth. At least, not all of it.

Tom would be safe as long as he remained grounded. She knew it was wrong to keep him so, with such an adventurous spirit. She just didn't want to lose him as she had felt would happen during these last few days. Despite the fact she knew he was safe and well, part of her still thought that something would go wrong.

It was worry, paranoia, and a whole load of other emotions warring with each other. Nothing could make it right, but these next few days would greatly help as she spent all the time with him that she could.

"There is no reason to believe anything about this being Talon Force members. The Championship is safe, and protection is being set up to help those who the attackers might go after. And for the next ques... Okay, I'll stop this for now and we'll go to some more tunes."

Pyra Summers of Radio Racer [03/3-0085]

The DSSC had been given to Lee so he could get Tom from the hospital. With him were the two mothers. Mrs. Hughs looked the same as ever when travelling in a vehicle more than eight meters from the ground, but the trip would be short and soon everything would be right.

Lee dropped the cruiser down to where he had last put it on instructions from the ground crew. Once landed, Mrs. Hughs bolted for the exit, Mrs. Johnson following quickly after.

Down in the hangar, Lee was impressed with the speed those of the spaceyard had worked. It was back to normal, with only a few small scratches on the other side that the Space Kicker had caused left to be dealt with.

Inside, Tom was sat up finishing a drink. One of the doctors was with him, standing and asking a few questions.

"I'm fine," Tom answered. "Fit and ready to go."

"That's what we like to hear," the doctor said. "Now, you mustn't dwell on what happened. That won't be good for your health. Just continue to work hard and bring the Champion name home for Saltare."

Lee waited for Tom's response. After a few seconds of Tom just sat with what almost seemed a conflicted expression, Lee answered for him. "We'll be having a small break but will be back up to space soon. We'll try our best to win."

The doctor turned to the group with a smile. "Whenever he's ready, he can go." He tapped the PMD he held, then added in a quiet voice, "He's made a quick recovery physically. It does seem there might be a bit of getting over the events that needs to happen, so I agree a break is best. Make sure he just relaxes for a few days with no worries."

"Will do," Lee said. He looked back to Tom as the doctor left to see that mild expression of conflict still on his face. "Come on, then. A nice walk to get you moving after the few days you've been here."

He stepped back so he could speak to his mother in a whisper. "You can pilot it back, right?"

"I remember the training, and it's only a short flight. I should be fine."

Mrs. Johnson moved off after saying she'll meet them all at home. Tom stood up, dropping his cup into the bin and followed her out the door. Lee and Mrs. Hughs followed last.

Outside the front entrance of the hospital, Lee looked up to see the DSSC fly overhead with just the slightest hint of a wobble. He looked down to see Tom also watching it.

"How is everything?" Tom asked.

Lee could tell there was something different about the voice of his friend. It sounded forced while trying not to seem like it. Lee also noticed Tom's left hand balled up by his side.

"Good," Lee replied.

"Good..."

Just the hint of relief in the voice that meant Tom hadn't wanted to discuss it. Lee would be keeping a careful eye on him.

The group walked it to the Hughs household, where Mrs. Johnson already sat. Four glasses of orange juice were set on the tables of the U-seat.

"Well, Tom," Mrs. Johnson started once all were sat down, "you've seen some action and survived through it. As the saying goes, that has strengthened you. Never let your thoughts go down the path of what-ifs. It's never good to do that."

"Thanks..." Tom said.

"Who wants to play a game of something?" Lee asked, attempting to move the thoughts of those events away.

Tom responded a lot more to the suggestion, even breaking into a smile. "Yeah, let's do it."

"How about a film?" Mrs. Hughs was quick to suggest. "Or a few episodes from a series?"

The Lightmorph Media Display lifted to a watchable state. Tom controlled the menus through his PMD. It was a new series that he'd chosen. Something to do with mysteries and a group who solved them while attending specialist education.

It was a funny thing for Tom to have selected, but Lee guessed it was just a way to avoid any thoughts of the last few days.

He found himself enjoying the episode the more he watched, and by the time a break was called they had got through four episodes.

"We can watch more tomorrow," Mrs. Hughs said. "For now, I think we ought to go out and have something to eat."

"Great idea," Tom exclaimed.

As Tom rushed out of the room, Lee had a quick thought and followed. Tom was already sat on one of the benches waiting.

"It's an enjoyable series, that," Lee started. "Had you heard anything about it before?"

"Nah, random pick." Tom had the air of being relaxed. He lounged on the bench with an arm over the back of it.

"So you'd want to be continuing it once we get back? You wouldn't want to be playing a game or heading elsewhere afterward?"

It was hardly visible, but Lee noticed it. The arm on the bench had tensed up, as though suspicious of where the conversation was heading.

"No." The voice was still the same, but with a hint of uncertainty. "I'm fine with watching the series."

Lee let the subject drop. He needed to not rush things. There had to be at least a few days where he didn't mention it to soften Tom up for what he eventually had to face.

There was just under ninety days until the Championship.

Lee had to give Tom all the time he needed. And for that to happen, Lee needed to forget about the Championship for the time being. Worrying about not being prepared would never allow him to keep quiet about getting back up into space, he knew.

There was one thing he could do. One he had said he would be doing. Once the meal had been finished, Tom was ready to get back and continue watching the series.

"I've got somewhere to be, but go ahead and enjoy it," Lee said.

He didn't want to be abrupt, but Tom probably knew where he was heading anyway, and outright saying it would just be another reminder of previous events that he didn't need.

"Tom not with you?" Matt asked.

"Still sorting through his thoughts," Lee commented. "He doesn't need reminders."

"You'll still be needing everything ready, right?"

"I'm giving it a week, then I'll be trying to get him back inside a control bay once again. If he gets in the air and finds no danger, I'm hoping he'll finally push through and expel whatever thoughts he's got that are blocking wanting to fly."

"Just be careful. I'd hate for anything to break the bond you two have."

"So would I." Lee knew he would be approaching the subject very carefully, and would only talk about it once there was an opening that Tom made.

"I'm going to enjoy the Championship this year. I do every year, and I never make it a point to win. For me, the Championship is meant to be a bit of friendly competition and a chance to make friends. We're all up there in space on that cruiser between events, why shouldn't we be having a chat and meeting new people?"

Rachel Carrington speaking on Radio Racer [15/3-0085]

It had been longer than a week.

Kerry had kept up to date with all the developments happening at the spaceyard concerning the Space Kicker, and the improvements on it were impressive.

It was a shame there had been no-one to test those improvements.

Ever since all repairs had been complete, the super cruiser had sat on their landing pad, with the Space Kicker still inside. It had been painted to be dark blue on Lee's request, and hadn't been touched since.

The two were away at school. It was the day they'd usually have a half-day for licence training, but what they'd be doing today Kerry had no idea.

Tom still refused to get up in the air.

Kerry walked up to the DSSC and opened the entrance. Climbing up, she looked inside. There the Space Kicker sat, awaiting some use.

She took a few steps forward. She still knew how to fly. She might not be as confident behind the controls, but knew exactly what she'd be doing.

She walked the rest of the way, pulled the viewshield canopy up, and settled inside. These new models really were different from the old ones. Holding the sticks in her hands, she reminisced about her escapades in a Braveheart model 'craft. She had only flown it between Hortii and Suati during her time as a courier, but she'd loved every moment of it.

Taking a deep breath, she waited a few seconds before engaging power to all systems. The screen was tuned to the status of the 'craft, with everything showing as one hundred percent ready for operation.

Reaching to the lever to pull the 'craft off the ground, it was then she remembered the docking grates were still closed and couldn't be opened except within the DSSC's control bay.

Sighing, she switched all power off. Not only would she need to head into the DSSC's control bay to open the docking grates, she'd also have to lift it off the ground and leave it unattended while she flew around.

Maybe sometime in the future she could get a new Braveheart and fly again.

The session had ended, with all other students dispersing out the door in twos and threes. They'd be talking to each other up until the point they reached where Tom sat. Each group that passed gave him words of encouragement – as they always had at this point since he became a competitor – but unlike the previous times this had happened, he didn't show any signs of recognition to them.

He had only been back starting this week. The overseers had allowed him a week to fully rest up and recover, and they'd also allowed Lee the same time off. They'd had two weeks away, and had been catching up with the work quickly.

Now the licence training session had arrived, which happened on every third-day of odd-numbered weeks of the afternoon. It was usually the time the two headed up to space to do more training for the Championship, but Tom seemed lost in thought today.

Almost as if he doesn't want to face anything, Lee thought. I've given it two weeks and not said anything. Now needs to be the time.

"Come on, then," Lee said in a cheery voice. "Let's get going."

Tom slowly looked up at him. "Where to?" he asked with the same slowness.

He waited until the tutor had left, then said "Home. Not like you'll be doing anything else."

"What am I meant to be doing?" Tom asked, and Lee realised he was mirroring the tone Lee had used. He hadn't meant to sound accusatory at all.

"I didn't mean anything," Lee was quick to say. "I just want to know why you've blocked the thought of flying."

"Who says I've blocked anything? Who says I'm not flying?"

"So... You are heading up to space?"

"Who said I was?"

It sounded like the problem was still there. He was still trying to deal with the danger he had been in. He was still in the land of what ifs. And had fallen for the most devastating one, it seemed, which had caused the block.

Lee tried a different tack as the two started heading for home.

"There's no danger to be going back up to space, you know. What happened was just a one off."

"You said that on the fifth day and look what happened on the sixth day. What if they had managed to get us on that fifth day? What if help hadn't come? What if... What if they had superweapons? What if-"

"Stop," Lee commanded. Tom fell silent. "You have to realise that safety measures have increased. Patrols have increased. No-one would try anything again with all of that."

"What if they did?" Tom said in a hard voice. "What if they had something outside of where all that security is? What happens if a new attack destroys me and others and the security teams are unable to do anything or pinpoint where the attack even came from?"

It took effort for Lee not to hysterically scream. There was no getting through at all. He wanted to help but had no idea what he could do beyond the reassurances he was giving. It was all true. He knew security had been increased to keep a watchful eye.

"The radar operators on board the Surveillance Cruiser are watching over everything happening up there," Lee tried again. "If they see anything suspicious, it would instantly be reported to the security teams who would quickly immobilise the suspicion."

The two were now out on the routes and quickly nearing Tom's home. This had to be done fast, but it seemed all he was doing was agitating Tom, and he felt he knew what reaction he would get once they were in sight of the gate.

"Do you even care what happens to me?" Tom asked, "or do you want to be up in space so much that you need to drag me along too?"

"That's not what I'm doing," Lee sternly admonished. "I am trying to help. Don't do this to yourself. Or to me."

"Doing what?" Tom scoffed, and without waiting for an answer sprinted to the connection and round the corner.

When Lee reached that point, the gate had already closed. He could easily enter the code and go for round two but felt it would be better to let Tom cool off.

Slowly he headed for his own home, and when he entered through the gate, he could hear talking.

"I'm sure Lee was trying to do his best," his mother said.

He didn't hear another voice and assumed she was talking to Mrs. Hughs on the PMD. He looked around for where she was and raised his eyes in surprise to see her sat on the edge of the DSSC's hangar.

"He's here now. Let me ask." Mrs. Johnson pressed something on the PMD and called to him. "What have you been saying to Tom?"

"What's he been saying about me?"

"Something about looking out for only yourself and not caring about your best friend."

That hurt. But it was Tom's warped thinking that had produced that result.

"I've been trying to help him, but he seems to have developed very strong feelings over this incident that happened and seems to have let it consume his thoughts in negativity."

Mrs. Johnson pressed the same button and raised the PMD up again. "Lee's been trying to help, but Tom doesn't seem to want it. I told him he shouldn't be thinking on the previous events, but he seems to have done exactly that." Her eyes flicked up to meet Lee's, then back down again. "We just need to give him more time, I guess. Maybe a softer approach..."

Lee didn't hear what was said, but Mrs. Johnson rolled her eyes at it.

"Yes, he is safe. There's nothing to say he's being specifically targeted, even if these last two weeks have yielded no more attacks. We'll talk more in the morning, or later on if needed."

The called ended. Mrs. Johnson climbed up from sitting and gave Lee a helping hand onto the hangar floor.

"Have you been in this all day?" Lee asked.

"Having a try of the facilities," Mrs. Johnson answered with an indication to follow. "It seems that during the repairs they finished

93

off the catering room. There was a note inside saying the only thing they need to do is add a divider into the lounge."

"Great. The only thing left is the bedrooms and whatever the forward rooms are to be."

"I've had a thought about that. The larger cruisers have maintenance stations, and this is big enough to have one."

"Makes sense. I'll see what they say next time I'm there. They'll probably be able to finish all that by the time Tom's in a better state of mind."

"Is that a touch of bitterness I sense?"

"Okay," Lee conceded. "I might have been a bit more aggressive than I should have in trying to reassure him that he's safe. I just can't measure how much he's really been affected because it's not a state of mind I've experienced before."

They were now in the catering room. It was small but serviceable, and several food items had already been put into the secure storage shelves.

"That's the reason you've pushed him away. Try again with the same attitude and you two will just drift further apart."

"Something I don't want to happen."

Lee helped with the food preparation, and once finished the two moved into the lounge to eat. His mind was on the situation with Tom.

There had to be some way to get through to him. There just had to be.

"There are sixty days left before the Championship starts. I'm going to be looking back at the previous Championships in the build-up to this one, and I'll be discussing it with those previous champions along with a few other guests. It's nice to look back once in a while. It helps build the excitement for the next event."

Pyra Summers of Radio Racer [31/3-0085]

More than two weeks later, the situation was now worse.

Lee had said hardly anything of the Championship, only ever referring to it in a way of a spectator rather than someone helping a competitor. The only thing that seemed to have done was drive Tom away from him. It seemed as though Tom still cared that he was a competitor of the Championship even if he still wanted to be nowhere near a spacecraft.

It confused Lee a lot. He had no way to deal with it, to get through to Tom.

Then a week ago, it had felt as though Tom had blocked Lee altogether. They'd even stopped walking back together, and when Lee had tried to walk with him Tom had quickened his pace. The next day Tom had changed his route to the school.

As Lee walked to the school, he wasn't surprised that this route had failed to find Tom on it. He seemed to be doing everything to avoid Lee.

Joining the stream of students entering the building he needed to be, Lee didn't spot Tom anywhere until right inside the classroom. The rows of tables had half been filled, with Tom sat in the middle of the front row surrounded by others. There was no reaction from Tom as Lee walked by, and he didn't turn around to see where Lee had sat.

As others filed in and took seats, the tutor arrived. The Lightmorph Media Display rose from the front table. The remainder of the students arrived and the class began.

Lee should have been paying attention, but he only felt a gnawing loneliness. The others around him were friendly enough but weren't who he would consider friends. He had a small bit of hope that Tom hadn't talked to anyone else either, meaning he still felt Lee was a friend. It was only the negative thoughts that stopped him communicating with Lee. Another reminder of what he was trying to forget.

It still wasn't helping Lee get over his own thoughts.

It felt all too similar to what had happened during their advanced education years. Except that time had been worse, Lee felt. There had been more at stake during that time.

It still didn't help ease the crushing loneliness.

"Lee!" the tutor called.

Lee blinked. He hadn't realised he had dozed off. He looked around to see everyone else had left – including Tom.

"Is there anything bothering you?" the tutor asked in a lighter tone. He looked concerned.

"No," Lee replied firmly. "There's nothing."

Lee looked into the tutor's eyes and could tell the tutor saw right through the lie. It was hard not to, with how different he acted these days.

The tutor said nothing more and let him go.

Lee hurried to the next sector that held nothing but the largest shopping centre of this county, stopping outside the entrance. It would be impossible to find him if he didn't want to be found, and Lee had no idea what he'd say to him if he did.

He sat on a bench eating the pasta pot he'd bought, thinking of ways he might be able to get Tom to open up. There had to be a way to do so.

Slowly he made his way back to the school and sat through the second session much the same as he had the first. They were more active in this session than the last, but Lee had nothing to really give.

He looked over at the group Tom had joined and watched the others mostly working away while Tom seemed lost in his own thoughts. When someone asked for an opinion on something, he'd give it, but he didn't offer anything without first being asked. His own group seemed to know his mind wasn't fully on task and left him out of everything.

Once the session ended, Lee had made a choice.

Tom had quickly left at record pace as soon as everyone had been dismissed. Lee followed as fast as he could.

Down the corridor and out the entrance, he looked left and right. Tom's red shirt looked like a beacon among the green of the grass. Lee hurried up to him.

"Hey," he called. "You want to do something?"

Tom didn't even turn. He just continued walking. Lee followed, knowing that being persistent might not be the best thing to do right now but wanting to try to force Tom to be open.

"Can you just tell me something? What if you were to fight your fears? What if you were able to overcome them?"

He didn't expect an answer, but he was trying to feed Tom's continuous thoughts of what if in a positive direction.

Why? Tom thought. Just leave me alone.

He still didn't know what to say to Lee. Had no idea of anything he wanted to say. All he wanted was to be left alone. He just wanted... He didn't know what he wanted, but it had to be better than trying to answer to Lee.

What if he got to space and was instantly targeted?

It was a thought that wouldn't go away.

What if he could fight... No. It wasn't fear.

What if he could overcome... No. Whatever this was, it was something he couldn't.

He heard nothing else from Lee and looked behind him before he could stop himself.

Lee had gone.

There remained an emptiness in him the remainder of the way back home. Inside, he sat down and let the events replay.

It was still the same.

But Lee wasn't the cause of them. He was the saviour. Tom knew he should be showing a lot more respect for Lee, but if the two were together, Lee would be convincing him to head up to space for training.

He didn't need that. Thus, he kept distant from his best friend.

The events replayed again in his mind. This time, he did what he'd been doing the past few weeks, and put Lee into those events that made him the cause of them. He convinced himself he didn't need Lee. He convinced himself there was nothing to be gained from continuing to be by Lee's side.

This time, though, it wouldn't happen.

What if he could fight... everything he was going through?

"Okay, so the 0050 Championship had a complete ruleset change owing to the popularity of the previous Championship. Those rules have held ever since, apart from a few small changes and of course the rotation and addition of new events. Do you feel such a change was the start of the increased popularity we see today?"

Pyra Summers of Radio Racer [09/4-0085]

Lee admired the rooms that had been completed on the DSSC. The two starboard side rooms of the upper level had been converted to bedrooms, with three beds per room and a small communal area linking them. The kitchen on the port side now had that divider into the lounge, which lined up pretty well with the ramp to get down to the lower level.

The forward rooms of the lower level had indeed been converted to a maintenance bay, complete with everything that the Johnsons had at their own maintenance bay for easy recharging and fixing of any 'craft within the hangar.

The only problem was that time for the Championship drew near yet Tom had been nowhere near the Space Kicker. It remained within the hangar untouched.

Lee hadn't wanted to take it out with no-one else to be with, but now the DSSC had been fully formed, he wanted to get it out to space to see how everything handled the entry and exit of the atmosphere. The Space Kicker was also still untested. He had wanted Tom to do the testing as he'd already flown it and would know the differences, but as time edged nearer to the Championship, it couldn't be left much longer.

He looked for his mother around the DSSC. She remained in the larger of the two bedrooms, looking at the communal area.

"I'm liking it," she said upon seeing Lee. "A little basic, but everything that's needed."

"Would you trade it for the house?" Lee asked, tone making it clear he wasn't serious.

"There's something we've missed in the design of this that would make it impossible to do so. No bathroom."

"Pretty sure the plans said there'd be one in this room..." Lee walked around and pushed doors open where needed. The fourth door that should have held a basic bathroom instead held another bed. "Ah. Someone missed that on the plans."

"It can wait until after the Championship," Mrs. Johnson stated. "We won't be using this for long periods anyway."

Lee turned and looked at her, thinking. He made his decision. If he was to convince Tom, this would go a long way in doing that.

"Would you be able to take control if I were to go up to space?"

"You're thinking of getting into that Space Kicker and testing the waters, aren't you? I'm up for that. Been a while since I've been up there."

The DSSC quickly made it up to space, and Lee was happy to see no mess within any of the rooms from the traversal. There was a lot to be said for gravity generators.

Inside the Space Kicker, he had a look on the board, taking note of where everything was located. The portside docking grate opened, and he sped outside into the void of space.

The Space Kicker handled better than he could have imagined. He'd been practising with a version two Rotablade during licence training, and if asked – that would be the one he'd choose as his own. The Kicker tested his resolve with that, but while it was good at speed, it had already proven defence was a weakness. While a second version would help with that, he still remained unsure.

And this currently wasn't even version two. It was effectively a prototype for a version two. That was the difference.

Without a plan of action, he ran through most of the systems. The mega power drive swapped in and ran without issue. All engines and repulse-pads had no issues either. It controlled perfectly and ran perfectly. Everything functioned as it should.

It should have been Tom sat within it enjoying himself as he always had.

"Everything's as it should be, and no-one has fired a single missile or CSP our way. Definite success."

"Will Tom see it that way, though? The way he's been?"

"He'll see sense in the end. If he still wants to be a competitor of the Championship – which I feel he does – then this block he's formed to flying will have to break. Even if he doesn't respond to my safety talk at first, I know he eventually will."

"Head inside and take back control, then. We may as well head back home if you're done."

"Returning now."

It had been a lot longer than Casey had expected. Tom still hadn't been up into space, and she was grateful for that.

She hadn't attempted to get him up to space, and though she knew relations between him and Lee were strained, she hadn't attempted to heal that either. It was almost as if she was back in the simpler times of five years' previous. If only Adam had been here as well.

Her PMD lit up with a call. She answered to hear Kerry's greeting, which jumped straight into asking if they could come over.

Kerry not being there for her was the only downside to recreating the past, since those visits had all but stopped as relations were strained between the two boys, and both had agreed not to arrange visits until that relationship had healed.

"How are you getting here?" Casey asked.

"We've been up in space testing the improvements," came the reply. "We'll be arriving in the DSSC."

Been up in space.

Casey felt a chill that had nothing to do with the temperature of the room. If they were coming from space, they knew it was safe and would try telling Tom that. She didn't want to refuse the visit, though, as she didn't want their relationship to degrade the same as the boys had.

"I'll be waiting outside for you," Casey informed, "but I have no idea if Tom will be willing to talk."

"We'll try anyway. See you in a bit."

Casey returned the PMD to her pocket and took a few steps toward Tom's room. She paused. Would it be better if he didn't know of the visit?

She turned and walked outside to watch as the super cruiser came in for a landing. It would be a surprise for him, but hopefully he'd respond better with a surprise visit.

It settled down on the landing pad, with a minute passing before the entrance opened to reveal Kerry. Climbing down, she came in for a hug as Lee climbed down behind her.

Casey led the two inside. Tom waited at the entrance of the kitchen. His expression said he wasn't happy they had company.

It also seemed a bit abrupt of Lee to quickly jump to saying where they'd been without a greeting.

"We've been up in space testing all the improvements done to both cruiser and 'craft. We came here to say there's absolutely no danger at all."

Tom walked around the U-seat to where Lee stood. He seemed to be working up to saying something. Giving a deep breath, he launched into what he had to say.

"Look. I'm sorry for being a complete idiot and being a jerk for ignoring you, but there's no way you can convince me that it's safe up there. I'm not getting into a spacecraft and I'm not going to space."

"Not even for the Championship?" Lee asked.

"The Championship will be safe. Everything before then isn't."

"You mean you'll be entering unprepared for what you'll be facing."

"At least I can duck out early and have it not mean anything."

Casey watched with apprehension, sure that it would break out into a fight. She looked to Kerry, who seemed to be doing some quick thinking.

"Then why enter at all?" Lee asked. He seemed about to continue, but Kerry cut across him.

"Tom. Think back to when you went to Donaldo. Was that not as dangerous as what you experienced? Were you not under as many if not more what-if situations, but even further away from home with absolutely no help whatsoever?"

"It was different then," Tom said with the air of convincing himself. "I was in control and could act as needed."

Casey felt he had a good point, but had to reason with herself she would agree with anything if it meant Tom would stay grounded. It was selfish on her part not to help him.

But what to say?

"You had control during the attack," Lee reasoned. "It just got out of hand and you needed help. The reality was that help didn't come as soon as you needed it, and control of the situation quickly left you. If help had managed to find you sooner, you'd still have had control of it."

"That your way of saying things could have been worse?" Tom's friendly outlook had vanished with those words, and Lee was quick to soften things up.

"Not at all. Just pointing out that control could have been taken from your hands on Donaldo and no-one would have known. At least during the attack, people were able to respond."

"When you put it like that..."

"Are you ready to take my word that you are safe and you'll have help if ever you get into trouble?"

A slight pause. "Yes."

"Are you ready to test out the Space Kicker and see what improvements have been made upon it?"

A slightly longer pause. "No."

Casey looked from Tom to Lee, then at Kerry. Looking back to Tom, she could see conflict within his thoughts. He'd been convincing himself he didn't need anything to do with flying for just over a month, though she felt it had been fear keeping him grounded. His fears had been put to rest, but he still felt them.

It was now a case of him fighting those fears – even if he had said it wasn't fear.

"We'll leave you to think on all that we've said," Kerry stated, pulling Lee back. "For now, we'll be going."

"Are you sure you won't stay for something to eat?" Casey asked.

Tom looked as though he was holding back from saying something. Lee looked as though he wanted to say more but knew when to admit defeat. Maybe time was needed to process what had been said.

Goodbyes were exchanged, with Casey following Kerry and Lee back out to the landing pad. She watched as the DSSC lifted off and headed the small distance to the Johnson's household, continuing to watch as it dropped in for a landing.

Once out of view, she headed for the door to head inside. Tom stood just within the frame, looking as though he had also been watching the journey of the super cruiser.

He noticed her approach and slipped inside. When she followed, he had already disappeared.

As she prepared a meal for two in the kitchen, she thought on what had been said and her own stance of things during the past month. She had been willing to sit on the sidelines, hoping that whatever was affecting Tom would keep him permanently grounded and never want to head up.

She hadn't been supportive of him. She hadn't been helping him. She had been trying to live a fantasy.

Adam, wherever you are, I promise you that our son will get as far in this Championship as possible, and I will help him however I can. I should never have been as selfish as I have been.

It was all that needed saying.

All Tom needed now was to accept that he wasn't in any danger and get back to training. She had a feeling he'd be more persuaded by her words, so when the food was prepared, she loaded half onto a plate and tray and took it to his room.

She found him lay on the bed with Radio Racer playing from his PMD – something that he had refused to listen to for a month.

"I brought some food," she announced.

Tom sat up quickly and took the tray from her with a smile. When he started eating, she steeled herself for saying what she had to.

"I haven't been very thoughtful of you," she said, looking for a reaction. Tom gave none, still enjoying the meal. She continued regardless, feeling that he was still listening. "I haven't been trying to help you at all. I just want to say I'm sorry. If you've had any negative thoughts about me, I can't say I blame you."

She waited again for a response. When none came, she turned and walked out. At the door, she heard Tom speak.

"I've not had any bad thoughts about you. Invite them over this weekend, and I'll stay friendly."

Casey stood with a smile and nodded without looking at him. She was convinced that he would soon be back in space.

"There's a lot of movement up in space now, as preparations are made. Two cruisers from Suati have moved into position near the Surveillance Cruiser, and a lot of security is now in effect. Things are heating up, and with just five weeks to go until the Championship begins, there's bound to be a lot going on up here."

Pyra Summers of Radio Racer [14/4-0085]

Tom hadn't said much to Lee – in school or out – but they were at least friendly to each other again. Tom hadn't said anything about the last month, seemingly slowly working at repairing the rift that had formed between them.

Lee didn't mind. It would happen eventually, so he let Tom work up to finally saying what he wanted to. It was clear that Tom now wanted to get back up to space and make up for lost time, but seemed unable to express that.

He hadn't expected it to come as early as this, though.

At the end of the session, the two walked out of the school together in silence. Lee turned to say something, but Tom beat him to it.

"We go straight to yours. We head out."

"Into space?" Lee asked, surprised.

"Yes. I'm ready."

Lee almost broke into a huge smile, but stopped himself, settling for a smaller, friendlier one instead.

"That's great. We'll take it easy at first, just to get you used to being in space again. We'll make this work."

"In the time left?" Tom asked.

Lee nodded. When he looked, Tom seemed to be struggling with something.

"Look," he finally said. "I just want you to... Just... Thanks, I guess. For putting up with me."

"I shouldn't have been so pushy," Lee stated. "We're both good."

"No, I mean it." Tom's voice now had confidence to it. "You saved me from the attackers and the only thing I did was push you away. I'm sorry and I can't express it enough how much I am."

All Lee wanted was his best friend back. He didn't need to hear what Tom was saying, as long as he was beside him again. There was no need to mention that though, so the two walked to Lee's house and the DSSC and prepared to lift off.

Tom certainly had fun flying once again, and Lee delighted in seeing Tom perform tricks as though he had never taken a month off from training.

There were a few new cruisers around, and Lee studied the designs for them. He always loved drinking in the Suati culture, and these cruisers looked as if they'd been built on Suati. It was the placement of the control bay that was the biggest clue. The cruisers of the STRDC had the tower above the main body to the rear. Those of Suati had a longer tower forward but with a shorter main body. He'd never been on one but wanted to explore.

After an hour, Tom docked with the DSSC and Lee took it down. The two were in high spirits.

"You can take the Space Kicker back to your pad if you want," Lee said. "I'll race you to get up to space tomorrow after school."

"You're on," Tom said with a grin.

He flung himself around his seat, Lee watching him all the way outside. Before he dropped the DSSC, he watched the Space Kicker land, finding a smile escaping him.

This was how it was meant to be.

Chapter 5 – Prelude to the Championship

"I often wonder what happened to those two. The fact they both managed to reach the final was impressive. The fact they didn't return to try and get a Championship to their name is surprising. I guess if they're still around, they'll be helping their young sister train to get to the final."

Christian Vizley speaking on Radio Racer [29/04-0085]

Tom couldn't believe that less than three weeks ago he'd been ready to dive out of the Championship at the first opportunity he got. He was back within the control bay of the Space Kicker and loving every minute of it. He couldn't believe he'd wanted to give all this up. He was back in love with the Space Kicker, but he felt this wasn't the Space Kicker he knew.

He'd noticed a few factors within the 'craft different from his previous experience. The material used was slightly heavier with a bit more thickness to it, making the 'craft need a bit more power under gravity for movement. The screen size had also been slightly increased – as had the entire control board. A few switches were also in slightly different places thanks to that size increase.

He'd took it all in stride and learnt everything about this new and improved version of the Space Kicker, but felt the response time in changing speed still needed adjusting even after several attempts at trying to get it as close as possible to how it had been previously.

There had been no attacks from anyone, so he and Lee had been left on their own whenever they came up to space for training.

Even if they weren't alone.

He'd become used to just seeing the Surveillance Cruiser around. A stationary cruiser watching over the happenings in space. Several other cruisers had since appeared, and he thought he recognised one from the latest update of Space Racer.

"Okay," Lee called. Tom looked out to where the DSSC waited. "You can come on in now."

Tom didn't reply, choosing to head straight for the DSSC's hangar. Training had gone well for another day, and being a fifth day meant they had been up here for most of the entire day. Lee had treated Tom to some of his own cooking, which had been an odd mix of regular meat-sticks and Suati spicegrass. Lee certainly seemed to be developing a taste for all of Suati culture.

As Lee took the DSSC back to the Hughs household, Tom checked for messages on his PMD to find an official-titled document from the STRDC.

"I've got a message about the Championship," he stated, slowly reading. "It's instructions for the event."

"And?" Lee asked.

"In two weeks, all competitors will be going up to the Sur-C."

"Fifth day of week seven?" Lee used the more technical date instead of the informal day and month format. "Does it give a reason?"

"Preparation and signing of all 'craft and support. New competitors are being put through first, with my name being one of the first overall."

"What's the final date?"

"Day six with only two names. Every name has an hour slot marked."

"That sounds like an awful lot of preparation per person."

"It might not take the full hour..."

Within the lounge of Tom's house, the two relayed the news of when they'd be going up to the Surveillance Cruiser for the start of the Championship. Mrs. Hughs looked a bit nervous but did her best to hide it.

"You'll soon be showing everyone how good you are," she said. "Let them know just how good the son of Adam Hughs is."

Upon saying that she looked close to tears, so Tom hugged her to show his love for both his mom and his dad. The emotional pain that his dad wouldn't be here to see him fly hurt a lot. He was usually good at hiding it, but today seemed the time to let it show.

It was then he realised something. His dad had said once that giving up should never be an option to following dreams. Tom had done exactly that. Or at least it felt like it, no matter what the cause of it had been.

❖

Darkness had fallen.

Kerry wandered the house, pacing from kitchen to lounge and back again. She had held it in for so long, but seeing the emotion that both Tom and Casey had shown over missing Adam had been too much. She had hidden her own hurt from them and suspected only Lee had picked up on it.

Once everyone else had turned in for sleep, she had come out here to let her own hurt out. Her Steve was out there. Knowing the name of the system and what the mission roughly entailed never helped with that hurt. It was a dangerous mission, for all of the fighters of the Craftile Armed Forces.

In the kitchen again, she stopped to pour a drink. She felt in control again. She had to remain in control. She had a feeling Casey would be needing her support tomorrow, and that support wouldn't be easy to give if she wasn't in control.

Soft footfalls reached her ears, followed by the sound of a door. Placing the cup down, she knew that someone had gone outside. Who that was she would find out.

Walking outside herself, she heard the slight grind as the airlock entrance to the DSSC opened. Around the house, she spotted a figure climb inside. She followed and climbed up herself.

Someone sat within the Space Kicker with its viewshield open. The light from the screen flashed across his face.

Tom.

When she walked up to him, he didn't look at her. He just stared into the screen. She looked at the screen to see the registered information of the Space Kicker that showed where it had come from. The information also included the designation code – A/41m2209.

The code had been transferred from the old Space Kicker, possibly on Lee's insistence. They both knew the code was important, as it translated to Adam's name and his birthdate.

"Hey," Kerry softly said.

Tom looked up, surprised.

"I didn't expect anyone else to be up," he stated.

"It's a raw feeling night for us all," Kerry said. "Those instructions just made it clear that – unless they were to arrive back soon – they won't see how good you are. But," she added, trying for some positive spin, "even if they don't, you will have a story to tell them."

"It'd be much better were I living the moment with him. And Mr Johnson. It just doesn't feel whole."

"We will be. I don't know when, but we will." Kerry reached out to switch the power of the Space Kicker off. "You need sleep. You've got to be on form for a new day of training."

"Yeah…"

Kerry followed Tom back inside.

"In a way…" Tom started. "I'm happy he wasn't here."

Kerry quickly formed a response to that, but Tom managed to beat her to speech.

"Happy that he never saw me giving up on a dream."

Kerry changed the response to something more comforting.

"I'm sure he'd have said it's a natural thing to have gone through with what happened. Ask him when he returns. Maybe with him by your side, he'd have been able to make you see enough sense that you wouldn't have given up."

"It's a thought…" Tom left her in a hurry.

Maybe she shouldn't have said that. It was another case of what-ifs, this time tied to a subject that was already a raw topic of discussion.

Returning to the kitchen, she formed the Lightmorph Media Display to a small screen, scrolling through the stored pictures until she arrived at one in particular.

The two families had celebrated the end of the 0080 Championship much the same as others had. This photo of all six people showed how much the two families had shared in such a short amount of time, and how much that friendship had grown.

She looked at Tom and Lee kneeling on the grass, fists together and smiles on their faces. Stood behind them were both Adam and Steve with thumbs held out and massive grins. Casey stood next to Adam, with herself next to Steve.

This Championship would end on a similar note, but no matter where Tom ended up in the rankings, it would never reach the happiness presented in this picture.

Not without Adam and Steve.

"I've got such a good time starting from tomorrow. I'll be meeting with all the competitors of the Championship as they register starting from tomorrow. Some of them I've already met, but quite a few remain unknown to me. This is the point that the Championship really starts. And now for the music of the day."

Pyra Summers of Radio Racer [40/4-0085]

"Come on. You haven't seen it. Don't you want to?"

"Yes," Lee said, "but do you really want to risk any damage this close to the Championship? This is no time for massive risk-taking."

"It'll be different this time. You'll be there to help me out of any situation that might arise."

Lee muted his audio pickup and gave a sigh. He should have expected it. Now that Tom had gained his confidence of flying again, he had been wanting to go back to Donaldo – even if he hadn't said anything. Now he was, and Lee had to admit to being curious as to why.

"Do you want to take the lead, or head back in and we'll go together?" he asked upon turning his audio pickup back on.

He heard Tom's surprise in his voice. "You mean it? No arguments?"

"I'm interested in seeing the planet, and I know better than to try and say no to you."

"Swapping to the MPD. See you there."

Lee almost exclaimed with a wait but just about withheld it. He'd give Tom a head-start then show him exactly how much speed a mini cruiser could give. He watched the Space Kicker accelerate away, then set his own computer for maximum speed. He pushed the handle all the way to full speed, watching as the actual speed quickly jumped to meet the set speed.

Then he swapped to the mega power drive.

A second delay, then it kicked in to produce a massive burst of acceleration that kept increasing. Lee watched the scanner to see his own blip pass Tom within seconds. After a few more seconds Lee felt he needed to decrease speed, otherwise he'd feel the sudden change once he swapped down to the kilo power drive again. He might have felt confident accelerating from maximum, but decelerating still gave him a funny feeling even at lower speeds.

Once there, he waited for Tom to arrive. He wanted them both to head down together. And he still wanted an explanation as to why Tom wanted to come here.

The Space Kicker decelerated to a hard stop on his left.

"That's a gut-punch." Tom's voice sounded as though he'd had his breath slammed out of him. He gave a cough and continued. "But worth it. So worth it."

"You okay?" Lee asked, unsure if this really was a good idea.

"Yeah." The voice came as a harsh rasp, seeming less raspy when he repeated what he had said. "Yeah."

"Now… What are we doing here?"

"Once we get down there, I'll tell you."

Tom accelerated away toward the planet. Lee quickly fell in behind him. The atmosphere looked wild, but that was nothing compared to below the clouds.

Bright red flashes were the storm. The winds were fierce. The light from the system's star failed to penetrate the dark cloud cover. He worked to keep the DSSC stable as it travelled around a mountain, keeping an eye on where the Space Kicker was as best as he could.

"Now, are you going to tell me why we're here?"

"When we first trained, I came here. Remember? Just a fleeting impulse. Returning is like... Well, it shows a sign of how far I've come. Being here at both ends of my training."

Lee found he liked that answer. It was a talisman of sorts, except the object was the planet itself. It was the real start of Tom's dream to be an explorer – having finally been to a new planet to experience what it offered. Lee guessed it would signify good luck.

The mountain had been passed, with another taking its place. This region of the planet seemed nothing but mountains.

He swapped to the status screen as another red flash blinded his view outside. The reading indicated that each flash seemed to be sapping power from the DSSC. He flicked the switch to prepare the atmos power drive. He then tried to get Tom's attention.

"Tom, check your status screen and report."

He looked back outside to see the Space Kicker still flying through the storm, managing a few close dodges away from the mountains.

"Okay, I've had my fun," Tom's voice sounded. "Returning now."

Lee noted his friend's voice sounded as though his fun had been cut short, but there was a time for playing around and this wasn't it.

Tom said he was in position to head inside the hangar, so Lee quickly lifted the grate up. Once Tom confirmed he was in, Lee let it close again.

The atmos power drive had found the required speed, with an indicator announcing it could be swapped to.

Tom bounded into the control bay, sitting down next to Lee. He had a joyous look upon his face. He had definitely enjoyed his time here.

Lee frowned as he looked back at the computer. A message had been received. He looked at the indicator saying the APD was ready, then back at the message. Activating the message, a voice speaking the Suati language had just one thing to say.

"Gata ah! Gata ah!"

Lee knew enough of the Suati language to know what that meant, but it was too much to expect just the two of them to be able to do anything. He traced the origin of the message to one of the mountains. Quickly he took the DSSC in that direction.

That rumour of the research station was true after all.

"I thought we were getting out of here," Tom exclaimed. "What was that message anyway?"

"It was a call for help," Lee stated. "I'm going to see what help is needed."

"So long as you're quick. Remember the power loss."

"I know."

Arriving near to the message origin, the reason the Suati on the base needed help was clear. Two 'craft were strafing around it, firing a continuous stream of lasers. This super cruiser had no weapons, and neither did the Space Kicker. They wouldn't be able to help.

Lee was about to activate the audio pickup to send a reply when Tom leaned forward.

"It is. That's the 'craft that attacked me. Quick! Go!"

The two 'craft seemed to notice the new arrival and stopped attacking the base. They turned around to face the DSSC and fired lasers as a warning.

Lee looked at the still active APD indicator, then made a choice. He accelerated toward the two attackers.

"What are you doing?" Tom asked in a panic.

"If you're right and those are the attackers who were after us, I expect they might want a round two."

That was confirmed when a voice sounded through the speakers.

"Give up already, or do you really need a new lesson?"

Tom certainly seemed to remember the voice as well. "What are you doing here? Is this where you've been since you attacked me? Harassing the Suati that live here?"

"We knew trying to attack you again wouldn't work. Security is so tight around there now. We took a chance hoping you'd be back here eventually, so yes. We have been harassing the Suati."

"Leave them alone. You've got us now."

Lee looked down at the scanner to see the two 'craft were now following them. Neither had fired yet, but it felt close. Lee cycled the APD to make absolutely sure it would be able to get them away fast. The calculations took seconds.

"We do. And you are never returning to take a chance at the Space Race Championship. You will never race again. All it would take is one shot. Are you prepared for that?"

"Try it," Tom said, looking to Lee.

Their eyes locked. Tom gave a nod.

Lee dropped the cruiser so that what should have been a disabling shot right between all four of the engines impacted on the top surface. The atmos power drive then activated, quickly accelerating the DSSC to rocket speed.

It faltered. Then stopped. It activated again for a few seconds. Lee didn't give it a chance to fail again and swapped to the mega power drive.

"We'll do this manually, then," he growled.

He knew the two attackers were still following, hoping to still get a disabling shot on them. Once out of the atmosphere, Lee did the one thing he knew would scare the two off.

Broadcast across most of the East Star and hopefully to the West Star so that Suati heard it as well was an emergency signal that requested help immediately. Everyone would pick it up, and that was the point.

After a few seconds, he turned it off. He'd made sure people would come.

Looking down at the scanner, he spotted the two attackers heading in the opposite direction. Their blips disappeared despite still being within viewable range. Wherever they were going, it was a secret.

"We're going back by a long route," Lee alerted Tom. "Those on the station will be able to explain everything, and it'll also keep a direct route clear for anyone answering that call."

"Fine by me," Tom said. "We don't need any awkward questions about what we were doing there."

"I'd have the answers. I just want to avoid the complication of having to give them."

"They have some nerve, though."

Lee looked up to see Tom as near to angry as he'd seen him in a long time.

"Who? Those two?"

"Yes, those two. Attacking innocents just to get to us. More innocents, I might add. Just what do they have against us, anyway? And how do they know I've been to Donaldo before? I've hardly said I've been there to anyone."

Lee had no answers to those questions. If he worked on the basis of all those rumours that they were Talon Force members, it still didn't make sense unless they'd had a serious grudge against Mr Hughs. But then attacking his son wasn't doing anything about that unless they knew for sure that he'd be returning to the bad news.

That gave Lee a little hope that at least both Mr Hughs and his own dad were still alive. Six months was still a long time for something to have happened, though. He still held that hope anyway.

As they looped around the star and made a direct route back to Hortii, Lee wondered if any help had arrived for the Suati of Donaldo yet.

"I'm out here on the hangar with remote access to the tunes as I prepare myself for meeting all the competitors of this day. All of those on the list for today are new to the Championship, so I'm going to be getting their thoughts and feelings on how they expect to do during the event."

Pyra Summers of Radio Racer [41/4-0085]

Clothes were ready and packed in the DSSC. Casey stood outside looking at it as Lee passed a few more things up to Tom.

It was the part she most disliked soon to happen.

She had never enjoyed space travel, or even being in the air, though that was probably due to a lack of experience even being a passenger. To get up to the Surveillance Cruiser, she needed to be on the DSSC as it travelled. She accepted that she'd rather be up in space getting caught up in all the action close by then sat down here on her own watching what happened. Thus, she could brave one journey.

"I think we're all ready," Tom called down.

"Great," Kerry said as she walked out of the house. "Everything is powered down in there, so we can move as soon as."

Once Tom and Lee had returned to the Hughs' house after training, everything needed from their house had been loaded into the DSSC, which had then travelled the short distance to the Johnson's. There it had stayed for the night until the morning, in which it now had to travel up to space.

"I'll get it prepared to move," Lee said, climbing up with a hand from Tom.

Kerry walked over to Casey and put an arm around her to guide her to the entrance.

"You going to be alright?" she asked.

"I'll be fine. I don't want to be stuck down here while you lot have all the fun. I'll push through my fears the same as Tom did."

"Good to hear," Kerry replied, indicating that Casey could go first.

The steps up were slightly awkward to climb, but she managed. It was slightly easier than the first time she had tried, though admittedly she had tried to rush up them that time. She waited for Kerry to climb up, then the two walked it to the control bay. Lee waited in the pilot's seat with his hands ready to take to the controls. Tom sat in the co-pilot seat, looking out at the sky.

Casey sat down behind Tom with Kerry behind Lee.

"Ready," Kerry announced.

"Lifting up," Lee said with a smile. "The adventure of a Championship begins."

Casey kept her focus straight, watching as the blue of the sky turned to black, feeling as though she wanted to shut her eyes and curl up somewhere until they were back within the blue. She held out, and soon Lee was announcing his arrival to those within the hangar of the Surveillance Cruiser.

The DSSC settled down in the hangar, with the two boys quickly heading down below. Casey still sat in her seat.

"That wasn't so bad, was it?" Kerry said with an encouraging tone.

Casey nodded.

After a few seconds, she stood up. Her legs felt slightly unbalanced, but she managed to walk back down to exit the DSSC and look at what was happening in the hangar of the Sur-C.

Tom and Lee were already talking to two men. They were confirming details by the look of it.

Casey walked over to the group to listen in. She tried not to look to either of the far ends of the hangar at the transparent blue-tinted atmosphere gauze. Beyond it lay the blackness of space again, and now she was up here she couldn't hide her nervousness. There was something about the never-ending void that scared her.

"Okay, that's all done, then."

One of the men shook both Tom and Lee's hands, then walked off. His position was replaced by a woman, who announced herself as Pyra Summers of Radio Racer.

She asked Tom about how he felt he would perform in the challenges ahead, to which he replied with confidence that he expected to make it far thanks to the guidance of his best friend.

"Now, I understand it was you who got attacked," she then started. "Is there anything you want to say about that?"

Casey stood back, not wanting to be involved, but wanting to hear what would be said. Tom seemed to have pushed through all of that stuff, but she had no idea if directly being reminded of the incident would crush him again.

"It was just a minor thing that I got through thanks to help from family and friends," Tom supplied. "I'm stronger thanks to what happened, and I know I can handle whatever comes my way."

"You sound pretty confident of success, that's for sure." She turned away from the two. "I'll be talking to Tom Hughs and his supporters a bit more soon, but for now here's some more music."

She turned back to face the group, pressing a few things on her PMD. "I still stand by what I said about you during the competitor announcements," she said. "You are a strong competitor. I'll allow you to see what your rooms are like, then come back here and we'll have a bit more talk."

She walked off. The remaining man then told the group to follow him. Their rooms were near to the hangar. The man explained that all competitors and their supporters had access to the best rooms for the duration of the Championship, along with access to one of the restaurants to eat for free with all the other competitors and supporters.

Once he had given them the access code, he left. Tom opened the door and looked in.

"This is much better than the room we stayed last time," he stated impressively.

The lounge area had a table to seat six, with six comfortable chairs around the outside. A small area at the back had clothes washing facilities and storage. Three doors on either side of the room held the beds and bathroom. Two double-sized beds, along with two singles.

There was something about it that hurt.

Tom stood looking around the hangar. The Space Kicker had been removed from the DSSC to have some modifications added to it, with a word that while it wouldn't take long to do, each 'craft had to remain under watch and wouldn't be able to be taken out again until the Championship started.

It was near enough to what had been in the instructions.

Tom watched Lee guiding the DSSC to the space he had been instructed to as he thought on the question that had been asked.

"I'm happy to be here," he said toward the audio pickup. "I'm not exactly sure what to expect, but Lee and I have been looking at what came before and basing our training off that."

"But what of this Championship?" Pyra Summers asked. "Even looking back at what came before, what do you expect from this current one?"

Tom looked around again while he thought. It wasn't that he was nervous about the interview, but he hadn't been thinking to the future and felt awkward to be admitting to that. Which was causing awkwardness in his answers as he felt he kept repeating things.

"Those cruisers out in space are there for a reason," he settled with. "And with the six of them I can guess that there might be some winding path around them all. Maybe we need to visit one for a challenge."

"That seems reasonable. Okay, so how would-"

"Excuse me," a female voice interrupted. "Can you tell me where I register?"

Tom looked to see a teen roughly his age. Around sixteen years old, he guessed. Pyra Summers didn't even mute the audio pickup or call a break.

"Always happy to be a help," she said. "You must be Sally Evans? The second on my list of those registering today?"

"Hmm," Sally intoned with a nod.

"You're early. Hold on a bit and I'll see about getting hold of the man in charge. Now, Tom. Back to the question."

"Tom Hughs?" Sally exclaimed. "Ace. You have a bit of a reputation where I live. Some of them are even rooting for you in the Championship."

"Really..." Tom mentally fought a battle of nerves and refused to let them win. "I don't know if I'll get very far but I'll give it my all."

"That's what we like to hear!" Pyra Summers exclaimed. "And that answered my final question. I'll leave you two to talk, then."

She turned away and wrapped up to swap to some music as she hunted for the man in charge to get Sally registered.

"Why are you early, anyway?" Tom asked.

"I've been up here a week already. My sisters said they'd be here."

"You mean the sisters who were in the final of the '75 Championship?"

"That's them."

A silence fell between them. Tom had no idea where to take the conversation, and it seemed Sally didn't either. He settled for asking the same one that the radio host had asked him.

"What are you expecting to happen during the Championship?"

"The first event to be a tough one and to just barely scrape through it."

"You're not confident?" Tom found himself asking.

Sally gave him an almost cheeky grin. "Who says I'm not?" That grin faded fast. "I'm just being realistic. Only a third get to go through to the next round and it's everyone for themselves. Only the skilled ones have much of a chance. I'm skilled of course, but against those who have been in Championships before? I'd have to be very skilled."

She had started rambling and realised that. Her eyes widened, but she didn't say anything more. She was nervous, just as anyone would be.

She looked as though she wanted turn away. As Tom formed a new conversation piece she turned and started walking. He looked blank for a second, then quickly recovered.

"Hey," he called. "We will do great. Both of us. Good meeting you."

She half turned to him with a thumb up and that almost cheeky grin back in place. The radio host returned with the man Tom had talked to before.

He looked around and spotted Lee walking toward him.

"Making new friends?" Lee asked.

"She seems nice enough," Tom said. "What are we doing now?"

"Back to our rooms."

Tom let Lee lead him, but as he followed, he turned back around. Sally seemed to have been allowed to register early. She was talking to the man, at least.

He felt confident at having overcome one factor of nervousness, but knew – just like Sally – he still had to overcome some nerves about the Championship itself.

"Everyone has now been registered, and I hope you've enjoyed the talk with all the competitors. Looking out at all those 'craft ready to be launched tomorrow is certainly getting me excited for what's to come, and I'll have the best seat in the house. I've heard a small rumour that one of those cruisers is holding a special something for one of the events. We'll have to see in the coming days."

Pyra Summers of Radio Racers [06/5-0085]

Lee had been drinking in the excitement of the event as much as Tom had. All the 'craft were lined up along the rear of the hangar for everyone to look upon. There was only one other Space Kicker out of sixty 'craft, which didn't surprise Lee one bit.

Despite being the newer 'craft, people would stick with what they knew. Since the Space Kicker was new, it was also the most expensive, so people would just spend their grams on boosting their old 'craft.

"There's a lot of Falcons," Tom commented.

"It's got the fastest base speed, and with a bit of modification can reach those speeds quickly," Lee informed. "It's definitely the winner's choice."

"So, what's with almost as many basic models?"

"Cheap to buy, cheap to maintain, cheap to mod. Not to a serious standard, I don't think. Although..." Lee walked down the row of 'craft. He stopped next to a basic 'craft that had seen a serious paint job applied – depicting a simple scene of nature with a blue sky and two trees. Tom stepped beside him to look. "This one appears to have little real work done to it."

"Aha-ha. That's what they all say."

The two looked around to see where the voice had come from. Lee was surprised when a woman rolled from underneath the 'craft. She stood up and offered her hand to them both.

As Lee shook it, he asked, "This is your 'craft?"

"Yes, the Nature Nest. The design always makes people underestimate what it can do."

The woman looked nearly forty years old. Lee hadn't expected anyone that old to be competing. It was then he placed the voice and the name of the 'craft. But Tom had got there before him again.

"Rachel Carrington," Tom exclaimed. "The artist."

"Got it in one."

Tom had fell silent again with nothing more to say, so Lee picked up again with the introductions. Not that he needed to.

"I know those names, alright. It baffles me why anyone would target a simple competition of all things. Especially if they're only going after one person. Oh, and I heard about the guy who's an ace on the game that he got banned from the tournaments held at games rooms."

"Yeah... It certainly has been eventful for us. What were you doing under there, anyway?" he asked, indicating the 'craft with a hand wave.

"The front claw's been playing up recently. Just wanted to make a small adjustment to make sure nothing goes wrong."

"You'll be at the Championship meal later, right?"

"Wouldn't miss it."

"We'll see you there, then."

Lee left her to continue working. Tom followed quickly, looking as though he was thinking something over.

"I didn't expect her to be that friendly, even after hearing her talk on Radio Racer," he voiced.

"Most will be friendly," Lee stated. "Some will only care about winning and will be distant. The ones to watch are those who act friendly but are just sizing up the competition and who they'll need to target to get ahead."

"That is so... comforting to know."

The extension on the so had been just too long for Lee's liking. "Just stating it like it is," he said, deadpan. He had a feeling Tom was being eaten by nerves. He didn't need reminders about how tough the competition could be. He hitched a smile on his face as they travelled to the next level down, saying "You'll be fine after eating something. We'll be happy no matter where you come. Just don't set a target. Treat it as a bit of friendly competition but do your best."

"Thanks..."

Tom was still unsmiling and half lost in his own thoughts.

The food court was a cheery place, and one Kerry enjoyed eating at – even if there were better alternatives.

The competitors had a group of tables to themselves. She could see Tom happily eating and talking to someone next to him. Lee had told her of his earlier unhappy side, but he seemed to be hiding that very well.

As she looked over all the competitors, she could tell who would be easy pickings for the unsporting award – not that there was one. She could pick up on those who knew each other from previous Championships, and those who were new to competing.

Only Tom seemed to exude enough confidence to pass as a previous entrant.

She turned to look around for Lee and found him talking to a woman who he'd described to her as one they'd met earlier down at the hangar. With them was a man a few years older than Lee who mostly seemed to be listening in to the conversation.

"This Championship," she heard Casey say. "It's going to be a fun event."

Kerry looked back to her food, took a bite, then up at Casey. "Hmm," she said. Then added once finished, "Tom will certainly have fun competing and we'll have fun being within the action."

"Within?"

"Don't you want to watch from out in space?"

"We can do that?"

"Any supporters with mini cruisers are able to take them out to watch from the perimeter line. For the free-for-all event, anyway. I'm not sure about the others."

"I'll watch," Casey said in a small voice.

"We'll be stationary so if you need a break you can run out of the control bay." Kerry knew how Casey felt about space. "Tom seems to be facing his fears. Now you should be able to face yours."

Casey looked down and continued eating in silence.

After a minute, Kerry looked around the food court again. Lee had met up with Tom, and both were talking to someone new. Tom's eating looked as though it had slowed, and that wasn't from the talking as Lee was doing most of that. His nerves were starting to show again.

She didn't want to think of him worrying about losing too much. It wasn't a healthy thing to do. She couldn't say anything about it at the minute, though.

Everyone had finished their food, giving the event organisers time to announce the starting time. 09:00 for the briefing and starting ceremony. Then everyone would prepare for the start of that first challenge, which would begin at midday – 10:00.

The organisers then said they were free to leave whenever. It came as no surprise that Tom quickly joined Kerry and Casey at their table. He didn't speak.

"You've got nothing to worry about," Kerry softly said. "You have the skill and you have the right equipment needed to give the others a real beating. No-one will think you're bad for falling out at the first hurdle."

"I would." Quietly stated, she might not have heard it at all for the talk that had risen all around.

"Don't you think that," Casey said. "You shouldn't think it."

"We'll see what happens tomorrow." Tom had closed his eyes on saying that. He opened them again to give the image of confidence. "I know I can do well."

"If you wish it, it will happen." Kerry recited the family saying.

A good luck charm could do wonders. It had followed good happening before. It would help Tom now. She wished him well, so he would get through the first challenge.

She hoped he also wished well.

"This is it. The opening to the 0085 Space Race Championship is moments away from starting. We've got the opening ceremony and announcements, then we'll be getting right to some action and I'll be covering it all right here live. Hold on to those flight sticks. This is going to be a wild one."

Pyra Summers of Radio Racer [07/5-0085]

Tom stood in the row of people facing the mini cruiser. Lee was attached to him as a support, stood to his right.

He had fought his nerves about this moment all through the night, had barely eaten anything for breakfast, and now stood here wishing he could get to some action and drown his nerves out.

The event organisers stood on top of the mini cruiser, waiting for the start of the event. It was seconds away.

"Welcome to all our competitors. To all our supporters. And to all those tuned in to the 0085 Space Race Championship. This year we have sixty competitors that need shortening to twenty before the real events start, and as ever it shall be decided in combat."

"Before we get to the event, we need to know just who is competing," the second organiser stated.

The names of all the competitors had been announced and Radio Racer had even talked to every one of the competitors, but the opening ceremony called for the formality of a roll call of both competitor and 'craft.

Sally's name was called, and Tom mentally jumped when he heard she piloted a Falcon. He had no idea why he did so. It was just a vague feeling related to the combination.

His own name was called, and upon hearing the designation code called out of his Space Kicker, he felt strength from his dad. He would do good in this Championship, and when he told his dad the story, he would be proud of his son.

Other names were called out. One such name was Brandon Golden, which Tom only picked up on as he used the same designation and 'craft as Tom used in Space Racer. A Rotablade — designation G/0ld5n.

With all sixty names called out, the first organiser took to explaining the rules.

"When each of you registered, the spacecraft you registered for use in the event was taken and modified with a single locked turret. That turret is able to be fired only once every thirty seconds, and holds an advanced tracking laser that will allow the scanners detailed telemetry per shot fired. Each spacecraft also had its computer tuned to recognise a hit from the laser, which will disable the turret and alert the person to pull out from the competition."

"Now," the third organiser continued, "we have thought of what if people try to stay in beyond their time, so the auto-pilot will kick in if they try to do so."

The first organiser picked back up. "There are four cruisers out in space forming a perimeter. This cruiser, as well as the Salty Sunrise, the Gata-Pron, and the..." The organiser exhaled as though he couldn't believe what he was about to say. "...Karzadono will be playing a part throughout all the events. Two other cruisers are awaiting their turn."

Tom heard the quiet, wistful "Wonderful" of Lee upon that name being said. He couldn't wait to hear the reasoning.

"All you have to do is remain active for as long as possible," the second organiser stated. "If you remain when the numbers have been whittled down to twenty, you'll be a part of the true challenges. And while no extra benefit comes from being first in this event, we know the crowds love to support the strongest, so do your best to come on top."

"Competitors! To your 'craft! Supporters! Take your positions!"

It was the rallying call to indicate the start of the championship.

Lee said a rushed "Talk on comms" and ran to the DSSC. Tom quickly walked to his Space Kicker. Inside, he lifted off and waited for Lee to get on the link.

He was one of the first out in space, and watched as the DSSC pulled away from the hangar and take up position between two of the cruisers opposite the Sur-C.

"Okay, you know I'm not confident in the Suati language," Tom said once Lee had wished him luck. "What's wrong with the name of Karzadono?"

"Well..." It sounded as though Lee was thinking of the best way to say it without actually mentioning the name outright. "The name of Donaldo is formed from two words of Suati. One of those words means storm. Now if I said that Karzadono is the informal way to describe a huge argument and the repercussions that come from that, can you piece it together?"

It took a minute, but Tom eventually understood the meaning. "Ah. What of the other name?"

"Well, I imagine that Karzadono is some form of cruel joke placed upon that cruiser, but thankfully the other name is much friendlier. You should know part of it, though."

"Gata..." Tom cast his memory back to the second visit to Donaldo. "Help."

"Pron is the Suati word for thought, bringing the full name of the cruiser to Helping Thought. Although I'd like to think it means helping idea in the context it's presented."

"I think I'll just stick to Salty Sunrise as my favourite."

Tom took the Space Kicker into a few rolls and spins, keeping track of the turret in front of him. It had been placed as far forward as possible.

He hoped it had very little delay once fired.

He felt the stomach-churning nervousness of an event soon to start. He knew he'd do well. As soon as he started, he'd be living the moment and any thought but the next second would be gone.

"Competitors!" a voice sounded through the speakers. Everyone would be hearing it, he knew. "Turrets active and event beginning in... four... three... two... Go!"

CHAPTER 6 – TARGETED HOSTILITY

"And the first event has started. Sixty spacecraft hunting each other down while looking out for danger from anyone else. Remember that the first shots won't be fired until those turrets are charged, but once they are we'll be seeing... Oh! It looks like several shots have just been taken, but will we see anyone going down this early?"

Pyra Summers of Radio Racer [07/5-0085]

His first shot had missed. Upon starting, he'd aimed a laser at a 'craft at random, then pulled away in case someone had a lock on him. He flew around the crowd, looking out at the mass of vehicles in the area, then dived back into the crowd to make a second, hoping this time to hit something.

He had just a second's warning as a Falcon appeared right behind him. He dodged to the side, watching as the laser flew by. He was glad to not have wasted time.

Pulling around in a tight curve, he looked down at the scanner. The designation looked like Z/x1916ec. The Falcon that Sally was driving.

Sneaky move, he thought. I'll pay you back for that one soon.

He powered up to maximum speed and took a zig-zag approach to the other side of the field. Sighting up on a basic model 'craft, he pressed the trigger to fire. The laser ripped across space to just miss who he had aimed at.

As that basic model turned away, a Falcon appeared right in front of him and fired. He quickly dropped, tightly turned and flew back the way he had come. He felt he knew the colouring of that Falcon, and it came as no surprise to him that it had been Sally's Falcon.

Just what are you up to?

He flew erratically as he came into a patch of heavy traffic. Several lasers came close to hitting but he remained safe. He made another tight turn and fired into the fray, this time managing to hit someone.

In seconds Sally was back on him and tried to get a lock. He continued his erratic flying, throwing the Space Kicker into a few rolls. Back within a patch of heavy traffic, he tried to lose her through it.

She fired, but while it wasn't aimed at him, she still remained on his tail once he emerged into the open again.

Go bother someone else, he found himself thinking.

He then had an idea.

Flying straight, he counted down seconds. When he reached five, he cut power to the engines as he started a flip. The zero-flip faced him in front of Sally and he pressed the trigger. Without seeing if he had hit, he powered the engines up again and sped away.

When he felt he could risk it, he looked at the scanner to see her blip still active. He noticed that the numbers of active combatants were slowly falling, but he still needed to remain in the moment.

The numbers weren't yet below twenty.

"How's it looking?" Kerry asked.

Lee sat within the co-pilot's chair looking at the scanner almost as much as he watched from the viewshield. Kerry stood behind him, having been to check on Casey. She hadn't lasted long before zipping off to one of the rooms. There really seemed to be a small phobia present there. Something Kerry couldn't help with.

"He'd be doing a lot better if he didn't need to keep an eye out for a certain someone," Lee informed, pointing at a blip on the scanner.

Kerry looked over his shoulder to see Tom's blip speed through a group of other blips, but another blip followed him through it.

As he pulled away from that group of blips, the one following him stayed on him. Tom's blip shifted to the side, stopped for a second as he made a tight turn and then looked as though he'd tried to fire back – the blip that had followed him had also shifted to the side.

They were two dancers twirling around each other for but a moment, but that moment seemed to stretch on, as the two blips continued to be near each other.

Kerry looked up through the viewshield to see the two come near. The Falcon fired as Tom started a turn, but he rolled away and underneath the Falcon. The Falcon flew away fast, leaving Tom open to someone else.

He fired first, managing to hit the other, but then the Falcon was back on him, forcing him back into a flying style of randomness.

"Isn't it against the rules for this to happen?" Kerry asked.

"Ah," Lee said. "But watch."

Kerry watched. At first, she couldn't see what Lee meant. The Falcon had fired yet again at Tom, who again had dodged out of the way. Mentally she counted down the time before the Falcon could fire again.

Despite still being on Tom's tail, the Falcon had deviated enough to fire at someone else. Counting down another thirty seconds, Kerry then watched as the Falcon fired upon Tom once more.

"It's only rule-breaking to aim at the same person twice," Lee said. "There's nothing that I can see for a situation like this."

"They need to do something about that."

"Not much they can do. Not like it's accurately trackable."

"How many remain on the field?"

"Forty-two."

"Don't get crushed," she wished for Tom. "Don't think about what came before, only what comes next."

"And whatever you do," Lee added, "don't lose sight of that Falcon."

Tom had decided that if Sally was trying to get him, he'd get her first.

He tried to force her into mistakes, trying to get others to take shots at her by continuously flashing past them. He didn't much care who took her out so long as she no longer presented a problem.

Another laser flew by, giving Tom thirty seconds to once again try to get her taken out. It didn't work as he planned, but at least he hadn't been taken out either.

I need to try this myself, he thought. *Everyone else is focused on other things. This has to be me.*

He'd already used the zero-flip, which he didn't intend to use again. There was one other thing he had yet to use.

Checking to see if Sally remained behind him, he set off up and away from any other distractions. Sally still stayed behind him, meaning she couldn't fire another shot at him without heading off elsewhere.

Twenty-eight... Twenty-nine... Thirty!

On that second, he pulled into a loop and dropped his speed slowly. Eventually he came to a stop, watching for any danger.

A Falcon rose on his right. Looking, he could see Sally inside.

She's not. It's against the rules.

He dropped the Space Kicker and pulled it up. The Falcon burst forward in sudden motion, and dropped down into the fray again, firing a laser into the fight.

Tom quickly corkscrewed the Space Kicker around to blast himself in Sally's direction, knowing this time he could get a lock and end her time in the Championship.

He was aware that he hadn't fired his own laser in some minutes, but he was saving it for Sally.

Who he had lost sight of.

"There she is," Lee exclaimed.

He'd been tracking both Tom and Sally on the DSSC's larger screen. The regular scanner was okay for distance tracking, but he really needed an area scan of the combat zone, so had swapped to one of the rear seats to set such up.

"Back where Tom had been," Mrs. Johnson said. "What is she up to?"

"Whatever it is, he shouldn't fall for it. He's smart. He'll round the others up and… What are you doing!"

The blip of Tom had followed Sally out to the open. The plan that Sally had been hoping to carry out had failed, but the counter of Tom's also missed its mark.

"If either of them had any sense, they'd be working on the others before calling it time. What has got them heated up like this?"

"Well, I can understand why Tom would even if he doesn't see it himself," Mrs. Hughs called from the room she remained.

Both Lee and Mrs. Johnson walked into that room to see a Lightmorph Media Display active and tuned to show what Lee had been looking at. She'd been watching the area footage that the Surveillance Cruiser provided for all people watching.

"Does it relate to previous events?" Lee asked.

"You can't see that for yourself? I suspect he feels targeted much the same as before. This is just his way of proving he can look after himself."

"I think it likely," Lee stated. "But then if that's how he's feeling, what of Sally?"

Mrs. Hughs reset the footage back to the beginning, activating the full array of data. At thirty seconds, Lee watched as Tom had been one of the first to fire. Randomly into the pack. The 'craft it had almost hit had been the Falcon of Sally's.

"No way!" Lee said, not believing what was being suggested.

"I find it hard to believe as well," Mrs. Johnson added. "We don't have any idea of the why, so we shouldn't think on it. Once the challenge is over, we'll see what Tom thinks of the situation."

"Either way, he's not going to be happy. Even if he gets into the top twenty."

Lee walked back to the control bay and sat down, looking for where both Tom and Sally were on the area scan. They were still within the dance.

Tom wrenched the stick to the side, dodging yet another laser from Sally. It was getting beyond a joke now and he wanted it finished.

He could see there were now just under half the amount of people in the area than when the event had started, meaning using the others for cover wasn't going to happen. He hated to admit it, but he wasn't going to shake his tail easily. He'd have to get on with the job of dealing with the others with it still following.

Employing a range of movements and speeds, he travelled around and took as many chances as he could to fire his laser. He wasn't even aware if any of them hit.

After a few minutes, his head was hurting from continuous twists and turns. He could feel tiredness starting to creep up on him. If he was going out, he wanted one more chance of taking out Sally first.

He stopped with the erratic flying, shaking his head to stem the pain. Sally had recently fired off a shot, though he couldn't remember how long it had been. This was being done on instinct.

Flying straight, he counted ten seconds. Sally was behind him, keeping directly on his tail. Pushing forward on the left stick, the Space Kicker angled down, and sure enough, Sally followed him.

He zeroed his speed as he bumped himself down, causing Sally to overshoot.

He fired.

Confirmed hit.

On both Sally and him.

He gave a frustrated growl, knowing it had been a risky move.

Flying to the outside of the zone, he looked down at his scanner. Only ten remained on the field.

His eyes widened in surprise.

He hadn't expected the numbers to have dropped so rapidly. The exultation of getting through only wiped the frustration for a few seconds.

As soon I can, I want the story of what she has against me. I could have placed higher if she hadn't been stalking me.

All the spacecraft and mini cruisers were back in the hangar of the Surveillance Cruiser, and Casey was happy once again to not be able to see the void up close. If she could, she'd remain on board for the rest of the challenges.

All the competitors were gathered. She and the Johnsons had barely had time to talk to Tom before everyone was called together. From his expression as he'd climbed down from the Space Kicker, she knew he had something to settle.

From where she stood in the group of supporters, she could see Tom on the right looking across to the line on the left with stony eyes. In the left line, she could just make out the same expression on a female roughly Tom's age.

The fight would surely be breaking out once the ceremony was over.

"First, we recognise those who tried and failed to gain a place on the roster of this Space Race Championship. Rows of ten, please."

The rollcall of names lasted a few minutes as two of the event hosts called out forty names. Four lines of ten stood in front of the hosts. They were told to turn and face the gathered crowd, who clapped and cheered to celebrate those who failed to make the cut.

"And now for those who are through," one of the hosts called as the forty competitors retreated back to their lines. "We'll start by calling the first lot of ten, then the second once we've acknowledged the first ten."

"Jackie Moore," the second of the hosts called. "Ryan Ross-Smith. Claire Beckett. Hayden Bell. And Brandon Golden."

"Dougal Sweet," the third host continued. "Dylan Hare. Sally Evans. Tom Hughs. Stella Sandford."

Tom and Sally were stood next to each other, and once they turned around, they were both pointedly looking away from each other with the occasional look at the other with a burning stare.

Once the crowd had finished with its cheering, the two stormed off in opposite directions to join the lines. The fire hadn't left either of them, with the stare of flames being in both.

Skyler Aquarion, Brian Sheldon, Trudy Nimré, Rachel Carrington, Graham Jones, Florence Petala, Bob Harrison, Adam McCoy, Katie Daniels, and Daniel Tampwick were the top ten, with Daniel being the one who had survived everyone.

The cheering died down again, with the hosts ending the ceremony.

"All competitors and their supporters are allowed use of the facilities given to them during the Championship, so those who were knocked out are welcome to stay and continue to mingle with those who remain."

"Tomorrow the real Championship begins, with the event briefing being at 09:00. The briefing won't be long, and the remaining competitors will be flying through space as soon as it ends."

"That's all for now."

The crowd started dispersing, with Sally having turned tail and stormed away. Tom made good progress in catching up. There was no way to find out what would happen between them.

Tom rushed through the crowd, eyes locked on the back of Sally's head. He jostled a few people, aware that some were trying to talk with him, but he didn't care.

Near the ramps down to the upper level of the cruiser, he managed to slap a hand on her shoulder to turn her around.

She didn't need much convincing to do that.

"What?" she stated sharply.

"You know exactly what." Tom managed to keep his voice level, though he wanted to shout it out with her. He didn't want the entire hangar to hear the fight. "Why were you singling me out?"

"Why were you singling me out?" she retorted.

"I wasn't doing anything of the sort. You, however, were onto me from the start, and never shifted your sights from me."

"I was ready and waiting to take someone out from the start. You forced me away from that opportunity."

"That's the point of the event. No need to take it out on me."

"You also tried to take me out numerous times after that."

"You took every opportunity to take me out."

"You stood the highest chance of winning. Can't blame me for trying to take out the best."

"You had a clear chance at plenty of others who have actually been in Championships before. You know nothing of me."

Sally turned around, quickly stepping away.

"Keep watching your back," she called. "As I'll be waiting for the opportunity to take it out."

Tom didn't follow, breathing deeply to calm himself.

"Forget about it," Lee's voice sounded next to him. "You won't get much sense from her if she's pinning all the blame on you."

Tom didn't reply. He knew Lee was right but still wanted to continue the fight. Where Sally had got to, he didn't know, but next time he met her he would make her see some sense.

"Come on. You need some good food in you. I'll treat you." Lee's voice sounded happy. "You did good, even against the pressure of a continual attack."

Tom took a few moments in responding. "As long as it's not the Taste of Suati again."

"It'll be a surprise, but one I know you'll like."

He wasn't sure about that, but anything to at least take his mind off his current feelings.

Lee's choice of food court had indeed surprised Tom, and he was happy to have taken his friend's mind off Sally – even if just for a while.

The four sat down, viewing the menus of available food. Lee knew what he would be having as soon as he looked and saw a single word. The others took a while longer, but soon a server arrived to take an order. He smiled upon seeing Tom.

"How delightful to have a competitor here. Celebrating the victory, are we?"

"It wasn't as much a victory as I'd have liked, but I'm happy to have got through," Tom said.

The server said nothing about the comment, instead asking around for the orders.

"Medium Suati Special pizza," Lee stated. "A medium Hunter's Hike pizza."

"And two Royal Combos," Mrs. Johnson added. "Oh, and four orange juices."

The server ran through the list to confirm it right, nodded, then walked off.

The conversation then turned to the Championship again.

"I shouldn't have to remind you how well you managed that event," Mrs. Johnson started, "so don't look back. Look ahead instead."

Lee looked at Tom. He said nothing.

"You're still thinking about getting back at her somehow." Lee could read that expression easily.

"I was robbed of a top ten finish thanks to her," Tom fiercely growled. "How do you expect me to feel?"

Lee felt he already knew the answer to this next question, but needed it confirmed for the group to hear.

"Just why is this so personal for you, anyway?"

"We were friendly with each other. We were getting on well." His voice rose slightly. "It was all a lie to get me to lower my guard."

"No," Mrs. Johnson said. "I've seen that type of person. Sally Evans is not that type of person."

"She's doing a pretty good impression of it."

"I'm not going to defend what she's doing, but there's something behind the why that seems to be controlling her."

"She wants to prove she can beat me," Tom said slowly, holding a hand to his head as though remembering something. "To prove to her community she's better than me."

"Say again?" Lee asked.

"She knew who I was because many people where she lives were rooting for me to win. She's trying to prove them wrong."

"Well..." Mrs. Hughs faltered. "There's nothing wrong with a bit of friendly rivalry."

Tom gave a slight hurtful glare at his mother, then looked away.

"There's nothing friendly about what she's doing," he strongly said, turning back to face them.

Lee willed no-one to say anything else as he quickly thought of some distraction. A small one came in the form of their drinks arriving. Lee took a sip from his as he continued thinking, and just as Mrs. Hughs seemed about to speak again, he had his question ready.

"What do you want this next event to be?"

"Something where I can put my skills to use. A simple race, maybe."

"Just a simple one? Nothing more complex so you can put some of those tricks to use?"

"A complex race where I can win."

No-one had much else to say to that, with Mrs. Johnson dispelling the silence by changing the topic completely. They talked for a good while about what they would be doing later on, with plans pretty much confirmed when the food finally arrived.

Lee's first taste of the Suati Special proved to be a delicious one. He tucked in with enthusiasm, relishing the way it had been baked.

He had to wonder why it wasn't served at the Taste of Suati and spent a few minutes as he continued eating mentally compiling a revised list of his favourite dishes from Suati.

It occupied him so completely, he didn't even wonder if the food had distracted Tom enough to wipe the thought of revenge against Sally Evans.

"I can't really say it was a surprise. I just knew I had to be aware of everything at all times, keep moving in a random pattern, and never slow down. There were a few moments where I felt it would be over, and a point where I was willing to risk everything for an easy takedown, but I held out. The final skirmish with Carrington was tough. I don't know how she's done it, but that Basic model of hers is more than just a piece of art."

Daniel Tampwick speaking on Radio Racer [08/5-0085]

Casey watched from the front of the supporters' crowd as the second event of the Championship was announced. Kerry stood to her right, also listening in.

"It wouldn't be called a Space Race Championship without some racing," the host stated. "You know there's races coming up, so we have a basic one to start us off."

"Though we call it a basic race, it will test you," the second host added. "Throughout the resting hours, a large area of space has been prepared as a racing arena. Checkpoint will prove who is the fastest as all competitors fight for first place in this daring race."

"It will start on Salty Sunrise, twisting around that cruiser, before moving on to the others that are positioned around," the third host explained. "We won't be saying more than that, as you'll have time to study the map. Only sixteen can make it through to the next event, so be fast, and be willing to push yourself to keep away from those knockout positions."

"Racers, to your 'craft!" the first host called. "Be prepared to swap to the Sunrise in two minutes. Supporters, you may choose where you will watch from."

Casey wasn't up to going back out into space, saying she'd watch from her PMD. Lee joined them as the two started walking away.

"As much as I'd like to join them out there and watch, I think it might be worth watching while the DSSC is still here in the hangar. At least that way we can still be together."

Casey found herself agreeing to that. As the three made their way to the super cruiser, the 'craft of the twenty competitors started lifting themselves and moving into position to make the short journey to the Salty Sunrise.

Inside the super cruiser and within the lower lounge area, Lee activated two separate LMDs. One showed a map that updated the positions of the racers in real-time. The other tuned to the live feed from the cameras with commentary by Pyra Summers.

Casey studied the map. It looked a complex route. All six cruisers were in play, with two closely positioned to give a really fun set of twists and loops.

Tom was an expert at the game of Space Racer, but this was the real deal. But this was also what he'd practiced most for.

He would do fine, and this time Casey wished for him to be in the top five. She knew he would get to the top five. He just had to.

"All the racers are now positioned in the hangar of Sunrise," Pyra Summers announced, "with the cruiser making its way to the starting position."

Twenty blips on the map slowly moved, with the first two checkpoints and one of the last also moving with it. Looking to the live feed, the image showed the cruiser settling to rest. It then swapped to another image showing the twenty racers waiting for the start.

"Everything is ready, with the final few checks being carried out."

The host then talked about the same area that Casey had noted earlier. Casey barely listened, feeling the anticipation of the event starting and how well Tom would do at that start.

If anything was worrying Casey at that moment, it was – how could it not end in a tangle of spacecraft parts and a giant wreck?

Tom looked dead ahead. He wasn't falling for no distractions.

He had an air of calm about him, almost of serenity. His right hand held the stick to lift, his left hovering over the switch to retract the landing claws. It would then be a quick change to different positions as he set speed and pushed the lever forward to fully let loose with it.

He might have been doing the movements every time he had taken off but never had he needed it done so quick. He remained calm knowing that the slightest fumble would cost seconds.

In a race, that mattered.

"Go!" a voice announced through the speakers.

Tom executed the take-off in just over a second. In another two he zoomed out the hangar seeing no-one in front of him.

He pulled up and around to face the tower of the cruiser, increasing speed for a few seconds, then pulling back to make the turn around the tower. The 'craft shook slightly as it sped up again, making for the front of the cruiser and the second checkpoint.

A Falcon slowly pushed into his peripheral vision. It had a different colour scheme to the one he was looking out for, so he paid no attention to it.

Dropping slightly in preparation for angling to the third checkpoint, he checked the scanner to see four more blips behind him.

Second checkpoint passed and nothing below him, he pulled back with the right stick to drop below the next cruiser. The Falcon on his left had managed to stay with him. On his right a basic 'craft quickly slipped into his vision.

The artwork confirmed it as Rachel Carrington.

A right turn after the third checkpoint meant she had the best line for it, though Tom wasn't about to let that worry him. He remained calm.

Through the third checkpoint, Carrington cut to the right immediately. The Falcon quick to follow. Tom continued for one second more before making a turn of his own, dipping slightly as he did so, and making the arc as long as possible so that when he hit the fourth checkpoint he still continued the turn. Pushing upward while still in the turn, he noted that while the two in front of him had passed through the checkpoint before him, they now needed to slow down to arc upward tightly enough to make the fifth.

He momentarily smiled at that small victory, then back to his state of calm. He took another glance at the scanner, rolled the 'craft and pulled in the opposite direction ready to cut a very tight corner.

A very small niggling thought invaded his mind.

Could he keep first for the whole race?

"So far, so good," Kerry stated, watching the map.

Tom hadn't followed most of the others with his racing technique. It was something Lee had mentioned to her once. Tom himself seemed unaware of it, but he did have a very good sense of awareness of his surroundings. He also had great skill within a spacecraft. Those two things combined gave him a great understanding of how to make the most of positioning himself to get the greatest speed from even the tightest of turns, as he had just proved once again with a weave on a straight that had transitioned into a very tight turn with very little loss of speed.

"He's a natural," Pyra Summers commented. "Is there anything that will slow him down?"

"I can think of one thing," Lee stated darkly.

Kerry looked up at him. He indicated to look back at the map.

Times had been added to it for Tom and one other. One of the blips had also become marked in a different colour.

"Heavily modified but within the legal limit, that Falcon is," Lee stated. "Sally Evans is catching up, with more than three-quarters of the race still to go."

Kerry studied the times as first Tom, then Sally passed through the eighth checkpoint. "She's gaining a second on each one."

"Where at the halfway point she'll be able to make a pass and use the boosted acceleration of her Falcon to get far away. The only reason she needs to catch up is due to a sloppy start."

The Falcon, already famed for its higher base speed, became near unstoppable with a boosted acceleration on top of that. The shield had probably been lowered considerably to be able to put all that extra acceleration to use.

Not that it mattered much at the minute.

"Tom still has a chance," Casey muttered. "He cuts time through his positioning."

Kerry smiled but said nothing. Tom was already fighting off two others. A third would be harder to manage.

❖

Tom had barely kept his lead position through those last few checkpoints, but now the real fun part came into sight.

The two cruisers that hadn't been named were close by, with Tom flying through the middle of them from up top. Cutting down below them, the next checkpoint waited some distance below. He chanced a zero-flip, hoping the others wouldn't manage to keep their speed so he could increase his own before they had a chance to overtake.

Facing the right way, he pushed forward on the lever to feed power to the engines.

A Falcon – in the known and despised colour scheme – cut straight across him, forcing him to drop speed to avoid a collision.

His calm had now evaporated.

He hammered the lever forward to increase his speed, keeping aware of where that Falcon was. It overtook him and settled in front of him.

He strafed left to overtake her. She shot off ahead.

Critical milliseconds had been lost.

He growled in frustration as he boosted passed another checkpoint, keeping a tight arc to quickly make up the distance he had lost.

During the winding course around the two cruisers, he had barely closed the distance and now had to settle for taking any opportunity he could to get ahead.

The route of the race barely touched the Karzadono – the cruiser coming up next – but it held what might prove to be the most challenging point of the entire race.

All three of those in front started slowing down to enter the hangar to the cruiser. Four checkpoints were located here, creating an S-bend that the racers had to navigate. Temporary walls had been constructed within to make speed worthless once inside. It needed precise movement, and if one was willing to push it, they could get some excellent positioning to overtake.

Tom smiled in grim determination, willing to take the risk.

He slowed down and flicked his landing claws out to avoid an even worse impact than the one he endured. The wall survived the impact with the Space Kicker, with it moving off quickly. The claws retracted, and a burst of speed moved it away to hit the first checkpoint of the S-bend. Making the turn as required, Tom flipped upside down as he shifted the Space Kicker to the left. Beyond the next checkpoint, he could see a Falcon just disappearing around another wall.

He followed the Falcon, risking a bit more speed to get closer to it for the next checkpoint. He manoeuvred to the inside of the turn, forcing the Falcon to the outside. Making sure she couldn't accelerate away, he positioned himself in front of her.

On the next turn, he felt a sudden unexpected force that almost crashed him into the floor. As he pulled to a complete stop to right himself, the Falcon zipped around the turn.

She had pushed right through him and almost ended his race.

Making the turn and out of the hangar, he pushed as much speed as he could hoping to catch up.

Not to Sally, but to fifth place.

"Foul play!" Lee shouted.

Everyone could see what had happened. The viewpoint from the cameras had picked it up clear as day. Though he didn't want to admit it, it would probably be viewed as a counter-move and allowed.

Tom had blocked her in that moment. Something he shouldn't have done.

"He's letting her get inside his head," he reasoned with a sigh. "He shouldn't be doing that."

"He'll do what he wants," Mrs. Johnson said. "But unless he finds his focus, he'll be losing more places."

"He knows he can't afford that, but he also wants to catch up and pay Sally back once again. He'll be feeling the heat too much to calm down."

"They shouldn't allow contact at all," Mrs. Hughs stated.

"Start saying you can't allow something, someone will find a way around it," Mrs. Johnson said. "The weapon of each 'craft can be fired, but it wouldn't do anything except slow the person who fired it down. And the counter-rule allows contact so long as the opposing person made a block."

"He was almost..."

Lee had a feeling she didn't want to say anything about being disabled or destroyed.

"If anything serious had happened, it would be called out," he assured her. "Tom reacted fast, possibly too fast for any assessment of how bad things could have been to be made."

"All we know," Mrs. Johnson added quickly, "is that he's okay, if a little upset and possibly even angry at having been forced to give away two positions. If he has any sense, he'll know that catching third place is a lost cause."

Lee looked at the map again, looking at where the top ten were. A few were lagging behind, meaning even if Tom couldn't catch up to fifth, he wouldn't be dropping below sixth unless he made a stupid mistake.

Which was entirely possible.

The race for Tom had become something he had never expected.

Used to winning races, the fact he had now lost one had opened him up to accepting that winning wasn't everything. It was something he needed to remember.

Having accepted that, he was now enjoying the twists and turns as each came, and had found his focus once again. And even though he had settled for just enjoying the race, there was still the matter of getting back into the top five.

Less than a quarter of the race remained.

The route had taken them far from the starting point which they needed to get back to. To get racers from one end to the other, a drive cycler had been placed at one checkpoint. It would be the only point where the 'craft were allowed to swap to the Mega Power Drive. It would also be up to the person of each 'craft where they swapped down again – so long as they did so before hitting the next checkpoint.

Since the speed would remain fixed, he had to make sure to keep his speed at the highest it could possibly be. Which would be a problem considering current positions. He had to make this work.

Keeping his speed as he flew near the Gata-pron, he hit the checkpoint and quickly swerved around the tower, employing the same arcing tactic he had before to again rise above the cruiser. As he hit the drive cycler, his speed read 02:20. Boosted to MPD, he struggled to straighten out and aim for the next checkpoint.

Taking a long deep breath once he had things under control, he counted to five slowly. On four, he swapped back down to KPD. On five, the drive had fully swapped and his speed slowed drastically just as he passed the second to last checkpoint.

Accelerating again to top speed, he quickly overtook fifth place, curving inward to take the last checkpoint. All he needed to do now was get inside the Surveillance Cruiser – the finish line – while also keeping ahead of the person he had just overtaken.

It was simple, except for the part where he needed to slow down. He zeroed speed meters from the atmosphere gauze, hoping that he could control the 'craft until it fully stopped.

It threatened to veer off the straight path twice, but Tom managed to fight it both times. With the Space Kicker now stopped, he let it idle in the air as he wiped his hands on his trousers, unaware of just how hot they had become.

He turned the Space Kicker around and dropped it. The landing claws made a slight tap on the hangar floor. He blew out a breath as he opened the viewshield, feeling a waft of cool air hit him in the face.

"Great work!" a shout sounded.

Lee had worked his way to the Space Kicker and had hopped into a sitting position on its right side. The cheers and the engines and all the other sounds had drowned out any noise of his.

"You did well," Lee continued. "But you need to control a certain thing."

"Don't tell me I need to stop chasing after Sally's Falcon, as I won't."

"I know you said it's personal, but it shouldn't be. There's no need for it to be so."

Tom said nothing. Lee wouldn't understand. While he didn't care about winning, he did care about proving himself the best against her. He wavered on the point but knew he had added two more things to the list of why he wanted to beat her at one of these challenges.

All the other racers had finished, with a slight pause as everyone gathered in the hangar once again.

Lee stood to Tom's right, awaiting the announcements.

"That was some great racing by everyone," the first host stated. "We have four people who have been knocked out, so we'd like to name them to celebrate how far they have come."

"First, we call the person who came last. Skyler Aquarion, and his Basic spacecraft."

"Giving the Space Kicker a bad name is Dougal Sweet, who came second-to-last."

"Brian Sheldon tried his best, but failed to make good use of his Falcon."

"Brandon Golden got overtaken at the last critical few meters in his Rotablade."

The four who were called stepped forward, forming a new line in front of the watchers. Brandon seemed to be fuming at his misfortune, which was something Tom also seemed to be doing. Lee's words seemed to have done nothing.

It was odd for Tom to even think this way. He never seemed to hold grudges against anyone, especially for something as simple as this seemed. But he also seemed set on this thought, and wouldn't be persuaded to budge from it.

The four accepted the applause and stepped back into the line.

"Though it matters little in this Championship, we'd also like to take a moment to celebrate those who made it into the top three."

"Daniel Tampwick came first. A second place for Rachel Carrington. Hayden Bell came third."

The clapping and cheering started up as the three stepped forward to accept it. Once it had died down, the hosts informed every one of the next event briefing. It would be held at 12:00, allowing everyone enough time for something to eat and to prepare for that next event.

"I need to speak privately," Tom said quietly.

Lee didn't respond, as their mothers had joined them. "To the room for a bit of a rest," he said. "I think Tom needs it."

Once in their room, Lee took Tom into one of the bedrooms, closing the door. Once it closed, he dropped the cheery outlook.

"What do you need to say?" he asked.

"I don't know how, but she's behind the attacks."

Lee blinked a few times, struggling to take that in. "Preposterous," he said.

"She has two sisters. Two females attacked us. They were acting on her orders, but when it became too dangerous, she told them to back off as she'd take care of it herself."

"Are you really going with that? Are you forgetting what they were doing on Donaldo? All that just to discredit you in her hometown?"

"It's likely."

"I'll tell you what I think. The two who attacked us were mercenaries out for a quick score. Or are you forgetting that we own the latest space-faring technology?"

It took Tom only a few seconds to disregard that as wrong. In other words – not his opinion.

"Why attempt to destroy, if that was the case? Why not capture instead?"

Lee knew he had to let the subject drop again. Not only was Tom's thinking on the matter distorted to fit his own agenda, he felt a silence from beyond the door that seemed unnatural.

"Okay, so... That it?"

"There's also the Championship itself. I feel I can't go on if I need to keep looking out for her."

"You will do good at this Championship, even with her trying to get you out. Don't think about her, and you have nothing to worry about."

Tom remained silent. Lee left him to think on those words and left the room. Both mothers looked a bit too unconcerned for his taste.

"He's just a bit worried about how he'll do," he told them both. "I've given him a few words of comfort."

"Here's hoping he listens to them," Mrs. Johnson said.

Lee sat down with them to watch the game they were playing. He thought of what Tom had said about Sally being behind the attacks. It made no sense and was absurd to think of, but he supposed that other absurd things had happened.

He still wasn't going to take the claim as a serious one.

CHAPTER 7 – CONFLICTING POSITIONS

"I'm... I don't even know. I have no idea what I feel. I could call out any number of people for why the event itself was unfair, go on a rant about the person who overtook me, but in the end, it's all down to me. I wasn't quick enough. I'll have done enough to get further in the next Championship, though. I'm definitely entering that one."

Brandon Golden speaking on Radio Racer [08/5-0085]

Once again, they were in the food court that had now taken on the name of Champion's Court. The competitors and supporters were talking about the race, with Pyra Summers flitting around asking people for their thoughts.

Casey enjoyed the food and the atmosphere but kept an eye on Tom. He had something on his mind, and it was obvious who that something was.

While talking with one of the competitors who had been knocked out, he had a habit of looking slightly to the right, where Sally Evans talked to a group of four.

Looking out for Lee, she spotted him close to Sally. He took no notice of her, instead being engaged with the conversation he had found himself in.

Kerry slipped back into her seat having placed two drinks on the table. She smiled as she looked up.

"There's a vote going around asking who people think will win the next event," Kerry said. "Tom's quite high on the rankings."

Casey nodded slowly, still keeping an eye on Tom.

"Nothing will happen," Kerry stated with certainty, guessing her current thoughts. "If anything were to happen, they could face expulsion from the Championship. I don't think either would want to risk it."

"It's not a fight breaking out here I'm worried about. It's what could happen during the next event."

"As long as Tom doesn't yield to the rage of an overtake, he should do fine."

"That seems very likely to be happening, though."

"I know Lee's tried to make him not see it as some personal war, but that's how strongly his mind is set on it. Maybe you could come up with something."

"I guess..." She had no idea what she would say, but the idea of it being a personal war for him was giving her some idea, and it resembled something she had told him before. There wasn't any point mentioning it now, though. She'd wait.

The food court started emptying, with people wishing each other luck for the next event. Lee ended his conversation, with Casey hearing that they'd talk more later. Lee really did seem to be enjoying being in the centre of the action, a lot more than Tom did. His conversation had finished earlier, and when Casey next saw him, he'd been sat at a table far from the action.

It was there he still remained.

"I'm just going to have a talk with Tom," she alerted Kerry, quickly having made a decision.

"Don't be too long," Kerry said. "We'll be going up in a bit."

Casey nodded as she stood up. Walking around the outside of the crowd, she easily managed to reach Tom.

"Are you okay?" she asked him.

Tom looked up and gave an indication to sit down. "M'all right," he mumbled.

"Don't be like that. This is an event that's meant to be a friendly competition. How would your dad like it if you spent most of it focused entirely on beating one person and shutting yourself off from everyone else? Go and be lively, revel in the atmosphere, and forget what happens in the events themselves."

"A bit hard to do that when you're being targeted."

"You aren't being targeted," Casey tried for reassuring. "It's only what you think is happening."

"I was cut off by her!" Tom's voice strained itself by trying to be loud and angry while keeping it low. "She wants me out. How is that not being targeted?"

"After this next event, try again. Don't be so confrontational, and maybe she'll see some sense."

"After she's done beating me senseless."

"Stop it." Casey's voice hardened slightly, something it hadn't done for years. "Forget her and forget what she's doing. Concentrate on getting through this next event your way. Don't let anyone else dictate your path. You have been given an opportunity. Don't spoil it by being someone you're not."

She had to pause herself, slightly surprised at what she had said. Was it what she felt? Deep down she knew it was. She felt different somehow, as though she'd unlocked something within.

Tom hadn't said anything. He stood up in silence and walked to where Kerry and Lee waited. Instantly that feeling vanished and worry set in again. Had she pushed it too far?

She stood up to follow and say more – apologising for what she'd said. She was brought up short when Tom turned around with the largest smile she'd seen him with for the last few days.

"Thanks for saying what I needed to hear. If nothing goes wrong this event, I'll do exactly what you said."

Stood in the hangar listening as the next event was announced, Lee felt Tom hadn't truly renounced all his feelings. It seemed like he was trying hard to block any thoughts of Sally Evans, and trying harder to be aloof and relaxed, but Lee could tell.

He could tell by the slight head turn before it snapped back. The way his grin would slightly falter. Tom's feelings on this seemed difficult to change. And if anything else happened, it would only get worse.

The event itself was named Retrieval. Four cruisers held an object that needed to be collected, but each object had to be returned to the Sur-C before another could be claimed. It would be a test of straight-line speed and able swapping between Kilo and Mega Power Drives.

Lee felt this would be something Tom would excel at.

Open communication was allowed between competitor and their supporters during this event, which allowed for some planning as Tom sat himself inside the Space Kicker.

"Okay," Lee panted as he ran for the DSSC, talking into his PMD. "Which of the cruisers looks far away?"

"Karzadono," Tom stated. "A massive distance away. Near Donaldo, in fact."

"And the nearest?" he asked, climbing up into the DSSC's hangar.

"Salty Sunrise."

Lee quickly made a calculation based on Tom's performance in training and what he suspected others would do. "Take the Sunrise first, then go for the Karzadono."

Inside the lounge, the two mothers already waited, watching the map and the positions of all the racers. Lee sat down and looked at the positioning chart that showed top-down and side views of all cruisers and racers. The Space Kicker would only have the top-down view.

"It should be an easy one to take," Lee stated, aware Tom hadn't said anything.

"Then why not last?" Tom questioned. "I wouldn't even have to swap drives."

"Exactly why you do it first. If you can time the changes right, you should be able to decelerate back to a KPD set speed as you enter each hangar – or even to a zeroed speed that you'll be able to land inside if timed right. That would give you a great advantage against the others, which is why you tackle Sunrise first."

The positioning of the Sunrise was forward and directly over the Sur-C. The MPD could be used to get there but would have to be cut short to get inside the hangar of the Sur-C on the return trip. Unless you wanted to perform a wide arc to pull the same trick off.

The call for the race to begin rang through the speakers and Lee watched all sixteen blips pull out of the hangar. Most seemed to be going for the Karzadono first. Lee quickly found and marked out Tom's blip, then did the same for Sally's. Tom had followed his advice to head to the Sunrise first, with Sally and two others heading for the Gata-pron. Only one other person had followed Tom to the Sunrise, leaving one cruiser with no-one heading to it.

Lee smiled at how right his prediction had been.

He didn't need much speed, otherwise he'd never make the swap back down quick enough. The Space Kicker quickly accelerated, with Tom's hand resting on the switch to swap back to the KPD, watching the scanner and counting down.

The Space Kicker hadn't even hit half of the set speed of 01:00 before that change had to be made. In that second as the drives swapped, Tom dropped the set speed.

The Space Kicker finished decelerating to 00:10 KPD just as he passed the atmosphere gauze. Directing the 'craft to where he needed to go, Tom landed it and quickly ejected himself from the seat. Sliding across the frame to place his feet on the floor, he ran to the man overseeing the boxes of items.

Picking out one of the spherical objects, he turned around to see a Galaxy landing. Running to his own 'craft, he climbed inside, placed the object between his legs, and lifted up.

Out of the hangar, he set his speed back to 01:00 and swapped to the MPD.

"I told you," Lee's voice sounded happy.

"Where am I on the rankings, then?"

"You are currently... second."

"Second?" Tom couldn't hide his surprise.

"A lot of people seem to have improved their drive swapping capabilities. The person in first seems to have very little delay between them."

Tom swapped back down to the KPD to make the turn into the hangar. As he guided himself inside, he noticed a Galaxy already landed. The pilot already at the hand-in point.

Landing his own 'craft, he carefully picked the spherical object up and climbed down. Rushing to the hand-in point, he heard three other 'craft coming in for a landing.

Tom handed the object over, mentally willing for the process to go faster so he could get back out. When he had the go-ahead to leave, he turned and sprinted back to the Space Kicker, hardly even noticing the Falcon next to it or acknowledging whose it was.

"Karzadono, here I come."

Swapping to the MPD as soon as he could, he aimed slightly down, managing his speed to give it all he dared for the longest journey of the four.

"Update for you," Lee said. "Two of those who came after you are heading for the other cruiser. I've pinned its name as Dark Ringer. The third is heading for the Karzadono, same as you. Most of those who went for the Karzadono first are starting to head back now, so be aware of incoming traffic."

"Thanks for the update," Tom said. "Dropping slightly so I can avoid them without loss of speed."

After another two minutes, he started dropping speed slowly ready for the swap back down to the KPD. He had it near enough zeroed when he made the swap and slipped smoothly through the atmosphere gauze to land a few meters from the boxes of objects.

Running to them, he quickly swiped a model of a spacecraft.

Turning around to start running back, he spotted what was coming through the atmosphere gauze at a high rate of speed.

The Falcon slammed itself down, the landing claws making a loud grinding as they skidded across the floor. The Falcon clipped against the rear of the Space Kicker which knocked it sideways slightly. The Falcon itself ground to a halt a few meters away.

Tom fought a mental battle between checking if she was alright and shouting her down for not being able to fly.

He chose the former, remembering his mother's words about not being confrontational.

The security of the cruiser were already there when Tom arrived, and had managed to pull the viewshield away. Inside, Sally Evans looked slightly dazed, but otherwise fine. She kept repeating to the security she needed no looking at and made to get out. Tom held a hand out. She looked up, halfway to taking it, then changed tack to place the hand down on the frame and lifted herself out.

"I don't need help," she said. "Get going!"

The security had dispersed, but Tom stood numb. He felt an empty shell, unaware of what he should be doing. When Sally arrived back and noticed him still stood there, she gave him a push and pointed to the Space Kicker.

"I'm fine," she repeated. "Do you care about staying in the Championship?"

The Falcon lifted off with him still stood next to it. It was then he remembered this was a race. Turning tail and running back, he hurried up and inside the Space Kicker, now with just one purpose.

Beating Sally Evans.

There was a problem, though. However slight a clip the Falcon might have given the Space Kicker, something had been affected.

"He's completely messed up," Lee said.

Kerry looked at the leaderboard, then down at the map. Tom had tried showing some compassion, and the way he described it was that Sally had blocked and provoked him. It hadn't looked like that on the view of the hangar that Kerry and Casey had watched.

Yes, the clipping of the Space Kicker had been bad. It had been a simple case of pushing too much.

Tom didn't seem to be seeing it like that. And now he was paying for it.

"The speed's definitely been affected," he complained through the link. "The changing between drives is getting slow."

Kerry checked on Lee's PMD that they were still muted to Tom. Then she turned to Casey. "Whatever you told him hasn't seemed to work."

"It was a simple mistake. He's blaming it as sabotage, no doubt. That seemed to be what he was going for until I talked to him. I expected it to have worked."

"It didn't anyway," Lee stated. "It was just a show. He tried believing in it himself, but he got himself wound up too much over it that he probably won't settle down until he's beaten her at something."

"That'll take forever," Kerry commented.

"Can I get an update?" Tom called. "How far ahead is she?"

Lee sighed. "Do you want to deal with it?"

"Sorry," Kerry said. "Your job."

It wasn't that she didn't want to deal with him, but coming from Lee it would sound better. As long as he knew what to say.

Lee unmuted the audio pickup and stated his position. Currently, Tom had fallen to the third quarter of people and was very close to going down to the fourth. He could pick up and just about make the second quarter if he brought his pace up. No mention was made of Sally's position.

"Okay… Almost to the Sur-C. Here's hoping I can do something good."

Kerry found herself a bit concerned about how that had been said. All the fight had gone from him. It sounded almost as if he didn't care where he came.

"Remember that some still need to go to the Karzadono. Most also need to go to the Sunrise. Depending on how they deal with both of those, you should build back to the second quarter just by continuing with your current pace."

"Noted."

Tom had nothing to say after that.

Kerry ran to the control bay to look out at the hangar. She watched as the Space Kicker slowed for a landing, expertly sliding underneath a 'craft that had just taken off to land.

Whatever his mood, the one thing he seemed good at was being aware of everything around him. Returning to the others, she looked at the leaderboard again. His position climbed a few places as his second object got catalogued.

"Which of the two cruisers are you going for now?" Lee asked.

"Which of the cruisers did she go to?"

It was obvious who Tom meant. "She's already done the Gata-pron, remember? Head there and leave Dark Ringer for last."

"Okay."

Kerry muted the audio pickup. "I hope he doesn't do anything silly trying to catch up."

"He knows what he's doing," Lee said.

When Tom had run a full system check through the health monitor, no problems had been reported. It was then he accepted that he had probably been creating even more reasons to hate Sally than he already had.

It still wasn't stopping those thoughts, but he felt he had a tight control of them. Lee and the two mothers were right. He needed to get rid of them. He had to do it gradually and not go adding anything else to the list.

Inside the Gata-pron, he collected the object needed and hurried back to the Space Kicker. As he lifted off, he gave another look at the map. He wasn't confident about being able to get into the second quarter of racers, but he'd be giving it a very good try.

He knew he was a conflicted pool of thoughts and feelings. Even he couldn't place exactly what he felt all the time, though he knew that for a few seconds he had indeed thought about giving up. That wasn't him, and he had quickly put the fight back into himself – carefully avoiding the topic he was still trying to avoid as much as he could.

He checked his position on the scanner and his current set speed, then called for another update. He still wasn't catching up fast enough, but at least he was no longer at risk of being knocked out of the Championship.

He swapped back down to the KPD, entered the hangar of the Sur-C, and noted the number of people waiting to get items catalogued. He sighed as he landed, and slowly pulled himself out of the seat. Item in hand, he joined the waiting crowd.

Faster than he had expected, he was able to get his item catalogued and climb back into the Space Kicker.

"Way to go. Just the Dark Ringer left." Lee sounded joyous. "Keep the pace. Don't ruin this now."

"I hear you," Tom said as he lifted. "What's the ranking looking like?"

"You've picked up two places, meaning you're now in the second quarter. Though there's every chance you'll drop one place and there's nothing you can do to stop that. Don't try to prove anything."

"I've got nothing to prove here," Tom affirmed. "Next event – that's mine."

In little time he reached the Dark Ringer, landed expertly, and dashed out and back in with the fourth object in hand.

Lifting up, he dodged to the side as a quickly decelerating Galaxy arrived on a collision course. Once outside, he swapped to the MPD and made straight for the Surveillance Cruiser.

On the scanner, he could see exactly what Lee meant about not being able to do anything about losing a place on the ranking. A Rotablade had pulled out of the hangar of the Gata-pron and within milliseconds had activated its MPD. Within seconds it had reached the speed Tom currently cruised at and passed beyond it.

There was no way Tom could accelerate any faster.

He didn't dare risk a late swap back to the KPD, and so slowed to an easy speed just before he hit the atmosphere gauze. He spotted the DSSC as he positioned himself for a landing and smiled at what stood on top of it waving.

Quickly he got the fourth object catalogued, and once he was able to, walked over to the DSSC and looked up.

"How'd you get there?" he asked.

"With difficulty," Lee replied. "But quickly."

Lee hopped down from the top onto the lower level, then slid down the sloped front to join Tom at ground level.

"You did good," he added. "Keep that focus for these next few events, and you could be in the final."

"If I manage to keep in the second quarter for these next two events, which I know I can."

The two hopped up to sit on the DSSC's hangar floor, watching as the remainder of the competitors landed.

"Look…" Lee said. Tom looked at his friend to see an uncomfortable expression on his face. Tom mentally gave a sigh, guessing what topic was about to be mentioned.

"I'm trying, okay," Tom stated. "I just need time."

"Time isn't what's needed here. It's an understanding that nothing is wrong. Just let it all go."

"It's a bit hard to see the first two challenges as anything but attempts to get me-"

"No. That's negative thinking."

"It's a negative event, though. Why try spinning it as a positive?"

"But that's exactly what you need to do." Lee's voice had a strength to it that made Tom think of the one he used when he'd solved a problem.

Tom remained silent to think things through. At first, he had been positive. A little cautious, a little nervous, but positive about the whole thing. Then the attack had come and everything had spiralled to a negative. He'd seen some positive eventually but had been half and half all the time. No positive allowed without a negative.

The Championship itself had allowed the more negative side to show through no matter how much he wanted to show positivity.

And what made the negative side worse was that most of them were simple or small things that were enlarged to be greater than they should be.

He needed to make sense of it all, but he couldn't be doing that here.

"Everyone has returned," Mrs. Johnson informed. "Everyone's gathering for the results."

"Great," Lee said, jumping down from the DSSC.

Tom followed a bit more slowly. The day would soon be over with these announcements, then he could relax and hopefully come to a more positive outlook.

The four of them moved into the crowd, with the two mothers joining the mass of supporters. Lee stood to his right.

"We have our results," the host called once everyone had gathered. Only one of the three was around. "And there seems to have been a turnaround of skill from some."

Tom only half-listened, but curiosity hit with that line. *Who must have fouled up worse than me?*

"From second straight to last is Rachel Carrington. That artistic 'craft of hers failed her in its drive swapping capabilities."

That surprised Tom, as he'd been sure that Basic of hers had been modified for everything. He had a feeling that being a Basic meant there were too many limits for such modifications. He'd be asking about that sometime.

"A slight loss of positioning from Trudy Nimré as she dropped further down the last quarter. Ryan Ross-Smith had a greater drop from the top of the third quarter."

Neither name meant anything to Tom. But he wondered who else had seen a great fall for that previous comment.

"And from first falls Daniel Tampwick, who started out good but messed up a few changes between drives. A problem that a few seemed to have."

The four who were being knocked out stood to face the crowd. It was time to see who had won this event.

"Just as some have declined, there's also been an improvement with quite a number of people. Bob Harrison makes a great improvement from the lowest position of the second quarter to take first. Claire Beckett moves from the third quarter into second. The same goes for Jackie Moore, who took third."

The three stood at the front to be applauded, then the final word from the host.

"You now have the rest of the day away from events. The next one will begin tomorrow at 09:00, starting with the event briefing. All I'll say for now is that your positions from this event will carry over to the start of the next. That is all."

The crowd dispersed, with Tom looking around for Rachel Carrington. She was surrounded by a crowd asking for details, which made Tom take a step back.

"Hey," a voice called from behind him.

Turning, he locked eyes with Sally Evans. Instantly he fought down the negative things he wanted to say, and managed a "Hey," in return.

Lee turned and stepped beside him. "How you doing after what happened?" he asked.

"Good. Just a simple case of mistiming things. I just wanted to say thanks for the concern you showed, but there was no need to risk the hit to your position in the rankings for it."

"It was... Well..." Tom felt unsure how to express what he wanted to. "I wanted to make sure you were fine." He couldn't continue, lost for anything else to say. Lee continued the thought.

"Looking out for each other is more important than winning. I'm sure you'd have done the same."

"Yeah, of course I would." She looked down at her PMD, frowning at a message. "See you around."

She left quickly, leaving the two stood watching her exit.

"She could do with some positive reinforcement," Tom stated. "She's a lot different in personality than when this thing started."

"At least you didn't lose it and have a go at her. I'm pretty sure you were close."

"I'm confident I'm getting no more trouble from her. Whatever I'm going through is nothing compared to what she is."

"We need to just take it easy for the next few hours. Keep our mind off the Championship."

"We're not going to eat at the Champion's Court, then?" Tom asked, thinking of when he might get to speak with Rachel.

"No. There's a lot of places to eat here, including places where we can eat and then get to something else. A little low-key sport, maybe."

"So long as it is low-key. I've had enough running for one day."

The food hadn't been the best, but Casey understood Lee's plan to keep Tom occupied away from the Championship for a few hours. Since this place had a bowling alley — a proper one not simulated through Lightmorph technology — it looked to be a good time.

She took a sip from her glass before standing up to take her turn. It had been quite an age since any of them had played, so they were all a bit rusty.

Tom was still winning, though.

"Nice one," Kerry called, noting the nine pins knocked down with one ball.

Casey missed the last pin with her next ball, and when Tom stood up for his turn, she noted his look of focus. She also noted Lee's smile and had a feeling he was up to something with this.

Tom swung his arm out to ready for rolling the ball. As he started the arc back forward, he took one step and wobbled slightly. His aimed messed up, the ball went straight for the gutter as he released it.

Swinging around, his eyes locked on Lee. Turning, Casey saw his arm outstretched with a small pin shooter.

"I am the enemy," Lee said. "I want to see you lose. What are you going to do?"

Tom picked up another ball, took aim once again, and this time Casey heard the faint click as the pin shooter ejected a tiny stinger. It struck Tom's leg once again, but this time Tom held onto the ball and lined up for the shot again. His quickened pace meant that he'd rolled the ball just as he got stung.

"Where did you get that?" Tom asked.

"From the owner of this place. I asked him for it to help you strengthen focus even under stress. You did good."

Casey had no idea how Lee had asked for it without any of them knowing about it. It just proved his skill in areas Tom had no hope of surpassing.

"You really think that would work?"

"We'll see, won't we?"

Throughout the next eight turns of Tom's, Lee continued firing the pin shooter. It did indeed seem to Casey that his focus on the objective had increased. He no longer seemed to even feel them after a few turns, and on his last two managed to quickly aim and roll the ball with no second tries or hesitation.

Casey took her last turn, ending the game. Her fifty points paled in comparison to Tom's hundred and forty-four. He had won the game even with the stingers hitting him, and Lee seemed to think that a success.

"Just focus on the objective and you can drown everything else out. You'll do good tomorrow. I can feel it."

"Could you have drilled the lesson in with something that didn't numb my leg?" Tom asked, rubbing his right leg as he leaned against the counter.

"It's a static pulse designed for training weapons," the owner informed as he accepted the pin shooter back from Lee. "You might have gone a bit overboard with the charge setting," he added as he looked down at it.

"Well, it shows how much he was focused on his objective, doesn't it?" Lee said. "He failed to feel anything."

"You have any idea what the next challenge is?" the owner asked.

"Nothing except that the positions carry over."

The owner turned to Tom. "Do your best. There's a lot of people wishing you well."

"Thanks," Tom said.

As the four of them walked out of the place, Casey hoped the lesson Lee had given Tom would last through the night. He needed to focus as he had during this game. As for Lee...

She wondered where he had learnt that lesson of focus. And how.

"It is a new day for our competitors, of which there are now only twelve. Yesterday proved that winning one event is never enough to secure a string of them, as something unexpected could be coming around the corner. Who are the final four going to be? We'll find out today with two new challenges."

Pyra Summers of Radio Racer [09/5-0085]

Tom had done some serious thinking during his resting moments, and even in his sleep through wildly shifting images of dream. He was going to prove, on this day, that he had the focus and the determination to overcome any obstacles and get to the final event.

All three hosts were back, with the absence of two of them from the previous event being down to something important they'd needed to deal with. It couldn't have been anything bad, otherwise the Championship would have been halted.

"This next event will test your reactions and your speed, but in a different way than a simple race."

"Simply titled Speed, a new route has been set out for racers to follow. This time, you won't be battling for position. You will instead be hunting down the fastest time."

"Each racer will start thirty seconds after the previous racer has launched, giving everyone enough room to manoeuvre through the route."

"The last place finisher of the previous event will start first, with the first-place finisher starting this event last."

The sorting of the 'craft then followed, with the racers being directed to form a line in the order they'd be leaving from. Two mini cruisers indicated the start line, with a timer ready to count down thirty seconds formed on the one to the right.

Tom felt confident about this. He'd finally be able to show off his true skill in handling a 'craft. Suddenly he felt good about where he'd finished in the last event. It placed him as the fourth person to launch out.

"First racer! Go!"

Everyone heard that command through their speakers. The countdown started as a Basic 'craft – the only one remaining – lifted itself and flew out the hangar.

The two Falcons in front of him moved forward slightly, placing themselves closer to the start line. Tom shuffled his Space Kicker forward. Looking down, he noted the route and the turns it would take.

He closed his eyes and let a breath out, trying to calm himself. Once again, he was preparing for the fastest take-off he could manage. His focus was on getting the fastest time.

Shuffling forward again, just one 'craft remained before he'd be lifting off from the line. Thirty seconds seemed a long time, and he'd have to sit through another thirty before he could launch himself.

Once the other Falcon was away, the Space Kicker slid to the line. Tom watched the thirty seconds count down, which seemed even slower than before. He lifted his hands from the controls to give them a shake, then placed them back to the controls with five seconds remaining.

Four... Three... Two... One...

On zero, the board flashed green.

The Space Kicker lifted and shot from the hangar. Pulling down, he spotted the first checkpoint he'd need to hit. The second one followed further beyond it, and as he rolled to get in position, he saw the third.

Accelerating to a faster speed, he passed the first, second, and third within seconds of each other. The fourth point continued the massive circle around the Sur-C, as did the fifth and sixth points.

The seventh set up a loop around the command tower, ready to head to the Sur-C's forward section. After that, it was a simple case of heading for the Salty Sunrise, then following a twisting route to reach the Dark Ringer.

As he hit the ninth checkpoint, a warning flashed on his board. The map gave way to the health monitor, where the danger was clear to see.

He gave a growl of frustration, then quickly buried it. He knew what he had to do, and giving in to the heat haze of frustration would just have him making mistakes.

And wasting the minutes he had before his power would be sapped away.

"Look at that Space Kicker go!" Pyra Summers commented. "It's going to be a tough one to beat – even for the Falcons."

Lee listened with half of his attention as he tracked the numbers. Once again there was no communication between competitors and support, meaning Tom wouldn't know he currently had the fastest time.

Looking at the map, it seemed that Tom would soon catch up to the Falcon that had launched before him. That would prove troublesome if he couldn't be guaranteed a smooth overtake.

The rankings were constantly updating as racers overtook each other's times by milliseconds. Three times were close to Tom's, but not one of them stood a chance of beating it.

A new name added itself to the list as the next person hit the first checkpoint. There remained six left to launch, with three of those being Falcons. And those would be a problem.

"He's increasing the gap between himself and the one who launched third," Lee stated. "He's serious about winning this."

"Well he would be," Mrs. Johnson said. "He wants to make up for the times things have gone wrong."

"Maybe your little lesson is working," Mrs. Hughs ventured.

Lee smiled. Maybe it was.

Tom had managed the tight, winding route between the two cruisers very quickly and controlled, aware his shield was draining fast. When he felt he could chance it, he ran the diagnostic program to find the problem.

It had quickly found static within his systems, which shouldn't have been able to get in. The improvements that had been made to the Space Kicker were supposed to have stopped it from getting in.

The diagnostic had at least notified him that all power wouldn't be drained the instant the shield zeroed. But it would drain at double the rate his shield was, meaning he still couldn't let off the pace.

Through the next checkpoint, he was now half-way to completing the route.

He eased off the power a bit to swing around the Gata-pron's control tower, aiming for the next checkpoint with the least amount of speed lost. Pulling up slightly, he took the Space Kicker parallel to the cruiser, ready for the entrance into the hangar and the tight manoeuvring it would provide.

Entering on the left side, he followed the route around the wall, tightly turned, and accelerated slightly before reducing speed again to make it through the very tight space.

Two seconds later the space opened out. Two directions presented themselves, and without even thinking Tom took the left side. Following the curving route to the hangar exit, he allowed a small smile from choosing the side that allowed him to keep most of his speed as he hit the next checkpoint by continuing that curve through the atmosphere gauze and into the darkness of space again.

Within sight was the Falcon who had launched before he had. His surprise showed visibly. He knew he'd been fast, but never expected to make up the distance that fast.

He looked down at his health monitor just as the last of his shield energy depleted. That was that. He had no need to be monitoring it any longer.

Swapping back to the scanner, he continued pushing his speed as much as he could. He'd never hit maximum at any point during the rest of the race, allowing about a minute and a half before he would be affected by the power drain.

He needed to make the most of it.

"Why isn't he overtaking?"

Tom had caught up, but instead of finding a quick way to pass the Falcon, he had instead dropped his pace to that of the Falcon. Kerry had expected him to just zip straight on by and chase down the one who had launched second.

"Maybe he doesn't feel the need to," Lee reasoned. "He could have seen how close he was to that Falcon and decided there was no way anyone else would catch up to his time. Even with a slightly reduced pace, there's still many seconds between him and the next time."

Kerry looked at the times on the leaderboard, and as Tom passed another checkpoint, the difference between him and second barely changed. She scanned the names on the list, seeing a few familiar ones near the top.

"The racer who first launched has now returned to the hangar," Casey shouted from the control bay. "Check the time."

Kerry scanned the map, and indeed the Basic belonging to Florence had returned. The time updated, though it didn't look an entirely competitive one. It was one that risked being knocked out from the Championship.

Looking to the map again, Tom and the Falcon he followed were roughly a minute out from finishing. The gap between the two looked as though it had increased. She locked eyes on the leaderboard, waiting for confirmation that something was wrong.

She didn't even need to wait that long.

"The Space Kicker that everyone has been cheering on and that has been the fastest throughout this event has started slowing down," Pyra Summers announced. "The gap between it and the Falcon in front of it has opened wide, with the time it managed to work for now slipping fast. Already it looks as though two times will be knocking it off that highest point of the ranking. Whatever problem Tom Hughs is facing, it might be the cause of him losing."

Indeed, as Kerry watched the times update, Tom's position dropped down once, then twice more. And all the while his speed slowly continued to drop.

❖

"Go-go-go-go-go-"

Tom continued repeating that single word, aware he was losing and that there was nothing he could do about it. He was trying to encourage the 'craft to keep what little speed it had left.

His maximum speed was dropping, and so was everything else. There was nothing else he could do, even if he wired the power pack from his spacesuit into the board – as Lee had done with the DSSC.

The second-to-last checkpoint was in sight, which led to a straight into the Sur-C's hangar. He had to make this count.

"Go-go-go-go-go..."

He passed the checkpoint. The Space Kicker now travelled at 00:10 KPD. There was a constriction in his throat.

"Go... go... go..."

He was meters out from hitting the atmosphere gauze. The Space Kicker's speed dropped to 00:05 KPD. His head wouldn't stop spinning.

He just about saw the atmosphere gauze fill his vision as he blacked out.

The security team were already surrounding the Space Kicker, but Casey shoved though them to look at her son.

Not again. Please not again.

She couldn't help but feel that Tom would relapse into a second bout of his fear of flight and space and the danger they both presented.

"Is he your son?" one of the security team asked.

"He is," Casey quickly affirmed. "He'll be alright, won't he?"

The viewshield had already been lifted away, with Tom being pulled out. A medic looked over him and nodded at her.

"Fortunately, he's only suffered a few seconds without a life support, so any effects will be minimal at best," the medic explained. "Even having been through such a thing before."

"What about mental effects?" Casey had to ask. "Last time he developed a fear of flight. It couldn't happen again, could it?"

"He should come back to us within the hour, so we'll know what mental effects have risen. We'll take him somewhere quiet to rest."

Casey said the best place would be the room they were staying at, so with a medical chair brought forward and Tom placed in it, Casey led the medic to the room where she and the Johnsons were staying.

Stay strong, she thought, looking down at Tom once he was transferred onto a bed. *Come out of this with a new resolve to win.*

CHAPTER 8 – GALE OF DETERMINATION

"That... was a finish. He's well, and that's all we know. The spacecraft is currently being examined elsewhere as the event continues. It was Tom Hughs who had suffered something similar before the Championship started, so here's to hoping he gets back on form and recovers quickly. He still stands a chance of winning, after all."

Pyra Summers of Radio Racer [09/5-0085]

He felt the comfort of the bed he had been using for the last two weeks greet him as feeling returned. Nothing felt broken. All was fine.

Thinking back on what had happened caused him little distress. This time, he had been prepared and had fought to keep bad things from happening. Mostly.

He hadn't wanted to overtake the Falcon that had been in front of him as he couldn't bear to think what would have been said had that Falcon then overtaken him when he was in trouble. And beyond that, he knew he'd alerted those on board the Sur-C to a problem without having to explain anything.

All the spacecraft would have been checked out at the end of the challenge, but that entrance he had barely managed to make seemed to have brought action straight away. At least, he hoped it had.

He couldn't even blame Sally Evans for this one. It seemed petty to even try. There was absolutely no chance that she could have done anything. It seemed stupid to be desperate enough to win that you would risk another's life to do so. She'd risked her own during the collection challenge, but he accepted that as a simple slip up.

He listened to any sound he could, trying to feel who else was in the room. He opened his eyes and looked to his left side. Sure enough, the medic he had felt sure was watching sat in a chair.

"Ah, you're awake," the medic exclaimed in a cheery tone. "Are you feeling fit?"

Tom shuffled back to sit up. "Better than I'll ever be," he replied. "I'm ready to get to that next challenge and win." A thought crossed his mind. "If... I'm still in?"

He was unsure if he wanted to hear the answer. He felt a slight nervousness and even a bit of fear that he'd been knocked out.

"Your effort managed to keep you in. Only at the very end did people start to beat that time, and not enough managed to do so. You almost fell into the third quarter, but the time you managed held."

The last of the second quarter. One off the top five. Joy bloomed within him and excitement at being able to get back out and show this had not affected him bubbled. His expression seemed to say all that, as the medic left him to be quickly replaced by his mother and Lee.

"I am so happy to see you up and smiling," Mrs. Hughs said. "I felt that maybe..."

"I'm looking at this positively," Tom responded. "I'm still in. Whatever attack this was hasn't worked. I'll be back out there as soon as I can to prove that."

"Great," Lee stated. He held his PMD up, pressed a button and said, "It's okay. Tell them the next challenge can go ahead as planned." He ended the connection and lowered the PMD. "They were waiting for word how you felt," he informed.

"So, the Space Kicker's working?" Tom asked.

"Whoever this is, they were clever. They somehow managed to attach a CSP into the framework of the Space Kicker itself and wire it to activate at a high speed. All the 'craft are under guard whenever they aren't being used, which is why security is stumped."

"No cameras looking?"

"Those had been dealt with, in such a way that no-one knew anything had been done until a true scan of the security systems was put into action."

"But it does work?" Tom asked again.

"The capsule that dispensed the static has been removed, all systems have been charged back up, and scans indicate that no trace of static remains."

A relieved sigh escaped him. "That's great."

Mrs. Hughs spoke up again. "The Talon Force connection has been made again, this time officially. But the records indicate those who were members have no connection to this."

"It's a definite mystery," Mrs. Johnson said as she entered the room. "The latest is that most of the Talon Force hardware went missing when they returned. That's now public knowledge, to alert everyone about the danger. The more interesting part is that everyone is accounted for, yet the training and knowledge of all this tech is still available. Somewhere."

"There's no need to worry about it," Lee stated. "This Championship is almost over. Security has now been strengthened, so no more attacks will be happening. Just concentrate on getting through this next challenge and doing your best in the final."

"I'm planning to." Tom rolled his shoulders to prepare for getting up. "Who did get knocked out, anyway?"

"Jackie Moore and Bob Harrison were two."

"That's a big drop in performance," Tom commented as he lifted himself up.

"Stella Sandford and Florence Petala were the other two. Adam McCoy took the top spot, with Hayden Bell and Claire Beckett making a return to the top three."

"The Galaxy models are proving to be stronger than the Falcon. Surprising."

"The next event begins in an hour. Should give plenty of time to get something to eat at the Champion's Court."

"Good. I'm feeling hungry after all that."

Tom seemed to really be getting into the true spirit of the Championship now, Lee noted. The two were sat at a table with several others, with Tom joining in with the talk. Those around were interested in hearing his take on what had happened, with Tom being a good teller of the story.

He even said he didn't want to be seen a fool from being overtaken once the problem had started.

"Everyone seemed to catch on pretty fast that something was wrong," Rachel Carrington stated. "The security guys were waiting for you to come in. As soon as you dropped in, they were on you instantly."

"I had hoped they would be," Tom said.

"I'm surprised at how fast you were able to go, even with the problem," someone else put in. A competitor that Lee recognised as having been knocked out at the qualifier. "You sure you aren't a secret professional racer?"

Tom smiled at that. "I'm just doing my best the way I know how. Though I am already a professional thanks to Space Racer."

The other gave an expression that resembled sarcastic amazement, then said, "You were so professional they stopped you entering the tournaments. How many wins did you rack up before that happened?"

"Too many to count," Tom replied after a few seconds of pretending to think about it.

That person left the table to grab some more food, with a few others also leaving. They all expressed certainty that Tom would win, with Tom shaking their hands as they left.

As Rachel Carrington got up to leave as well, Tom asked her about when she had been knocked out. Lee was also interested in that.

"Oh, it was just a complete oversight. I'd travelled up in a mini cruiser and hadn't needed to swap drives for so long I'd completely forgot about them. The slowest it clocked was around five seconds before the MPD started up. Can't really complain, though." She held her hand out for shaking, to both Tom and Lee. "Go and show how great you are. I'll be watching."

She left. Lee looked around the food court, seeing it mostly empty. There was one person slowly walking to them, and it looked like she wanted a word.

"Hey," Sally Evans greeted nervously.

This should be good, Lee found himself thinking.

Tom whipped around to face her, but the fight immediately left him once he did. "Hello," he managed awkwardly.

"Look. I know we've had some issues with each other," she stated. "Things that maybe we both could have controlled. However, I want it to end. We shouldn't be fighting, trying to one-up each other. Fresh start?" It looked as though she had tried one of her cheeky smiles, but it came out as more a nervous grin.

Lee waited for the answer, knowing what he would say if he were Tom.

"I probably inflated the issue more than I should have," Tom said with a sigh. "We're the youngest here. We should be looking out for each other."

He still hadn't agreed.

"Are you suffering any problems with that Falcon of yours?" Lee asked. "Lagging in drive swapping, or just the drive operation in general?" He had no idea why Tom was stalling, but conversation was better than silence.

"Not that I know of. Like I said before, I just pushed too hard." She looked back to Tom. "Okay, I admit to wanting to win out over you, and... in the qualifier..." She looked around, spotted no-one close by. "I did target you after that first near miss. I wouldn't have minded that, but our exchange after the qualifier..."

"Yeah..." Tom muttered. "I... Fresh start..." He then repeated in a stronger voice, "Fresh start. That's what we need. I'm sorry to have shouted at you. I admit to taking things a bit too personal."

Now the cheeky grin really did show itself. "Great! See you in the next challenge, and don't get knocked out."

She ran out, still smiling.

"Well, that's sorted," Lee said. "She's happy, and so are you."

"I still say she doesn't mean it."

"Do you need a reminder not to go down that route again?" Lee said sharply. "You've made up. Giving things a fresh start. Don't make this a repeat of the first time."

"Oh, don't worry. I'll give her a chance. I won't jump on her for a little thing, either."

"That's alright, then." He looked at the time on the wall above the serving counter. "Few minutes before briefing."

As they headed for the hangar, Lee ran through the challenges so far and what could still happen. A standard race and a time trial, as well as a more unusual sort of race. Then he remembered the hint on Radio Racer about something special in one of the hangars. Nothing of the sort had come out to play, and it was time for another one of those unusual races.

Then he remembered that the mounted turret that had been fitted to each competitor's 'craft hadn't been removed. At least for those still in the Championship. Then there was something his dad had said before he'd gone to war. Something about a prototype spacecraft that held more than one person.

If all that added up, the competitors were in for a fun time.

There remained a minute before the announcement for the next event. Kerry looked at both sides of the hangar and failed to spot Tom and Lee. Looking to the gathering of competitors, she noted the back of a head she knew.

They'd somehow slipped into the crowds and joined the line. Maybe she just hadn't seen them come in.

The announcement of the next challenge started, and it sounded like a great test of skill. This one was named Accuracy, and involved a prototype 'craft named the Dragonfly. The largest spacecraft built, purely for the Championship – or so the crowd were told.

Steve probably shouldn't have told them about it, but just as he'd shared a few snippets of info about the mission he had undertaken, he'd also shared a bit about the Dragonfly.

This model of spacecraft held three people, each in their own pod. Each pod was diamond-shaped with a large middle diamond and a slightly smaller one to each rear side. These smaller pods held a massive array of weaponry, and as she listened to the hosts of the Championship continuing to give the details of the challenge, she recalled a few of those weapons.

The competitors wouldn't be told of them, she felt certain. It would be a surprise to them, that they'd have to overcome as they tried to hit the Dragonfly with their own weaponry three times.

That meant they'd once again be using that mounted turret that had a thirty second recharge time.

Tom had proven he could hold his own against another fighter in combat in the first challenge. She had hope that he'd do the same here.

The prototype 'craft would show itself at any time from any hangar of the cruisers that formed the arena. Tom flew the Space Kicker in a wide circle to get as close to the hangars as possible, noting that two others were doing the same thing.

He had a feeling the pilot and gunners within that Dragonfly would be aware that some would try getting the jump on them, but he had no idea what sort of weaponry it could use.

All the competitors had been told was that the turret charge would be reset if they got hit by any of it. Which made Tom think there was a lot.

As he passed the Gata-pron, he spotted the Dragonfly move out from the Dark Ringer and instantly fire off some sort of flash on both sides.

Everyone seemed to move as one and lock onto that position, hoping to get the first hit on it. Tom was close, but not as close as some of the others, who underestimated what a powerhouse it was. It picked them off, stopping them from firing their turrets.

Sally and her Falcon arrived next, following from the side as the Dragonfly dropped into a dive. As she lined up, the Dragonfly started to spin. As Sally fired, it pulled away from the dive.

The pilot was doing a great job of flying it, and Tom was sure the three within it were communicating as the next competitor flew in from above to be stopped as the Dragonfly tilted one of the gunners up to fire.

While they were busy with that, Tom managed to fire at it while the two were face-to-face for exactly a second. He flew past it close enough that proximity warnings sounded, but he looked down to see a confirmed hit.

He gave a smile and nodded slightly, pleased at the result. One down, two more hits to get.

Tom had got a hit on the Dragonfly, but one other had as well a few seconds later. Lee watched as the leaderboard updated to place Katie Daniels below Tom.

Lee was aware she was the only one who had entered a Braveheart model into the Championship, and it had proven itself to be a worthy 'craft. She had managed to always stay in the second quarter. She hadn't been one to mix from what Lee had seen, but then he'd hardly seen her in the Champion's Court.

"I see Tom's hanging back now he's got a first hit in," Mrs. Johnson stated. "Good to see he's not rushing in."

"Why wouldn't he try for a second hit so soon?" Mrs. Hughs asked. "It's been longer than thirty seconds. He's got the charge for a shot."

"It's not about getting the shots in as soon as the gun recharges. Watch."

All three watched as one of the Galaxy 'crafts flew in for another shot, with the second Galaxy doing the same from a different direction. The portside pod fired at the first, with a bright flash coming from the starboard one. Both Galaxy's flew by without firing.

Mrs. Hughs still looked blank, so Lee filled in.

"Even if you can get close enough to fire, there's still a lot to consider. Such as what that Dragonfly can use against them. Those bright flashes you see are, I think, nullifiers. They disperse any energy weapons and can also disorient anyone who directly looks at them for a few seconds. Powerful things, but they take a lot of recharge time. Since these ones don't have to operate at full strength, that recharge time is drastically reduced. There's also the regular laser cannons on a rotating axis, and things we haven't seen yet. Those are what Tom is looking out for."

"You mean he's hoping the others will force the Dragonfly to show those things so he knows what to look out for."

"In a way, yes. No doubt he'll try and take advantage of opportunities as he always does."

The leaderboard updated again as Sally managed to avoid a flurry of lasers. The nullifier had fired slightly too late to stop the hit.

Lee watched as Tom flew in. The lasers fired, but he'd already pulled away. Someone tried taking advantage of that, but a new weapon showed itself. The Dragonfly tilted slightly so the portside was raised above the starboard pod's viewshield. A continuous laser then fired from it, hitting that 'craft, then quickly sweeping around to hit every 'craft within range.

Both Tom and Sally had tried taking advantage of that by keeping to its underside, but an explosive charge ejected from the Dragonfly's underside and imploded before either could line up a shot.

"This Dragonfly is wild," Pyra Summers announced. "It's like a weapon's factory with the amount of things it can do. But these competitors are not slowing down in trying to get a hit."

Lee swapped the live images for a tactical map and looked at the movement of all eight competitors compared to the Dragonfly. Tom had flown far away again, possibly in an attempt to surprise it when it got near to him.

The map showed that two people had attempted to hit the Dragonfly, with both failing. A third attempt by Adam McCoy was successful. Sally then tried to get her second hit on it, and succeeded as well.

Lee frowned.

"Something wrong?" Mrs. Johnson asked.

"Probably nothing, but the starboard-side gunner seems to be getting a bit slow to react. But then whenever anyone else gets within range, the gunner is back on form."

"Can't trust anyone. No doubt a bit of favouritism is showing."

"I just hope Tom knows what he's doing."

The Dragonfly shouldn't be expecting this, Tom thought.

It had got close enough that he was able to strike. He flew in, ducked down and around it fully aware that both nullifiers would be firing, then zero-flipped and fired just as the lasers started coming his way.

Confirmed hit.

A thirty second recharge and he'd be able to get back into it. But...

He'd been aware that Sally had also got in a second hit, a bit too fast for his liking. Now she seemed to be aiming for a third, aiming again for the starboard-side.

He had to stop her.

Boosting forward, he aimed for the starboard-side too, aware that his gun still hadn't recharged but wanting to force a reaction from the Dragonfly.

He had almost reached the Dragonfly when it rolled around firing lasers from the portside pod. Sally quickly realised what was happening and pulled away from the Dragonfly, which had performed a half-loop and fired another explosive charge. Tom had tracked its movement.

His turret was now charged.

He couldn't mess this up.

He stayed out of range, keeping track of it but never posing a threat. He looked around, noting as best as he could where the others were positioned. The two Galaxys made for another attack. One of them managed a hit, the other got caught in a nullifier.

He tried not to think of anything, drawing on a focus he had discovered the day before at the bowling alley.

One shot. One hit. Victory.

He had to make this count.

Spacecraft were now coming from both sides, Sally once again aiming for the starboard-side. She seemed to think that whoever was in that starboard-side pod would allow her to get a hit.

It was reckless, but he needed to act now.

The Dragonfly dropped into a dive and started spinning again. Tom knew that it would try the same trick it had performed before. He was ready for it.

He stayed slightly behind Sally as she fired. One of the nullifiers flashed. Instead of pulling away, she dropped speed slightly to come alongside Tom.

One of the Galaxys made a move as Tom increased his speed. The second nullifier flashed. Out of nowhere, Katie Daniels appeared and fired to score a hit, barely missing both Tom and Sally as she flew away.

The Dragonfly pulled out of the dive. Tom tracked and fired, then immediately regretted doing so. He hadn't got in close.

He pulled away hoping to get around to the front again, then changed his mind and flew up a bit. He increased his speed to maximum, aiming for the direction the Dragonfly was in.

He flew past it quickly, performed a zero-flip, then noticed the Dragonfly had fallen for the bait. It hadn't deemed him a threat and had instead tackled two other 'craft that were aiming straight for it.

As he started moving forward again, he noticed Sally's Falcon aiming once again. He could do nothing. And further beyond was Katie Daniels, also closer than he was.

The Space Kicker accelerated fast for where he hoped the Dragonfly would move to next when faced with what it was. It curved to the right, Sally fired, it shifted left and performed a tight spiral down. Katie Daniels fired but the starboard nullifier caught the laser.

The Dragonfly then straightened out just as Tom reached it to fire his winning laser.

He had a victory to his name.

He held back his cheer. It could wait.

He flew to the perimeter the cruisers marked, near to the Sur-C where he would wait and watch.

Casey looked at the leaderboard. She blinked.

Lee had put the live images back up, and she had watched Tom pull off that opportunity. She hadn't believed, but the leaderboard showed it had happened.

It had just updated to show Tom up top with three hits.

"He's got first!" Lee yelled in celebration.

"Tom Hughs has done it!" Pyra Summers cheered. The Radio Racer host had certainly taken a real liking to him. "He's performed excellently throughout it all, but only now has he been able to show just what he's capable of. Well done to him. And it looks like our second place is here."

"Katie Daniels," Lee announced before Pyra could.

The three watched the live images to see who would get third, and sure enough, Sally Evans managed a hit on the starboard-side.

"I still say whoever is in that starboard pod is biased to her," Lee commented.

"I'm sure there will be talks with whoever that gunner is," Kerry assured. "Nothing we can do about it, but from the looks of things it doesn't matter too much anyway."

Adam McCoy had just got his third hit, with the other four still only having one hit each. A definitive ranking meant those four would still be duking it out with the Dragonfly until only one remained.

The celebration of Tom's victory wouldn't start until he was back with them, but even then, it would be subdued. While he might have taken first place, it was still only as good as a first-half finish – meaning he was cleared for the final challenge.

No matter where he finished, though, a proper celebration would still be had back home, where hopefully a trophy would be within the picture.

If only Adam could be within it as well.

The event had dragged itself on for another fifteen minutes. The four remaining hadn't been as quick to score hits, and the Dragonfly had remained as relentless in stopping those hits as it had always been.

Now all eight were back within the Sur-C's hangar for the announcements. Tom watched as the four that had been knocked out stood in front. Claire Beckett had been last, with Graham Jones, Dylan Hare, and Hayden Bell being in seventh, sixth, and fifth respectively.

Then it was time for the winners.

The top four were announced. When Tom heard his name as number one, he felt a bit giddy as he walked forward. It hadn't fully hit him just what he had done. He knew he'd done it, but it still felt like it hadn't happened to him.

He stood with a nervous grin as the crowd cheered. He spotted Lee waving his hands in the air. His mother clapped with the rest. And Mrs. Johnson shouted through the crowd "Go, Tom!"

The celebration died down. The four walked back into line. The hosts took the floor again.

"The final challenge is here," the first said. "Every challenge before this has been announced just before it starts. This one we want everyone to be prepared."

"Tomorrow there will be no challenges to give the final four a rest before this momentous challenge starts."

Tom felt excited at what the challenge would be. It had to be a big one, otherwise there wouldn't be any need to hype it.

"Now, safety has been our number one priority in setting up this challenge. We are aware of what strain it will cause to the competitors, and as such have designed it in a way to be as easy to follow as possible."

Get on with it, Tom thought. What is it?

"And so, for the first time ever, the Space Race Championship is to use the asteroid field as a racing route."

Silence followed the announcement, and Tom felt his excitement pop and drown him in fear. No, they couldn't. They wouldn't.

"Throughout the last three days, our scouts have been within the asteroids, marking up several paths through it. We don't want to cause too much stress, so the route has been lit, and the support will be a part of this race as they shuttle the competitor from a finish to the next starting point."

They have done it.

Tom knew he shouldn't be scared, but he'd never wanted to go near those rocks again. Now he was going to race through them.

That just means I'm prepared, though. I can do this. I can follow the guides easy enough. It's just a case of not straying too far from that route.

"You did great," Lee said, snapping him out of his thoughts.

"I had a few moments where I felt I wouldn't be able to grab first, but it worked out."

He then mentioned about the starboard-side gunner, but Lee quickly hushed him.

"Not now. You need a rest after all that."

Tom had a feeling they'd be talking in private within their room.

Fine with him, as he didn't feel like facing crowds after the announcement of the final challenge.

His confidence at winning had fallen off almost as fast as he'd gathered it.

Kerry had a feeling she knew why they were back in the room and wasn't disappointed when talk turned immediately to that starboard-side gunner. She herself felt there wasn't much to talk about, and it seemed pretty self-explanatory as to reasons.

What she wanted to hear about were Tom's thoughts of this final race. They were no doubt conflicted, but talking it out would help.

She listened to their discussion about that gunner for a while, then put in a final word designed to break it up and move the subject away.

"I'm ready to give it a shot," Tom said uncertainly. "Even with the guiding lights... Those rocks really messed me up last time."

"Last time you weren't at your best," Kerry stated. "You shouldn't let that experience affect how your performance will go this time. This time, you will be at your best." She gave him a reassuring smile.

"I've got a day to relax. Nothing should go wrong. I'm just... still not confident about it."

Lee chipped in. "You have the confidence for it. You're slipping back into negative thinking. Anyway, I'm sure you'll find that confidence at some point."

"Maybe..."

He still had a look of uncertainty, so Kerry thought it best to steer to yet another topic. She suggested doing some activity they hadn't done before, just like the bowling of the previous evening.

"Race through a maze?" Lee proposed with a sly smile.

"You'll only lose," Tom said jestingly.

"Challenge accepted."

The two then ran out of the room. Kerry stood processing the quick exit they'd made. She looked around the room to find Casey had also gone from the room.

"Don't even give me a chance..." she muttered as she walked from the room.

"Since this is a day of rest for the competitors, it would be wrong of me to go and arrange a full day of chat with them about how they feel the Championship has gone so far, right? Right? Well, I've gone and done so anyway, starting with the final four. I'm very interested in particular about the happenings related to the Space Kicker. Stay tuned and have another song."

Pyra Summers of Radio Racer [10/5-0085]

Tom hadn't expected Pyra Summers to be in Champion's Court, but there she was ready and waiting for the competitors.

Tom walked toward her to ask something, then noticed the sign beside her that answered it. The interview would begin after they'd had something to eat.

"Just a little informal chat," she informed, noticing Tom looking at the sign. "Nothing much to worry about."

Tom walked to the counter to collect some food, then chose a table at random. He'd come down early, so very few were here. As he slowly ate, he listened to the commentary that Pyra gave between breaks in the songs.

Lee and the two mothers arrived. They made no comment about the radio host until they were sat down. Tom repeated what she'd said to him.

"You'll be made a famous star out of this," Lee said. "If you want it, anyway."

"I don't think I'd want to get such attention."

"Everyone'll be talking about you for a while, but until you enter again you won't get that much. Doesn't even matter if you get knocked out at the first challenge, you'll still get respect as one of the elite."

Tom looked back to where Pyra Summers sat, thinking about fame. He turned back to his breakfast after a short while, but no sooner had he started eating again then a voice cut across his thoughts.

"Hey, you." Tom turned around again. Sally Evans had come to greet him. "Never got a chance to say great work on that victory yesterday."

"Thanks," Tom said. "We both did good to get top three. Although... No, doesn't matter."

"You think I paid off a gunner to give me an easy time?" she stated, smile now gone.

"I was going to say that you were probably the better pilot."

"I just saw an opportunity and took it. You did the same. Except you had a tougher time of it." Her smile returned. "You are the better pilot."

"Thanks. Now go and get some food and see you at the interview."

"I'm ready and waiting."

Tom watched her walk to stand near the food counter, then turned back to his own food.

"You two really managed to put the past behind you," Lee said. "Wonder if we'll see more of her after the Championship?"

"Who knows. Where is she from, anyway?"

"Minamwood," Mrs. Johnson stated. "One of the smaller towns up north."

"I thought that was one of the farming communities?" Lee asked.

"One of the border towns, so in a way it is."

"How did you know that?" Tom asked.

"I've been looking at the details of all competitors. There's some great information about all of their past Championship entries for those who have, and a lot of graphs making comparisons and other things."

Tom had completely forgotten about the official information board for the Championship and how much information it would be giving. A look at Lee said he wasn't alone in that. They both were more interested in getting stuck in rather than looking at the detail.

Once the four had finished their food, the two mothers said they'd head back to the room and listen in. Tom and Lee walked over to where Sally Evans already waited. Both Katie Daniels and Adam McCoy arrived a minute later with their second supporters. Tom found it slightly odd that Sally was the only one who didn't have anyone beside her.

Pyra Summers held her hand out for silence, then said, "That was Aversion to Life by The Rogue Misfits, with another song by them to follow after this announcement. All four of our finalists are now gathered, so our chat will begin shortly. As we prepare, take a listen to this next set of songs."

She muted the microphone on her PMD, quickly put three songs into the play queue, then looked up. "We'll be sitting in comfort and quiet over in the private section of this place over there." She indicated behind and to the right of her with her head, then stood up. "I'll say more once we're comfy."

She led the group to one of the round tables, where ten chairs waited for them. Tom sat down with Lee taking the chair to his left; Sally taking the one to his right.

Once everyone had sat down, Pyra ran through what would be said and told them all to relax, saying again that it was just an informal chat and nothing to worry about.

She placed her PMD on the table and connected it up to receive a signal from the 360-degree audio pickup device placed in the centre of the table. She then looked up and gave them all an encouraging smile.

Pressing a button on the PMD, she said, "Welcome back everyone, and here I am with the final four and their support. We'll be talking throughout this next hour and beyond about the Championship and everything that has happened, then we'll look to this final event."

Lee had little to do to start with as Pyra Summers questioned Katie Daniels. Their previous talks were referenced, with thoughts of then and now being a theme. Then Adam McCoy got questioned, who had little to say.

"I'm sure you'll have more to say soon," Pyra said, "once we move onto the Championship itself. Next, we have Sally Evans, who... I thought you had supporters?"

"They had to go somewhere today, but promised they'd be back tomorrow."

"Your sisters, right?"

"Yeah, they've been a good help in getting me ready. They do seem to have been busy these past few months, but they still made time."

"That's good to hear. Now, there's been talk of you and Tom having a rivalry during this Championship."

"We have," Sally said, turning to Tom and flashing her cheeky grin. "It's been fun to have someone to have a friendly fight against."

"And you Tom, despite all the problems, have managed to pull out a win. How does that feel?"

Lee waited for Tom's answer, wondering how much he would say. It took a few seconds for his answer to come.

"Great and unexpected. I had hoped to have got a win earlier, but so long as I got through, I was happy."

Lee smiled at that answer. What else could really be said live without diving into the wealth of detail?

The interview continued, with the support being introduced, then a two song break before the real talk began. Lee had a lot to say, but was more interested in Sally. At first, she hadn't minded being questioned on her sisters, but as the conversation continued and the talk reached what her sisters felt about her performance and the challenges of this year, she started faltering.

He wondered whether her sisters were really helpful to her at all. It didn't seem right to say anything while this live event was going on, but he did feel that they weren't as close as she was making them out to be. There certainly didn't seem to be a tight natural bond.

He wasn't going to bring it up, since it seemed unfair to do so, and it wasn't really his place to do so anyway.

"This final challenge, then," Pyra Summers stated. "Through the asteroids. How are we all feeling about that?"

Katie Daniels was the first one to speak. "I'm up for it. Nothing I can't handle."

"I'm going in and out faster than everyone else," Adam McCoy added. "I don't have time to look at rock."

"Ooh. Confidence. I love it. But what about our younger competitors? After all, you've already been inside the field, Tom."

"An experience I didn't care for," Tom said. "And something I didn't much want to repeat." A forlorn expression briefly appeared on his face as it lowered, but when he looked up again his eyes blazed with an icy intent. "That's not to say I won't give it my all. Besides," he added with a smile, "following a guide on top form is a lot easier than groggily flying randomly to find a way out."

"Fighting words that show someone isn't letting the past get in the way. What about you, Sally? How do you feel about those space rocks?"

Sally remained silent.

"It'll be okay," Tom said to her. "You've got nothing to worry about."

"I'm not nervous," she muttered. "I'm not nervous."

She certainly looked it.

"But if you three can do it, I can do it."

But Lee was convinced she was just saying that. She was hiding it well, but Lee could see her breaking down slowly. As though she was thinking exactly what he had been thinking about her sisters.

"There's a lot of security looking out for problems on the route during today, so you won't have any problems with getting lost," Pyra Summers informed. "There is absolutely nothing to worry about. I can understand feeling a bit scared, though. However, all of you will do good in this last event. And no matter what position you come, you were good enough to reach the final and that's all that matters."

"Definitely," Katie Daniels said.

"Absolutely true," Tom added.

"We'll be seeing which of you four manage to come out on top in the challenge tomorrow. It's been good to have you here."

Everyone thanked her for the enjoyable chat and moved off as Pyra announced that she'd be getting a few of the other competitors for a talk later on.

Back into the main area of Champion's Court, Lee checked the time to see that it was nearing mid-day. He looked around, noting Katie Daniels and Adam McCoy had already left. Tom and Sally had already sat down near the food counter.

"I'm scared about going into there," Lee heard Sally say. "As good as I am..."

"You can't lose confidence in yourself," Tom said as Lee sat down beside him. "Look at what you've done to get to this point."

"That's just it. I have basic skills that anyone can learn. I don't have the skill that you have. That the others have."

"Don't sell yourself short," Lee cautioned. "You'll fall apart and wrap yourself in doubt, possibly leading to you wanting to drop out."

"I'm not doubting myself," she said, but looking panicked. "I'm not dropping out."

She got up from her chair and ran out of the room.

Tom looked at him with a thoughtful expression. "She'll be okay, right?" he asked.

"I'm sure of it. She just needs a bit of time to get used to what she's got to do. I'm surprised you aren't cracking up like her at the thought of going into the rocks."

"I'm fine with it. As I said, I'll be on top form, and no-one will be hunting me down."

"Good. Keep positive."

"She's the one who needs that advice," Tom said, looking to the exit where Sally had gone.

Lee looked that way too, seeing the two mothers entering the food court. They congratulated the two on the interview, then started talking about tomorrow, when the Championship would be over.

Lee found himself thinking of Sally Evans and hoping that she'd be in a better state of mind for the race. If he ran into her at any point, he'd certainly try to help her.

He had a feeling he'd be better at it than her sisters were.

CHAPTER 9 – ASTEROID ADVENTURE

"Our final race. Our final challenge. No matter what happens here, it has been a fun event. All preparations have been made, and the competitors are waiting for the start. Just one final word before they do, though. I'm not meant to have favourites but plenty of you have been voting for Tom Hughs to win. We'll see just whether he can pull another victory from that Space Kicker of his."

Pyra Summers of Radio Racer [11/5-0085]

Kerry felt nervous anticipation for what was about to start. She wanted Tom to win.

She couldn't be out and watching even if she wanted to. This was a race that used both 'craft and mini cruiser, after all, and Casey had once again stated she didn't want to go out. Especially since they'd be within the action.

Fortunately, for this final race, plenty of screens had been placed around the hangar for people to watch, along with numerous seats so they didn't have to stay standing. The two had claimed chairs near to one of the screens while remaining close to where the mini cruisers waited for the start.

Those four mini cruisers were in a line close by the hangar exit. A countdown in red showed how long until the race began. Kerry hoped the best for Tom, wishing he could win. If he could get another win for this final race, celebration would be fierce. He'd have shown his strength in victory.

But even if he didn't win, he had still managed to reach this point. Only a select number could ever say they had reached a final of the Space Race Championship, and for Tom to have done so on his first try was a massive show of skill.

The same could be said of Sally Evans, who did seem to have calmed down a bit. From what Lee had told her the day before, Sally seemed to have been panicking a lot about this final race and hadn't felt confident in sharing what was on her mind. There had seemed something else he'd teetered on saying, but had chosen not to.

Kerry had a feeling it had related to the interview, but that it didn't matter much. Unless it was about what she'd heard the two talking about before relating to her sisters, in which case it was just baseless accusations.

A minute remained.

Casey had been able to hide her anxiety about this final challenge. She hadn't believed at first that the hosts had been serious, sure they were just joking around.

But it had happened, and Tom was once again heading into those asteroids.

No matter what Tom said, she still felt seriously worried that something was going to happen. It was dangerous, reckless, and foolhardy to be going into those asteroids, no matter how many security precautions there were and how safe they said it would be.

She had held off trying to stop it and had even come to terms with the challenge itself, even if there was still concern for Tom and Lee's safety. For everyone's safety, she felt.

The route itself showed up on the screen they would be watching. Casey stared at that route – which showed six paths through the asteroids that needed to be completed in order with a different colour marking the paths that the mini cruisers would take between those paths.

The map made it look simple, but that would be far from the truth. Tom's experience of the asteroids last time had told her that even if he was on top form and following a guide, he'd still be working hard to navigate through and would get worn out quickly. Even if they were allowed a rest while the support in the mini cruiser ferried them to the next point, there was no returning to top form. She expected that all the racers would be tired and slower to react near the end, which would probably explain why that last path was the shortest of the lot.

She looked back at the mini cruisers, nervously expectant for when that timer hit zero and the race would begin. She wanted Tom to win. Of course she did. But she worried about how he would go about getting that win and how fast he'd be heading through those rocks.

Thirty seconds remained.

Lee had given Tom a talking to, saying that he should concentrate on navigating safely and not trying to be the fastest. If he needed an advantage, the DSSC should easily manage to get him back to the group if he fell behind or get him further ahead than he already was.

Tom, it seemed, hadn't heard him. Sat within his Space Kicker, he had communication with Lee, and again he asked, "Is it time yet? I'm ready to fly fast and win."

Lee rolled his eyes, looking up at the timer counting down.

"Just be prepared to get safely through the asteroids," Lee said. "I'll be waiting to give you a boost between your sections."

He'd seen Sally during the very small briefing, and she looked slightly better. Her supports hadn't been with her, but she had barely entered her own mini cruiser when it had taken off and moved to the point it would be starting from. Lee had taken that to mean they were inside.

There had still been a slight look of fear to her, but Lee would expect that to be the nerves she had about what was to come.

"Okay," Lee called suddenly. "Timer is almost at zero, be prepared for a fast lift off."

The Surveillance Cruiser had moved to be close to the first point. As soon as the mini cruisers had left the hangar, the 'craft of the competitors would launch from the hangars of the mini cruisers.

That gave Tom and him an advantage. All mini cruisers were two levels high, but the hangars of every previous model were awkwardly positioned – either having a forward-facing entrance or having an entrance above instead. Both would mean the other three wouldn't be able to move fast while the 'craft flew out.

Zero seconds remained.

"Remember, we've practised this," Lee said as he quickly handled controls.

"I'm ready to roll."

The DSSC lifted itself. The other three mini cruisers were lighter, so had that advantage. Power hit the main engines to propel the DSSC out of the hangar. Lee aimed straight for the asteroids, calling "Go, go, go!" to Tom.

He watched on the screen as Tom lifted with engines already at power, slowly inching to the rear of the hangar as he zoomed out of it from the port side.

"Clear!" Tom called, and Lee pulled the DSSC into a dive to head for the point he needed to be to wait.

Tom had heard what Lee had said about flying safely, but he'd been talking as though speed and safety were opposites.

Tom knew better.

The lights that guided the way were attached to each of the rocks across a far width, meaning you couldn't get lost even if you tried. It was easy to follow them, even as he flew around them.

He'd thought that, but he was losing a bit of confidence in navigating and had dropped speed slightly. The guiding lights might be showing the way, but the disorienting effect of the asteroids meant he lost sight of which way he was meant to go.

He'd flown beyond the guiding lights without realising, and whizzed around a larger rock to see the lights again, quickly putting himself within them once more. Checking the scanner, which marked the direction he needed to be going, he found he at least was still pointing the right way.

Nothing eventful happened other than the lead he had gained had slowly been destroyed. While he remained in first, both Katie and Adam were right behind him. Both were better at dealing with the disorientation from flying through the asteroids, it seemed, whereas Tom had made plenty of small mistakes.

He flew out of the rocks, quickly sighted up on Lee's position, and flew in that direction. The scanner showed that both Katie and Adam had emerged from the rocks a few seconds after he had.

The hangar of the DSSC was looming near. Tom breathed in and placed a hand on the speed lever. He flicked the switch to bring the landing claws out, then placed that hand back on the stick just as he entered the hangar and brought the lever inward to him.

As his speed decreased drastically, he slammed the Space Kicker to the hangar floor, shedding speed even faster. He felt the bump ripple through him and shoot a second of pain into his head.

"I told you not to do that," Lee admonished as the DSSC set off for the next point. "You have to keep yourself on top form for as long as possible."

"It's the quickest way of landing," Tom said. "The others are catching up."

"And what did I tell you? We have the advantage. You'll end up damaging the claws if you keep doing that."

"Are the others in their hangars yet?"

Tom felt restless energy beating at him. He wanted to get back out as soon as possible. Just sitting and waiting didn't feel to him as though he was progressing in the race, even though he knew they were moving to the next point. He also wanted to keep ahead of everyone else in case he made more mistakes.

"The other two mini cruisers have just set off, but neither has our speed."

"Two? Where's Sally?"

"Still within the asteroids, though from the map it looks like she's coming out within seconds."

Tom felt that Sally was having a hard time of things. She had little experience and seemed to be guessing her way through nearly everything. As such, he could imagine how terrified she would be of trying to navigate through these rocks.

Lee had mentioned his theory of how her sisters hadn't done enough to prepare her for the Championship, and Tom had found he agreed with it.

In the qualifying challenge, she had mostly avoided everyone else through luck. She hadn't been ready for his moves of evasion. Then she had nearly crashed during the collection challenge trying to enter the hangar at speed. She'd had it easy during the accuracy challenge, and with the speed challenge she'd had little to worry about.

However, he couldn't take pity on her if he wanted to win this race. He had what it took to win, even if he wasn't as good as the other two in staying on target.

"We have arrived at the second route," Lee announced.

Tom didn't waste a second. He pushed the lever forward to power his speed as he lifted from the hangar floor.

Once again within the rocks, he felt for sure this time he wouldn't lose his way. He tried not to waste time going around larger rocks, instead aiming for smaller clusters. This route was slightly longer than the first, and he found that he managed himself well.

The only thing was that his winding route to avoid the larger rocks meant he had let both Katie and Adam pass him. He felt a slight concern that he might be letting the gap widen if he continued with his current tactic, even if the DSSC could help him catch up slightly.

He looked out at the field, pulling the Space Kicker back to what he imagined as the centre line. One of the larger asteroids filled his vision. He pulled up and rode over it, then ducked under another of the larger asteroids. He then dodged sideways from another.

A scattering of smaller rocks littered the exit from the second route, and as he left, he felt a small glow of hope that he'd manage the rest of the routes just fine.

He checked his scanner to see the mini cruisers of the other two racers leaving. He found it odd that the mini cruiser of Sally was nowhere around. He knew for certain that she hadn't passed him, but it should be at this point waiting for her to arrive.

Landing in the DSSC, he asked Lee about it, who confirmed that she hadn't overtaken, but was slowly catching up.

"I haven't seen her mini cruiser all while I've been waiting. It was the same at the last point as well."

"Are there meant to be cameras watching the routes the mini cruisers take?" Tom asked.

"I wouldn't be surprised if someone was watching, but it wouldn't be available for the public to see. This is about the racers, after all."

Up in the control bay, Lee watched the map to see that the other two mini cruisers had stopped at the next point he was fast approaching. Both Adam and Katie were quickly leaving.

The mini cruiser of Sally was taking a long, slow arc to reach the point, it seemed. He'd be keeping an eye on it as he made his way to the end of the third route. It could easily be that whoever was inside was keeping pace rather than rushing to the point like everyone else.

"Okay," Lee called. "Slowing down as we approach the third route. Good luck."

Lee swapped the scanner to the camera within the hangar, watching Tom pull out. He then set off for the end of the third route, swapping back to the map and focusing on the mini cruiser of Sally's. It had just met up with her.

As he continued to travel, he continued to watch.

"There's something wrong," Tom called to him.

"What?" Lee asked, still keeping his eye on the map.

"Everything's just gone dark."

"How?" Lee's voice snapped to a more serious tone. "You can still see alright, can't you?"

"The asteroids are in sight, but there's no guiding light. Something's happened to them."

"All of them?"

"All of them."

"Be careful, and keep an eye out for everything." Lee tried paging the emergency contact on the Sur-C. "There's definitely something going on here."

The Sur-C emergency contact was busy, though Lee had a feeling it had been put offline for the duration of the race. For whatever reason.

He hoped they were at least attempting to find out what was going on.

On the Surveillance Cruiser hangar, Casey worried.

Most of the cameras on the third route had been taken out, with the map being the only thing shown until the racers made it out of the offline area. The map had marks on it to show the disrupted area. Some of the fourth route had also been disrupted.

People around were talking, wanting to know what was going on. All of the people who had been sat around this screen had disappeared elsewhere, since it was clear there was little racing to be seen.

Casey remained, as did Kerry. Both were showing signs of worry. They were both hoping their sons were fine.

Casey barely noticed as two people sat behind them as she turned to Kerry. "Why is there not anyone out there? Why hasn't this been called off?"

Kerry looked at her but seemed unable to answer.

But she did get one.

"We don't want to alert anyone that they've been found out," a voice behind her said. "As soon as they land, we'll be ready to pounce upon them."

Casey turned behind her, intent on finding out more.

She froze.

Sat behind her was the man she had been wishing to return to her for almost two years. There he sat, with another who she recognised and who Kerry dearly loved, a burn across most of the right side of his face, smiling at her with all the warmth of the galaxy.

Adam had returned.

She felt tears building in her eyes, and quickly brought her hands up to wipe them. She felt Kerry stand up and move the seats so she could get to Steve. Casey then did the same to pull Adam into a tight hug that expressed the eternity of hurt she had felt at being parted with him.

It didn't matter that they were in a large hangar full of people who could be watching. All that mattered was that reunion of husband and wife.

After a few minutes, they broke apart. Kerry was the first to break the silence and bring everything back to the current situation. Casey wished she hadn't, as she wanted to live in the moment forever, but recognised there would be plenty of time for love when the Championship was over.

"What was that about not wanting to alert anyone?" Kerry had said.

"Well..." Adam looked to Steve, who nodded his approval. "We've been back a few days now, but it was kept quiet. The security here has been compiling the details of two suspects who have been targeting two people."

"Tom and Lee," Kerry offered.

Steve nodded as Adam continued. "They didn't have much to go on, but then we returned a day or so after the Championship began. And that's when further trouble started."

"We know exactly what's been going on," Steve added. "And why. We just need to get the two responsible cornered. Which is why things are being allowed to continue."

"But the boys..." Casey blurted out.

"Are fine," Adam reassured. "Tom's got skill. I'm proud of him. Lee has skill too, the way he's managing that super cruiser."

Casey felt her eyes water up again. She was being silly, worrying. He had skill and knew how to use it.

He'd be fine.

She felt the heavy weight of worry ease at finally having Adam back.

Tom checked the scanner again to make sure he was on track. Lee had confirmed he had arrived at the end of the third route, so Tom was using his position to guide him to the end.

Sally was still somewhere behind, and hope of catching the two in front had completely vanished. He'd tried to keep as straight as possible, but it had been impossible. He was just glad he had at least been pointing in roughly the right direction.

Around the asteroids he flew, now with a guide driving him forward. When he felt he was nearing the end, he looked all around and found a few of the guiding lights were on a few meters to his right.

He didn't merge with them but flew the last few rocks to come to the end of the third route and rushed directly to the DSSC.

He hammered into the floor of the hangar once again, which brought an admonitory comment from Lee.

"I don't care," Tom moaned. "I just want this to be over with."

"I can understand that," Lee agreed. "Just don't slam down like that. I know this is the final event, but you need the 'craft on top form as well as yourself if you want to survive out there."

"I just hope the guiding lights are still on during this fourth route."

"They should be. This far out, they should be."

After a minute, Lee announced they had arrived at the start of the fourth route. Tom flew out of the hangar, happy to see the guiding lights active.

Knowing he wouldn't be overtaken; he kept a more sensible pace heading through this route. He could feel a slight tiredness to his movements but was at the point of not caring at all.

As was going through his mind at all times, he just wanted it finished. He'd been confident of winning. Confident that his prior experience — even if he had been lost — of flying through the asteroids would help him. But even with the rests in between routes, he was now feeling the same as he had that last time.

The situation was different. He was fine, in almost every way. But it was being on edge, continuously having to keep moving, that was chipping away at his good spirits. He'd hit the point of not caring if he won, but he knew it wasn't due to the large gap between the other two racers that had made him feel like that.

Continuing to push the Space Kicker around asteroids of various sizes, he shook his head. He'd seen... something. But was unsure of what it might have been.

Diving around a large asteroid, then zigging through a few smaller ones, something caught his eye once again.

He slowed the 'craft slightly, still keeping it moving and still keeping aware of everything he had to go around. But he was also on the lookout for anything that didn't belong.

He caught sight of another something. He knew it was moving, and away from him. But he was well aware that there were multiple of them and any one of them could spot him and... do what?

How could he prepare to evade something he couldn't see? Even if he couldn't see them, he knew he didn't want to remain near them.

Increasing speed, he flew up and over the nearest asteroid and continued pushing to the edge of the guiding lights and stopped.

Spinning around to face the viewshield to the guiding lights, he scanned the area that was now above him.

Swimming around within the guiding lights were shadows. He couldn't make out anything else about their appearance. The way they moved made it look as though they felt attacked by something and were on the hunt.

Tom activated his engines again to put as much distance between himself and the angry shadows. He could feel his heart thumping against his chest. Whatever they were, they seemed to know what they were after.

"Lee," he called into the audio pickup. "What sort of creatures live within the asteroids?"

He heard his voice come panicky and tried to control his breathing to relax himself as he continued driving for the end of the route.

"Within?" Lee answered. "I don't think there's any sort of creatures within the field."

"Well there are, and they seem to be after something."

"That's unsettling. Just concentrate on getting out of there and to me. We'll report it once this is over with."

"Okay. I think I'm away. I can't see any more of the shadows, anyway."

"I'll try to contact the Sur-C again. Just keep me updated on where you are."

Tom breathed out an affirmative. It was all he could manage.

He'd dived around a large asteroid, and something had flown in front of him. He'd hit it, and his engines had cut out and now it was looking at him.

It looked like a giant spider. A body with eight legs, longer and thicker than a normal spider had. Those legs looked as if they rippled in a non-existent breeze. As though there were no bones within them.

The front two of those legs lifted up, and slammed down hard on the Space Kicker. It spun uncontrollably as Tom tried to focus enough to reignite the engines before he ended up even more damaged.

Or crashed into an asteroid.

A second strike hit the Space Kicker, and Tom looked up as he hammered the ignition switch back and forth.

The creature was trying to wrap those legs around the Space Kicker.

A burst of power lit the control board back up, and as Tom shot away from the creature, Lee's voice filled the control bay.

"What's going on? What happened?"

"I've had a good look at those creatures," Tom said. His voice was high pitched and rough. "I don't want to again." He gave a harsh cough, almost messing up a turn as his left hand shook.

"Just concentrate on getting far away from them and to me. You don't need to worry about anything."

"But what about-"

As Tom thought about her, she seemed to have thought about him.

"Emergency! Help required! Tom, if you're out there, help!"

Lee seemed to have heard it as well.

"Are you prepared to go back within them and help her?"

"I need to be," Tom said, voice somehow strong.

"Go, then."

Tom didn't need telling. He flipped around an asteroid and powered back the way he had come, glancing at his scanner to see the emergency signal had appeared and was dead ahead.

He might not care about winning, might have become listless to the whole event, but he knew that helping someone was the right move no matter the circumstance.

And if someone he knew was being attacked by some unknown creature that seemed to have deadly intent, he knew he would try to get them away from that danger. It was what Lee had encouraged him to do and what his dad and Lee's dad would do.

So, he would do it.

The hangar had become more active again as people flocked in to watch the struggle between Sally and these creatures from space. To them, it must have looked a great bit of action, but Kerry knew some of them would see it for what it was.

A desperate struggle to survive in a situation that needn't have happened.

"This is their work as well?" she asked Steve.

She could hardly believe that her husband had returned. She'd been as shocked as Casey had at the voice that had answered them and relieved to find the two mostly unhurt. Adam had suffered worse, and she wondered what could have burnt his face so much.

Now they'd returned, there'd be plenty of stories to tell.

"This is their work, yes," Steve replied. "But it does seem to have backfired. We'd hate for anything to happen to her, but we can't pass up this opportunity to capture them."

"Surely the regular security forces that helped Tom out of a spot of bother before should be out there," Kerry stated. "We here can see everything that's going on, after all."

"That's true, but any security forces out there will make them run as soon as the race is over," Adam replied. "We were told about their last major attack upon our return. They fought on until they'd completed what they set out to do, then fled."

"As typical of Talon Force," Kerry said. "But it's already been confirmed that all of them returned and are accounted for."

"Not all of them," Steve informed. He looked around. They were alone. He checked a result on his PMD, then continued talking in a slighter lower tone. "Two remain unaccounted, and they remain that way because they were never registered."

"No official ranking meant they came and went as they pleased," Adam added, "able to command Talon Force members under their lead to do things that were never agreed or accepted by the chain of command."

"And that's where this all starts, isn't it?" Kerry inquired, putting pieces of the puzzle together. "You were a part of the team that brought them down."

"In a way," Steve said, with a slightly uncomfortable look. "Their status as unofficial commanders meant they could disappear for weeks on end and we'd have no record of it." He checked on his PMD again before continuing. Kerry figured he was keeping up a continuous scan for any listening devices. "However, we bumped into them during a fight on board a cruiser."

"They'd turned against you?" Casey gasped.

"They were helping the enemy, yes. When we finally captured that group of Talon Force members, we sent the entire lot of them back here. There'd been a guard making sure they didn't escape again, but somehow they did."

"Did your men guard against just that group of members or the entire force?" Kerry asked.

"Just that group," Steve said with a sigh. "We have to accept that it was a contingency of the entire force. They were disbanded, but we've learnt they did it themselves. The word had been put around that the remainder of the CAF had seen to it that they were, having learnt of what went down at the Zilthex system. Now, we know they had inserted their own agents into the CAF to control things to get that result."

"So all the 'craft that were thought to be destroyed..."

"Are still out there somewhere. That's why this operation is so important. These two we're after know that location. We capture that mini cruiser, we'll know that location."

The increase in noise alerted the four to something happening. As they looked at the screen, they heard Pyra Summers announce, "It looks like the Space Kicker is going on the offensive to tackle those creatures and help out a friend. It doesn't matter that he won't win with actions like that. He's got the spirit of a solider, that one."

Indeed, the Space Kicker had now joined the Falcon of Sally's in the swarm of creatures. It was shifting itself around to smash the creatures out of the way and open up a clear path for Sally to go through.

"He really is channelling your spirit," Steve jested to Adam. "He's showing a massive amount of bravery in doing that, and he's using your style to do it."

"He has the courage," Adam stated. "Although I'm pretty sure he's using your style. I wouldn't be crazy enough to bash my enemies out of the way like he is now."

"That was only once," Steve replied in a mock-hurt voice, and both burst out with a shout of laughter before quietening and becoming serious again. "I just hope he doesn't drain his shield energy too much in doing that. I'm sure he'll be needing it."

Lee listened to Tom's voice as he took command of the situation. He would have dived right in there himself, but he knew the DSSC was too big to fit through some areas, and if he rocked the asteroids around too much he might awaken more of the creatures, or even something worse.

So, he waited at the end of the route, hoping that the outcome would be a positive one.

"Go! Go! Go!" Tom called. "Move it before they swarm back to us!"

Tom had opened a channel to Sally but left the link between himself and Lee open purely so Lee could hear exactly what was going on. It made for a messy way to handle things, but at present, it was the best Tom could handle. He didn't have time to be switching between two connections when a second's distraction could cost him.

Lee felt a surge of pride at how well Tom had handled the situation so far. While he couldn't see what was going one except via the map screen, from what he had heard on Tom's end made him realise that Tom had been using his 'craft as a weapon, trying to get those creatures to follow him instead of Sally.

For some reason, the creatures were intent on capturing that Falcon.

"You need to turn off all external signals," Tom was saying. "It'll cut us off, but I'm sure that's why they seem insistent on you. I can't think of anything else." A pause as Sally must have been saying something. Lee imagined she was calling him crazy to be suggesting such a thing as she needed a third eye to direct her. "If they leave you alone after you turn off all signals, gun it straight for the end of the route. If they don't, keep heading to the end anyway. That way we can bring the firepower of the Sur-C onto them." Another pause. "I don't like it either, but we need to get out of this. Fast."

Lee waited a few seconds, looking at the map. The signal that marked where Sally was winked out. "I can confirm all outward signals are lost," he reported to Tom. "How's it looking?"

"Those that were closest still seem to be on her, but the others look to be dispersing. I've still got a few on me, so I can't exactly say."

"Follow your own orders and get out of there, then. Just hope they won't follow beyond the largest of the rocks."

"On it."

Both were silent, except for the occasional growl or groan from Tom. Lee looked out at the asteroid field, wishing for them both to be alright.

He noticed that the mini cruiser of Sally's support was waiting just within it.

He felt it only right to alert them to what had been going on, as they didn't seem to care. That mini cruiser could have reached Sally to help her.

Closing the link to Tom, Lee set up a direct signal that would reach the mini cruiser that was waiting.

"Do you realise what's been going on?" he stated. "I've been directing the help that has had to rescue your sister from this super cruiser, and you're just waiting? Why aren't you helping?"

The message sent, he opened the link to Tom back up and reported what he'd just done.

"Good," Tom replied. "They need to answer for why they aren't helping. It's not right. They should be helping even more than I did. Do they just not care?"

"I would assume not. I guess we'll find out why once this is over with."

"You plan to confront them?"

"I do."

"I'll back you up on that. I can see that Sally is just about to get out of the field, and I'm right behind her."

"I'm ready to get you back inside and end this."

Once Tom was inside, Lee powered the engines to maximum speed. The final two routes were near the edge of the field. As he checked the map, the final route — the shortest — disappeared from the map.

A message flashed up on the screen.

"Right," Lee called. "It seems this whole ordeal has been noticed on board the Sur-C. They've just axed the final route with a message saying they don't want to cause any more stress to the racers, mentioning that the final route seems pointless to go through."

"Great," Tom said. "If only they'd have axed the fifth route as well."

"My guess is the other two racers have already finished that fifth route, but the organisers want to make it fair for everyone — at least in terms of routes travelled."

"This should be a simple route, anyway. I'm sure I can grab third. Heard anything from Sally's support, yet?"

"Nothing. Seems they really don't care."

"Figures. Seems we were right about them."

"Their thinking is completely messed up if they think they could win without preparing their sister for the event. Unless..."

"What?"

Lee held his silence for a few seconds more. What he was thinking was even more levels of wrong. It wouldn't do well for Tom to be hearing it.

"This is your last stop," Lee said. "Happy racing."

"Unless what?" Tom said as he lifted the Space Kicker out of the hangar.

"It's just baseless thinking. Careful how you go."

Tom had entered the asteroids. Lee took the DSSC into a dive, noting that the mini cruiser of Sally had stopped to let her out.

He didn't feel it right to go into thinking that Sally's sisters had been trying to cheat her through the entire Championship, but the more he looked at the events that had happened, it looked very much like they had been doing exactly that.

"This isn't right," Tom said uncertainly.

Lee stopped thinking back to the events of the Championship and fitting everything into his theory. Turning his attention to the present, he asked, "What isn't? The guiding lights are still active, right?"

"Everything's working, but... There was... I can't even explain it."

"Try." Lee hoped there wasn't something worse now after the competitors.

"It looked like a laser, but orange. It was flicker-"

The connection had dropped. Lee didn't have time to start panicking before Tom's voice returned.

"I'm hit! I'm..." Lee felt Tom was trying to find the right word to describe what had happened. "...hot. Burnt."

"Where?" Lee had now become very curious. What sort of a weapon could burn things in space?

"On the very edge of my starboard side. It definitely looks like it's been burnt away. And everything had overheated for a second. A third orange laser then tried to hit me but missed."

"Hopefully it can't follow. Whatever it is. You're still able to get to the end?"

"No damage apart from that burnt area. I really don't want it to spread. But whatever it was did wipe all my shield energy, so I'm not going to push it."

"Just get to the end safely. I'll be waiting."

Lee continued toward the final point, wondering again what sort of a weapon could burn things in space.

The cameras had shown that super-heated laser strike at the Space Kicker and Casey was horrified at what she had seen.

"It's not a laser like anything we know," Adam said. "At least, no-one here, at any rate."

"It's something the Zilthex created," Steve added.

"But..." Kerry seemed unable to grasp the reality of it just as much as Casey. "But... How?" was all she managed.

"We don't fully understand," Steve said, "but we're sure those two do. And that's one more reason for capturing them."

Adam looked to Steve with what Casey thought of as a questioning look, which Steve replied to with a stiff shake of the head. It seemed they knew more than they were letting on, but Casey expected they didn't want to worry either her or Kerry with the details – however bad they were.

The viewpoint on the screen swapped to show the Space Kicker once again. The entire starboard side was now coated black. Whatever had hit it seemed to be burning away the entire body of the 'craft.

Or at least trying.

"They're desperate, it seems," Adam said. "Superficial burning of the 'craft means that weapon hasn't been fully charged."

"It can still present a problem. It's still got to be hot, but it slowly seems to be losing that heat."

Casey looked at Kerry to see the other wearing a frown.

"I don't get it, though," Kerry said. "This weaponry is hot. Super-hot. Those two are human. How can they be handling it?"

"That's what we need to find out. However-"

Steve cut Adam off from saying any more simply by pointing at his PMD. Casey looked once more to the screen to see that the mini cruiser that held Sally was quickly approaching the Sur-C's hangar. The DSSC of Tom and Lee not far behind.

They'd lost third place, but Casey no longer cared about that. She was just happy that Tom had survived the asteroids and everything that had been within them.

The mini cruiser hit the atmosphere gauze. Casey noted that three people on the other side of the hangar were slowly ambling forward.

Talking, looking for all the world as though they had no objective or destination in mind.

She looked to her left and found three others admiring the 'craft that were scattered around that had the same look.

The mini cruiser landed, and all six instantly pounced into action.

It was then that Casey realised the mass of people that had been in the hangar hadn't just wondered off aimlessly because the race was getting less interesting. No less than thirty others then pounced, weapons whipped out of secret holders and aimed at the mini cruiser.

The grate at the far end was starting to be closed. As soon as the DSSC had slipped through, the other hangar grate closed. Someone directed it away from the mini cruiser that was now surrounded.

Away from the action that was sure to take place.

As Adam and Steve walked forward, Casey felt a flood of nerves hit her again.

CHAPTER 10 – THE PHANTOM SISTERS

"As much excitement as has been going on, I really wasn't expecting this. It looks like we'll be finding out who has been attacking this Championship and they'll be done for good. A fight looks like it might break out, but I'm sure the CAF will make sure nothing serious happens."

Pyra Summers of Radio Racer [11/5-0085]

Tom landed inside the DSSC's hangar for the final time. He took a long, heavy breath of relief and leaned as far back in his seat as it allowed.

He stayed like it for a few seconds more, just happy that he had got through such perilous trials.

Popping open the viewshield, he felt the heat radiating from his starboard side. Standing and leaning over the side, he let the heat of it wash over his face, amazed that it had still not cooled to a normal temperature but thankful that the heat hadn't messed him over any more than that brief power loss.

Climbing down from the port side, he ran to the control bay and sank into the co-pilot's seat. He watched the asteroids as Lee took the DSSC back to the Sur-C, happy he was no longer within them.

"We'll get the Space Kicker fixed up good as new," Lee said. He then looked at Tom. "You did better than anyone would have expected."

"Just get us back to the Surveillance Cruiser so I can have a nice, long rest," Tom said lazily. "Then we can celebrate."

"As you say, Champion."

Tom looked back over at Lee, an exasperated expression forming, and saw a grin cracking on his friend's face.

"It's what everyone will be saying," Lee stated reasonably.

Tom found himself smiling at that.

"Yeah. Famous for avoiding a terrible fate. Not something I wanted, but I'm sure some good will come from it."

"And for pulling off that spectacular rescue."

He knew it to be true, but there seemed no reason to say anything to it.

The Surveillance Cruiser now in sight, Lee angled the DSSC to quickly get inside. The speed of it lowered drastically before it hit the atmosphere gauze.

Tom then noticed several things.

The grate at the far end had almost closed. The mini cruiser of Sally's was now surrounded by armed guards. The hangar itself seemed empty of nearly everyone except those guards.

"Well," Lee said, following the guidance of someone directing him to a place to put down. "It looks like we might find out just what all this has been about."

The DSSC now landed, Tom felt the tension of all that had happened come to him. He didn't want to move but was curious at what was going on in the hangar. He stood slowly up and started walking out of the control bay.

At the exit, two guards waited.

"How serious is it?" Lee asked from beside him. Tom hadn't realised he'd followed.

"Unsure as yet," one of the guards replied. "It depends on if a fight will break out."

"Are we allowed out?"

"We know you're curious to hear what will go on, but we can't allow you to be in their sight when it goes down. We'll go as far as the exit, but not out of it."

"Okay."

The two guards led them down to the hangar level, and once at the port side hangar exit, they waited. A voice met their ears.

"There are plenty of armed soldiers out here. If you don't come out, we will force you out."

"We're already out," a female voice called. "And we can burn this place to ashes."

"Up on top!" a shout rang out.

Tom imagined all those weapons now being pointed up as the guards took a few steps backward to get the female in sight.

"You wouldn't do that," the first voice replied calmly. "You can't do that."

"How do you know what we'll do?" a second female voice called out. "You wouldn't want to risk it by making a move. Especially since we have a bargaining chip."

Tom looked to Lee, confused, but Lee seemed to have figured it out. He uttered a soft "oh, no" in a worried voice.

"Sally," he then added, and finally Tom understood what Lee had figured out.

It was the same two who had targeted them before the Championship had started. The same two who had tried twice to injure them. He couldn't bear the thought that they'd tried killing him.

It was these two that had possibly convinced Sally that he was a danger to her success, slotting another piece of the puzzle into place. Was it possible that one of them had also got a gunner position in that accuracy challenge?

"If you have your sister with you, you can't possibly be thinking of taking her hostage. She's your family! Just let her go."

"Let us go," the first female replied. "Let us go, and you can have her. If we have to blast our way out of here, we will."

"Get off me!" Sally screamed. "You're not the sisters I know. Let. Go!"

"Do as she says," another of the guards commanded. "She doesn't have to be hurt. You've as good as said you don't care about her."

"We can do what we want. We have all the power. And we want to leave. So we will. With our sister, so you won't blow us up as we do so. Not that you'd be able to with a cruiser imploding all around you."

221

The guard clapped slowly. "You really think you can get away? With what? Talon Force might have trained you to take extreme action, but you have nothing left you can do."

"I really shouldn't have missed last time, Hughs. Fortunately, this time, I won't."

Whatever happened next, Tom never heard a discharge of a weapon, but he did hear plenty of shouts. What struck him most was the surname that had been stated.

His dad couldn't be back. Could he?

When the guard spoke again in his clear calm voice, Tom recognised it at last.

He had returned.

"We can keep playing this game as long as you like. You missed me completely. I am prepared to get up there and tackle you, as are all of these soldiers, but I ask you to consider your options and surrender. You have no way out."

Silence followed.

"You have a plan, don't you?" Lee whispered to their guards.

"We do," one of them assured.

Tom took a step closer to the exit. He wanted to lean out and see what exactly was happening. The silence made him think it was something bad.

"We can't just be doing nothing," Tom said when one of the guards pulled him back.

"As much as I'm impressed by your skill in that Space Kicker, you have no idea what will happen if you were to step out. It's what they're waiting for."

"That's why we guided you far away from that mini cruiser," the other guard added. "So you wouldn't be in sight."

"How far?" Lee asked. "Is there any position in which it's clear to move from this super cruiser?"

"Not that I can think of... Maybe the other side. But you can't go out."

"If they are driven to a last resort, whatever it is they want us for, by being inside here, we could easily end up worse than the Space Kicker's looking."

The two guards considered it, and Tom could tell that Lee's reasoning had got them. One of the them ran to the other end of the hangar and looked out. That guard waved them over.

"They aren't looking this way. If we're quick, we can run to that red mini cruiser nearby and hide."

The guard looked out again, then dropped down to the hangar floor. He then waved again to tell them to move quickly. Lee sat on the edge and dropped.

Tom took a breath, ready to do the same, when he had a thought.

Turning back to the Space Kicker, a wild idea was forming. Dangerous, foolish, but worth a chance.

The remaining guard seemed to realise what was going on in his head. He grabbed Tom's arm and pushed him toward the exit.

"Keep them distracted. I can do this," Tom said.

"Our priority is your safety," the guard sharply stated. "You'll ruin our plans."

"I can't just do nothing."

The tiredness within him had disappeared, once again filled with that energy of wanting to help. Wanting to get stuck in the action and help someone who needed it. He wanted to help Sally once again.

But he realised that his plan couldn't work unless he knew where everyone was. But then he thought to what had been said.

"I'll be the distraction, then."

"No," the guard said, tightening his grip on Tom's arm.

"Are you going to surrender?" Mr. Hughs' voice asked the two sisters. "We will keep you grounded and head inside that mini cruiser with force."

"Have they gone inside it?" the guard asked the other. He got a nod in return.

"Please just let me try," Tom said.

"To do what?" the guard questioned. "There is nothing you can do. We have people already inside that mini cruiser, disabling everything within it. They will do everything they can to rescue your friend."

Tom gave a sigh, relaxing his tense body. "I trust you, but I want to be out there doing something."

"I understand that, but we cannot allow it."

Tom sat at the edge of the exit and dropped to the hangar floor, with the guard following. They ran to the mini cruiser where Lee stood out of sight of the two sisters.

"Do you have contact with those inside the mini cruiser?" Lee asked.

"We can hear but not speak," one of the guards replied. "They haven't returned to the control bay. There's been no fighting inside. Seems they haven't left the hangar of that mini cruiser. No-one is able to get inside it to see if they are still there, though."

"How many spacecraft could that hangar hold?"

"Two at most."

"What if it wasn't a second 'craft?"

The guards exchanged thoughtful looks. "You mean a small land vehicle of some kind?" one of them asked. "There's room for one. But it wouldn't have the..." The guard then pressed something on his left wrist and spoke into his shoulder. "Get access to that hangar however you can. They have even more Zilthex tech than we realised."

Tom heard some of the guards start to climb up the mini cruiser. He took a look around their hiding place and watched as a vehicle lifted from it.

That vehicle rose above the mini cruiser and the guards that were now stood on top of it. Long, thin, with a wider rear end that must have held a power core of some unknown type. And it must have been connected to the overly large weapon emplacement that was attached to the underside that was as long as the vehicle itself.

"Disable it!" came a shout.

The hangar was full of the sounds of discharging weapons and strikes upon the vehicle.

"We need CSPs!" came another shout.

"We'll wipe the cruiser's power!"

"We need someone to ram them," Tom said. "Force them to the ground."

"We can't," one of their guards stated. "We don't have anything that'll do so."

Before the guard could stop him, Tom had charged back in the direction of the DSSC. He climbed into the hangar, making straight for the Space Kicker.

Once sat within it, he quickly lifted and flew out into the Sur-C's hangar, rising higher than the vehicle. He imagined the shouts of surprise at what he was doing, thought he could feel the worry of his mother and the shock of his father, but his focus was fully on his objective.

Now in the air, he could see that Sally was with her sisters, being restrained by one while the other piloted the vehicle. A quick scan showed that the weapon – whatever it was powered by – was almost fully charged.

He needed to be quick.

The Space Kicker shot forward. Just before he reached the other vehicle, he angled downward. Slamming into that vehicle knocked him around hard, but he still managed to kill his forward momentum.

The sister piloting hadn't been prepared for such a move, with the vehicle still idling.

Tom directed the 'craft to shift itself downward. As far as it would go as fast as it could. The force he felt trying to resist meant the other vehicle had now reacted and was trying to get away, but that was the wrong thing for it to have done.

When the Zilthex vehicle shot forward, the wide rear end caught on his now extended landing claws. Still under power, it swung upward and shot to the ceiling. Having slammed into that ceiling, it lost all power and fell to the floor.

Upside down.

Tom brought the Space Kicker into a landing nearby. As soon as he popped the viewshield open, hands grabbed him out.

"That was a dangerous thing to have done," he found his dad saying. He looked stern. Tom waited impassively for what was to come next. "But I'm so glad you managed to take charge of the situation like you did." His dad then smiled. "Perhaps you'll become a squad leader someday."

"I just wanted to help," Tom said. He looked behind him at the Zilthex vehicle. "Sally's going to be alright, isn't she?"

His dad looked at the place Tom was. "She should be."

The vehicle swarmed with guards, with hands reaching in to grab at the people inside. The two sisters were dragged out and cuffed. Sally was handled more carefully, lifted out slowly from the vehicle and guided away from the hangar.

Tom hoped she would quickly recover. She was strong, he felt.

But some things couldn't be overcome so easily.

Lee watched the vehicle fall, impressed with how Tom had formed a plan and made the sisters slip up.

As the Space Kicker landed, Lee thought on the name that had been said. Hughs. Tom's dad. Since the two fathers were usually inseparable, Lee knew that his own dad had returned as well. A great excitement welled up in him that they'd be a whole family again.

The two families whole again.

"You're doing great for yourself," a voice said behind him.

Lee turned, his smile growing wider upon seeing his dad. "We've both been fighting a war, it seems."

Mr. Johnson put a hand around Lee's shoulders, thanked the guards and gave them orders to look after the prisoners. The two then walked out into the open, watching as Sally was guided away by medics.

"They were responsible for everything, then?" Lee asked.

"More than you probably realise. I'm taking you to your mother while I sort the squads out with Adam, then we'll join you and talk this whole thing out."

Lee had no objections, as he could see Mr. Hughs doing the same with Tom. The two mothers stood up from the seats they'd started in, having been screened among two squads also sat within the cluster of chairs.

Lee was hugged tightly by Mrs. Johnson while Tom had the same done to him by Mrs. Hughs.

"Oh, how I'm glad you're safe," Mrs. Hughs wailed. "Even if I knew everything was going to be fine – that I wished everything was going to be fine – I'm still happy that's exactly what happened."

"Go to your room," Mr. Johnson advised. "Get some rest. We'll sort everything out here and call in on you when the final ceremony is ready to happen."

The four of them walked slowly out of the hangar and across the corridors to their room. Once all had sat down, Lee had to ask.

"What's going to happen to Sally? Does she have any other family?"

The other three looked up at him with clear uncertainty pasted on their faces.

"I'm sure someone will take her..." Mrs. Hughs said.

"And what about her third place within the Championship? How will what's happened affect that?"

"She deserves it," Tom stated blankly. "But everyone will try to push it onto me."

"Are you sure?" Mrs. Hughs asked.

"Will it be seen as a fair win is what I want to know," Mrs. Johnson added.

"It would be unfair if it wasn't," Lee strongly stated. "She had no idea what they were up to."

"Let's put all this to the side for now, and get some rest. We'll see come the ceremony."

Tom stood up and wandered to the direction of his room, with Mrs. Hughs doing the same. Lee sunk further into his chair and closed his eyes.

He hadn't realised he'd dropped off to sleep until he was shaken awake. Opening his eyes, his dad stood over him.

"You'll be late for the ceremony, you know."

"How's everything?" Lee asked as he slowly stood.

"The two sisters have been locked away, everything they had has been taken from them, so they are no longer a problem."

Lee walked to the door with his dad following.

"Sally is recovering, you'll be glad to hear, and is waiting for you at the ceremony. She's currently in the care of one of the medics who will be taking her to live with her. She'll be close by to us, so visiting her won't be a problem."

"That's great to hear," Lee said. "I just wish we could do more to help her."

Tom entered the room with Mr. Hughs as Mr. Johnson replied, "As long as you keep up the visits, you'll certainly be helping her." Mr. Johnson then looked behind him at Tom and beckoned him to join them. "You two have helped her more than you realise, and she knows that. She trusts you both."

"It's friendship she needs," Mr. Hughs added, "and you two have been the support she hadn't been getting from anyone else."

"She told you this?" Lee asked.

"Yes," Mr. Johnson said with a nod. "We had to sort her out with her new home, and she told us about how she should have realised her sisters hadn't been helpful to her. We asked if anyone had been helpful, and both your names were mentioned. It might not seem much, but you cared what happened to her."

The four of them walked out of the room and headed to the hangar. Lee then spoke up again. He wanted to hear his dad's opinion.

"I think she did know that her sisters weren't looking out for her. That's why she was so defensive of them. She didn't want to admit it."

He mentioned the finalists talk on Radio Racer, to which Mr. Johnson said that they'd heard it. They had expected her sisters to be on it – or at least one of them – to present a public image of support for their sister.

"I still don't fully understand it, though," Tom said as they reached the ramp up to the hangar. "Why didn't they just stake out the town and destroy our home if they just wanted to get revenge on you?"

"We'll talk about that soon," Mr. Hughs stated. "For now, just enjoy the ceremony and be with your friend."

Lee admired the energy that seemed to be within the hangar. The crowds of watchers had returned, as had all the competitors and their supporters. Three of those competitors stood at the front before the stage where the hosts stood.

Sally waved to them as soon as she spotted them approaching. Lee smiled as he waved back, and he and Tom quickened their pace slightly to reach her.

"How you doing?" Tom asked.

"Good."

There had been a slight weariness to her tone, and he was glad Tom didn't push further with the questions.

She then added, "Would it be possible to travel down with you and stay for a while?"

"I'm sure that would be fine," Lee said.

"Yeah, we can enjoy the celebrations together," Tom added.

"The ending ceremony will begin," one of the hosts announced. "If everyone would like to take their seats."

Lee looked behind him to see Mr. Hughs and Mr. Johnson settling down beside the two mothers. He also spotted Pyra Summers at the side of the seats, wearing a headset with an extra audio receiver pointed out toward the hosts. He then took a seat in the front row.

After a few more seconds, the hosts began.

"This Championship has been a fun series of events, but it has also been stained by the actions of two sisters. Those actions proved to be dangerous, but didn't hit their mark. For that, we are thankful."

"Before this Championship can end, our finalists need to be awarded with their prizes. In fourth place, the person who overcame the trials that were set against him and managed to reach this point even in spite of them – Tom Hughs!"

Tom walked onto the stage and took hold of the fourth-place trophy that had been handed to him. He faced the crowd to thunderous applause, and Lee felt he detected a bit of anxiety in the face of his friend, and a great relief as he stepped back off the stage.

"In third place is another new face, and someone who pushed herself to stay in the pack – Sally Evans!"

The crowd cheered for her, though it was more subdued than that for Tom. Perhaps noticing this, one of the hosts added, "We have agreed that she holds no account for the help her sisters tried to force upon her, and welcome her up on stage to collect her prize."

Tom turned to talk to Sally. Lee couldn't hear what was being said, but it seemed that Tom was trying to convince her to head up. He took her hand and a step forward. She tentatively took one of her own, with the two climbing onto the stage together.

She accepted her prize but seemed very uncomfortable to be doing so. While the applause and cheering continued, she escaped back down off the stage. Tom followed her back into line.

"In second place is someone who has done their best to stay within the top fourth of competitors, just letting his guard down at the end – Adam McCoy!"

Once Adam had accepted his award, Katie Daniels was announced as the first-place winner. She accepted her prize with a lot more joy than Adam had.

The hosts then talked about the success of the Championship and of growing it further, wanting to hear of ideas for improvements and refinements for the next one in five years' time.

"We thank all the competitors who showed great enthusiasm for the event. We thank the supporters who helped the competitors throughout."

"Thank you to all those who have been watching or listening from wherever you are, whether here on the Surveillance Cruiser or our beloved planet."

"We'd also like to thank the Space Technology Research and Development Corporation and the Suati Spaceworks for their involvement and the supplies they have allowed us to use. And special thanks this year go to the Craftile Armed Forces for their action when it was needed most."

"We hope you have enjoyed yourselves. We wish everyone a safe journey back home."

The applause broke out again, with the dispersal of the crowd starting. Lee quickly joined Tom and Sally.

"I don't deserve it, though," she was saying. "It should have been you."

"You do deserve it. I might have handled myself massively well in the situations I was put in, but that's not what the Championship recognises." Tom looked to Lee with an appeal in his eyes.

Lee quickly took the hint. "You did better. You said when we first met that first-time competitors rarely make it to the final, yet here you both are. You should be happy to have got to the final, no matter where you placed."

"I'd have felt better had Tom got third place."

"How about we forget about who came where," Tom suggested. "We both had fun. We both reached the final."

Sally looked slightly happier about that, seeming to take it better from Tom.

"Are we all ready to get going, then?" Mr. Johnson asked.

"All three of us are," Lee said. "Everything packed?"

"Done while you were asleep by me and Adam."

"Even my stuff?" Sally asked.

"We'll be heading to your new place first," Mr. Hughs stated. "See that you're happy with it."

"Great."

Lee located where the DSSC had been moved to, with the others following his lead as he walked toward it.

Kerry looked up as Adam, Steve, Tom, Lee, and Sally entered the lower lounge area of the DSSC.

"We heading back home, then?" she asked.

She stood up as the others started walking to the ramp. Steve replied with a nod of his head. At the upper lounge, Sally and Tom took seats, with Adam splitting off to find which room Casey had settled in.

In the control bay, Lee took the pilot seat and started handling the controls straight away. Kerry settled into one of the rear seats, with Steve sat beside her in the other.

The DSSC took off smoothly, with Lee directing it out of the hangar quickly. He then shot toward Hortii. His smooth handling raised a new comment from Steve.

"Thanks," Lee accepted. "Where is this new place of Sally's then?"

"Same sector as us, on the connection with Crimson Wings."

"That place only had a small landing pad when I last flew over it. Will we fit?"

"There should be a temporary extension over the grass."

"I can see it."

Kerry raised herself slightly higher to see, but could only see their own house.

The DSSC smoothly slowed itself for the landing, and as Lee lowered it down, Steve commented, "I would never have thought you'd manage something like this. I haven't had any experience with one of these super cruisers yet, yet it feels completely natural to you. You really do pick up things fast. I sure have missed you."

He ruffled Lee's hair, then turned to Kerry. "I missed you both. I'm pretty sure there'll be no major action required of us, so it'll be back to home defence."

"One thing I'm going to miss is this," Lee said as he powered everything down. "I'm sure the STRDC will want it back."

"They do want it back, but I'm pretty sure you've been assigned as a tester for it."

"Me?" Lee asked blankly.

"You've done such a good job of handling it," Kerry said with a smile. "Who else would be able to feel the differences they make?"

"True. Let's go gather everyone and take a look around Sally's new home."

Lee exited the control bay quickly.

Kerry held out her hand for Steve to take. When they both stood up, they walked slowly to the lounge, which was empty. Down in the hangar, Kerry saw the Space Kicker with its burnt side and wondered if the spaceyard would allow Tom a second one without payment. It seemed unlikely, but with all that had happened to it, she wouldn't be surprised if he did get yet another free replacement.

Hopping down onto the landing pad, Kerry watched the three teens exploring the outside of the house.

"There'll be some changes happening to this place, I expect," Steve said.

"How so?" Kerry asked.

"Well now it's got some new occupants, you don't think it'll stay the same, do you?"

Kerry looked at him, thinking things through. "You mean this is also a recent purchase?"

"Of course. We had a background check done on Sally, just to make sure. Her sisters are the only family she has. She'd been in an orphanage for more than five years when her sisters returned and took her back."

"It's good of you to be helping her this way." Kerry gave Steve a kiss on the cheek and put an arm around him. "I'm sure she's much happier with Tom and Lee."

"You can see that easily. Shall we check out the house?"

Kerry allowed herself to be directed inside, where Sally seemed to already be planning the design of the house's furnishings. All the rooms were triangular in shape, fitting with the overall shape of the house.

Adam and Casey wandered inside, also checking the house out.

"It's about as large as our house," Casey stated.

"Slightly larger, I would guess," Adam said. "Though we have a larger landing pad."

"I suspected you were here already," someone behind them said.

Kerry looked behind her and noticed the woman who had entered behind Casey and Adam. Steve turned around to greet the new arrival.

"You couldn't miss us with that cruiser on the pad. You'll be okay here?"

"We'll be fine."

Sally seemed to realise that her new carer had arrived. She had stopped by the entrance to what seemed to be a bedroom. Slowly she walked forward. Kerry saw Tom and Lee leaving that room as Sally merged with the group.

"Hey," she said with a smile.

"Hello, Sally. I'm Lisa," Lisa held her hand out. Sally took it and a handshake was shared. "You can continue to be with your friends while I get things sorted around here. Your things are in the entrance lobby, so take them to a room and I'll make sure that one is yours."

Sally quickly walked to the lobby, saying a thank you as she passed Lisa. She returned with two backpacks and took them to the room she had been viewing.

She returned to the group and said another thank you. The two shared connection details for their PMDs, then Sally gave a cheery "see you later" to Lisa and walked out.

Tom and Lee quickly followed.

"Anything you need, just ask and I'm sure we'll be able to provide it," Steve said to Lisa.

"I will. Have fun with your celebrations."

The four adults left Lisa to look after the house and headed back outside. Tom and Lee were sat on the hangar floor while Sally took another look around the outside of her new house. There was an excited flair to her movements that Kerry took to mean she was very happy with how things had turned out.

"Back to ours, then?" Lee called.

"Back to ours," Steve replied. He gave a sigh. "It'll be good to see the household again."

It was a quick journey to the Johnson household in the super cruiser, and Casey had to agree it was the better of the two houses to go to. It was closer to where Sally now lived.

The three teens quickly took off as soon as the DSSC had landed, which Kerry had wanted to do, and she heard Steve commenting about her piloting prowess.

"You still never want to learn to pilot a 'craft, do you?" Adam asked.

Casey looked at him and winced again at seeing the burn. Whatever had caused it had created a large scabbed area on his face. He didn't seem to mind, but it still caused her discomfort to see it.

"No," she replied to his question. "I'd get too nervous and end up crashing into something." She paused for a second to work up to asking, "How did you get that burn?"

"Those weapons you saw the sisters handling are Zilthex tech. The ammo they use is super-heated. I got grazed by one of those lasers. It did hurt at first, very painfully hurt. It hurt until I passed out from it, and spent about a month out of the action."

Casey jumped up and hugged him.

"I am so glad you survived that!" she wailed. "It sounds like a horrible two years!"

Adam hugged her back, saying, "We managed to win and return. That's all that matters."

She felt he'd rather not speak any more about those experiences, and after a few seconds more she let him go and relaxed slightly.

"Are you ready for the photo?" Steve popped his head into the room to ask. "We'd better get to it quick."

"Get everyone ready," Adam said. "We'll be out."

He listened to the footsteps fading away, then said, "You don't have to worry any longer. Nothing dangerous will happen from now on. No more war. I'll be here for you." He closed his eyes and breathed deeply. "Now let's enjoy ourselves."

Casey nodded her agreement, following him out of the room. As they passed through the lounge, she noticed the two trophies lying on the floor. Neither Tom nor Sally seemed to care much for them.

Outside, Sally was talking to Tom and Lee as the camera was being set up for the photo by Kerry. Casey and Adam joined the teens.

"Okay," Kerry said. "The camera's ready to roll. Where's Steve?"

Steve walked out of the house with a muttered, "Just as I remember it."

"Tom, Lee, and Sally at the front, with the four of us at the back," Kerry instructed.

They all took up their positions, with Tom and Lee either side of Sally, large grins on their faces. Adam and Casey stood behind Tom, with Steve and Kerry stood behind Lee.

"Ready, and set," Kerry said.

Two beeps from the camera and the photo was taken. Kerry pulled out her PMD and looked at the photo on it.

"That's a great one," she commented. She held it out for the others to see.

Casey noticed that Sally had put her thumbs up and had an even wider smile than the two boys. She smiled upon seeing it and nodded her approval of the photo.

"If everyone's happy, let's get inside for some food."

Tom and Lee took Sally around the various rooms of the Johnson household, and it wasn't long before they started up a game of Four Point Fight between the three of them within one of the lounges.

The food was brought in as the game heated up, and soon all four parents were watching just as Sally managed to take another of Tom's pieces.

"I was asking for that," he said.

He looked at the board, locating where all the pieces were. They were playing on the four-locked mode, so everyone always had four moves to make during their turn.

He moved his two remaining pieces to be close together as away from the action as he could, hoping to draw someone into a trap. He had to admit it looked too obvious that the others probably wouldn't fall for it.

Lee still had all four of his pieces, having been barely moving and making a much more effective trap. He moved one of his pieces four spaces to form all his pieces as a triangle.

It seemed he was now going for the attack.

Sally retreated two of her pieces back one while moving the third near to the point of Lee's triangle. Tom moved his two pieces closer to Lee's as well, keeping them close to each other but away from an attack.

After another two rounds, Tom had lost all four pieces, with Sally down to one. Lee still had two.

"You're a great strategist," Sally commended, moving her piece to an easy takedown.

"It's just a defensive play," Lee admitted. "Which works against full-on attackers very well," he then teased.

The three shared a quick laugh, with the adults also smiling at the fun had. The food was eaten quickly with more talk happening about the Championship and the other competitors.

Soon after, it was starting to get late.

"It's been a lot of fun," Sally said with a smile. "I really should be going, though."

"We'll walk you back," Tom said. "Have some more time to talk."

"Great."

The three of them left through the gate and out onto the walkway. Hardly any traffic came up this way, but as they turned the corner, it seemed one of the households was having a party as a large number of vehicles were parked across the walkway, filling out the entire space.

"Not again," Lee exclaimed.

"Is this common?" Sally asked with a slight hint of worry.

"No, it's not common. But at large events, such as the Championship, that family always has a huge after-party celebration and invites more people than they have space for. There's no point trying to get around all that. We'll take the path through the green space."

Staying as close to the Johnson household border as they could, they followed it onto a path that opened out to a lot of greenery. On the other side of the path was the border of the household where the party was being held. A few loud voices could be heard from within.

"It's..." Sally fumbled. Tom looked at her. She looked slightly uncomfortable. "It's been... great. Being with you. You've both made me happier – than I have been for ages. Thanks."

"But something's troubling you," Lee said.

"I... It's just been good, being with you... that I'm hoping my new home can be just like yours is." She looked sad, and her voice reflected that as she added, "I haven't had a true family for more than five years. I just want it to be a happy one."

"It will be," Tom said. "You'll have us two as friends no matter where we all are. And that carer of yours seems like a nice person."

"I'm happy to have you as friends." She tried for one of her cheeky grins, but it only half appeared on her face. "I just wasn't expecting it to blow up so fast."

Tom understood.

"You did right to denounce them. How did you end up back with them?"

"They tracked down the orphanage I was at. Since the biological connection was there... It was an instant process. I don't know any of the details of what they were or anything. They just arrived after about five years away, took me back with them, but..." She shook slightly. Tom put an arm around her. "They just let me live with them. Since they took me, I haven't been in any education. They suggested I enter the Championship, and since I had nothing better to do, I did. But I had no idea what their plans were!" she then cried. "They weren't even around half the time, and they only ever taught me the basics of flight. I wanted to not bother with it, but they kept pushing for it!"

The fact she was opening up about all this meant she trusted them, Tom realised, but the fact her sisters had still been around had probably stopped her whenever she had tried. When he thought back, he could remember two occasions in which that had happened. She had probably struck a friendship with them from that first meeting. Anything better than what her sisters had been like.

"What they did doesn't reflect on you," Lee said. "You just admitted that you had nothing to do with their plans. Everyone can see that. Don't think you are bad just because you're related to them."

They had reached the end of the path through the green space and were back on the walkway. They stopped just before it, looking up at the traffic flying overhead.

"You are my family now," she said quietly. "Those two are no longer my sisters."

"What about..." Tom tried thinking about how to approach the question.

"Your parents were good people?" Lee asked.

Sally remained staring at the traffic.

"Don't feel you need to answer," he added softly.

"They were," she finally said flatly. "What happened to them wasn't." She added in the same flat tone, "Thank you for walking me back. I'll see you tomorrow."

She slipped out from under Tom's arm and walked to the gate of her new home.

Tom and Lee stood a few seconds longer, watching as she entered, then turned back up the path to head to their home.

"She'll be fine," Lee said.

"Yeah... She'll be with us tomorrow and we'll have more fun. You think she'll join our school?"

"Maybe. We'll see."

"And what of her parents?"

"I have a feeling our dads might know something about that."

Lee's assumption was correct.

When the two entered the house, Mr. Johnson was waiting for them. Wordless he directed them to the lounge they had been in earlier and indicated they should sit down.

"How is she?" he asked.

Lee related all that had been said during their walk. Mr. Johnson nodded when he finished.

"Yes, it was horrible," Mr. Johnson said. "They'd been in contact with Talon Force and were already in talks with joining up. They just wanted a little convincing. The reports from that day stated that the accident had been genuine. Everything appeared to be so. The sisters have been very chatty since their capture, so we know everything they've been doing."

"They revealed everything?" Lee asked, astounded.

"It surprised us, too. That's why we're now keeping a closer tally on all former Talon Force members. There's something about it all."

"So, what happened?"

"Their parents worked a shop. They were to have a repair done on the solar collector. Instead of a repair, the collector had a slight malfunction which overcharged the electrical current being sent into the shop. The resulting current then electrocuted them both when they walked into the shop to open it up."

"So how is that genuine?" Lee asked.

"Because when the town's collector had been shut down and all energy drained from the one in the shop, the electrician was also found dead. His records were brought up and it was found he wasn't marked with any previous wrong-doings. The collector in question had been an older model, and it was assumed that he had made a slip up. The sisters say someone from Talon Force had been the one to mess it up enough that it needed the repair, making sure to overcharge the output. Easily done on one of those older models, as the things were pretty unstable at times anyway."

"Shouldn't it have been turned off?"

"The older ones never could be turned off. That's also what made it seem genuine. A lot of research had gone into that attack."

"So they offed their parents and were impressed with the efficiency of it," Tom stated with disgust. "No wonder they joined up after. They were already partway there."

"It was part of a plan to make them disappear. A few days before that attack, they'd left home. No-one knew where, so Sally had gone to the orphanage."

Mr. Johnson rubbed at his eyes. Tom saw that he did look tired.

"Then they showed up with Talon Force," he continued, "during the Zilthex System War."

"That doesn't make sense," Lee spoke up. "That lasted two years, having only just finished up. They'd have only been in training for three."

"We can only know what they've been telling us. If I had to guess, they had already proven themselves to be accepted on the mission. They'll be held for life anyway, where we can hopefully get more from them."

"Have they told you where all their hidden tech is?" Lee asked.

"No. And that's another reason to keep an eye on those formerly of Talon Force."

"Did they tell you what they hoped to achieve by staging the attack on Tom? Aside from a bit of revenge?"

Mr. Johnson sighed. "It's all a bit delusional where that's concerned. They say they were hoping to destroy the entirety of the Space Technology Research and Development Corporation by lessening the public's faith in them. And discrediting the Craftile Armed Forces by associating them with that failure. It could have worked had they all been working together in the shadows, but that was never to happen. It could never have happened, which is why we think they accelerated that plan for their own ideas and a bit of personal revenge."

He stood up and wiped at his eyes again.

"I've said all I've got to. Tom, you'll be staying with us tonight. Get some rest, both of you."

He then left the lounge.

Tom and Lee looked at each other, wide-eyed. Tom felt they were both thinking the same in that they were lucky things had played out how they had.

And that Sally had escaped worse treatment than what she had got.

❖

"Winning the Championship has been great for me. I just wish there were some more serious racing events to take part in. I know I've got the ability to win whatever comes my way. I do think things could have been different had that Evans not been trying to disrupt things, and that I'd have really been able to get a serious three-way race instead of just two. I don't believe she had no idea what was going on. She should have been held accountable."

Katie Daniels speaking on Radio Racer [14/5-0085]

Three spacecraft waited together at the start line within the cruiser's hangar bay. The improvised line was nothing more than two mini cruisers parked either side of the three 'craft.

The first 'craft was a Space Kicker – designation M/2209k. Dark blue in colour, it looked like a pentagon that had been stretched from one flat side to be long in shape. The second was a Braveheart – designation I/w7b. Oblong in shape, it had a larger front end than its back. The pink colour contrasted brilliantly against the pale blue of the hangar floor. The third 'craft was a Falcon – designation P/f2m5. Green in colour and another that was oblong in shape, its front end thinned out into a rounded point.

The two mini cruisers flashed their lights, and the pilots of the 'craft lifted them and shot out of the hangar.

The Space Kicker had got an early lead, with the Falcon not far behind. They flew through the first checkpoint, angling upward to hit the second. The Braveheart followed behind.

After two more checkpoints, the 'craft entered a hangar that ran the full length of the cruiser it belonged to. The Space Kicker continued at full speed, managing to avoid the few mini cruisers dotted around by skirting the walkways near the ceiling. Both the Falcon and the Braveheart slowed down slightly to take a safer route through.

The Space Kicker shot out of the hangar with too much speed, having to shed it to make the turn. The other two 'craft easily made the turn to hit the checkpoint that was attached to the side of the cruiser.

The Braveheart took the lead, putting on a burst of speed in the hopes of keeping it.

It was then that the game was paused.

The walls of light dispersed, allowing the players to see each other. Lee looked over to Tom with a questioning look. Tom nodded at Sally.

She was once again on the edge of breaking down.

She had arrived earlier looking distraught, asking if either of them had been listening to Radio Racer and believed what was being said. Since neither of them had, they asked what she had heard.

There had been plenty of people making remarks about her having been in charge of her sisters and having used them to try and win. The truth was out there, yet some didn't believe it – even some of the competitors who she had been competing with.

They had reassured her that nothing would come of it, since the security teams knew the truth, and she had calmed a bit. They had invited her to play some games to get her mind off things, but every so often she had paused the game and been close to crying.

It was clear she couldn't get it out of her head.

"Shall we leave this and go for a walk?" Lee suggested.

"I'm up for that," Tom readily agreed. "Some air might help you to clear your head a bit," he then suggested to Sally.

She had her eyes closed and shook slightly, then nodded her head.

Outside, they walked through the park, onto the walkways and found themselves at the spaceyard. The journey had been quiet, but when Sally saw where they were, she asked, "Why here?"

"To see a friend of ours," Lee said.

Inside the spaceyard and the sales desks, Lee found Matt finishing up a sale. Once the person he was dealing with walked away, he waved the three over.

"Let's take this chat elsewhere, shall we?"

He led them out of the building through a different exit, through another building, and Lee set eyes on the super cruiser that had been his for just over two months.

"This has been sat here with nothing to do except be examined," Matt stated as they walked to it. "It was made a bit too large, we think. But I guess that's not why you're here."

"Do you know who I am?" Sally asked in a small voice.

"I do. I've also heard what people are saying about you. You don't need to listen to them. If they don' want to listen to the truth that's very clearly visible, that's on them."

Lee could tell that she still wasn't fully reassured.

"What about attacks against me? Proper ones."

"If it comes to it, it will be dealt with by the security teams. Just don't let what they say get to you. You know you weren't involved and that's all that matters. As I said, they are the ones with the problem if they don't want to accept the truth."

"But extreme matters-"

"Will be taken care of. You have two great friends who know the truth. They'll protect you while you're with them, and your carer will do the same when you're with her."

"What if I'm out and on my own?"

"Don't think on what they say. If they start getting aggressive, ignore them. But while a small portion of this population will still hold it against you, by the end of the month most will have forgotten. If you're still worried, just stay with these two until then."

Lee could tell she wasn't fully convinced but was willing to believe it.

"If you wish it, it will happen," he said quietly.

Sally, he was sure, was using her own version of that to settle her mind.

"I guess you all are right about that," she said. "I'm holding you to your word, though." A smile broke out on her face, which evolved into her cheeky grin. "I can't keep thinking negatively, and so I won't. They can say what they like about me, and I'm not going to care anymore."

Lee felt that keeping the mood light would help. "I believe we had a game we were in the middle of? One where I was winning?"

"You were winning?" Sally asked mock-surprised. "I thought I'd already overtook you?"

Tom joined in. "Don't think I won't take the lead back. I'm just giving you an easy time."

"Sure you are," Sally sarcastically stated as the two started walking back the way they had come. "You just don't want to admit that you messed up."

Lee followed behind with Matt as the mock-argument continued.

"Thanks," he said. "Me and Tom alone couldn't break her from those thoughts.

"Ar, no problem. Come back some time. That super cruiser is yours to fly any time."

"Thanks again."

Lee joined Sally and Tom, who were stood just outside the sales hall continuing with their teasing. Lee turned and waved to Matt, who returned it as he returned to his desk.

Then he joined in with the teasing as the three of them walked back to his home, assured that all three of them would remain happy throughout the rest of the month.

"And that is Radio Racer off the air for another five years. It's been great to be catching up with all the news, all the competitors, and living in the hype of the Championship. The competitors have all been lovely this year, and they rose to the challenges well. It's tough to have to say goodbye for another five years after these three months, but there's plenty for me to be doing in the meantime, and I'm sure the same can be said for all of you. I look forward to seeing any newcomers to the next Championship, as well as the returning faces, but it looks like this Space Race Championship is... over."

Pyra Summers of Radio Racer [17/5-0085]